John Richardson Wilkinson

Canadian Battlefields

And other Poems

John Richardson Wilkinson

Canadian Battlefields
And other Poems

ISBN/EAN: 9783744771993

Printed in Europe, USA, Canada, Australia, Japan

Cover: Foto ©Andreas Hilbeck / pixelio.de

More available books at **www.hansebooks.com**

CANADIAN BATTLEFIELDS

And Other Poems

BY

LIEUT.-COL. J. R. WILKINSON

PRINTED FOR THE AUTHOR BY

WILLIAM BRIGGS

TORONTO

1899

PREFACE.

In submitting "Canadian Battlefields and Other Poems" to a discerning public, I realize it may be marred by many errors; the harp may not always be in tune—some chords may jar upon the fastidious ear. Rhythm and harmony may not always present that mysterious appeal to the soul that approves, and proves the worth of all. Yet, withal, I feel that some thoughts and emotions of patriotism, love of home, the song of nature, the mystery of creation, and the impenetrable depths of infinitude, may be found and approved.

The subtle voice of nature, the voices of love, home, and country, have ever appealed to me, and impelled me to sing my humble song. And thus, in doubt and uncertainty, I cast it out on the world—the reading, critical public—asking that the pure, white veil of charity may conceal its rough edges and inequalities.

> Seek but to benefit thy fellowman;
> Let smiles, not frowns, his rugged path assail;
> Better with blinded eyes his faults to scan
> Than let the sin of wrong and scorn prevail.

J. R. WILKINSON.

Leamington, 1899.

CONTENTS.

CANADIAN BATTLEFIELDS

AND OTHER POEMS.

WHAT SHALL I SING ?

WHAT shall I sing, I prithee, O Muse ?
    For song burns my bosom to-day ;
And it flows o'er me like a wave o' the sea,
    A dream-wrought, subtle melody.
Shall 't be of the wondrous present,
    This scientific, restless age ;
Or cull from the field the centuries yield
    Rich gems from history's page ?

Shall it be of stern war and the cause
    For which millions of men are slain,
And heroic days with glory ablaze,
    Dear freedom and honor to gain ?
Shall I sing of the stars of heaven
    That forever their orbits keep—
Beautiful, serene stars of heaven,
    Gemming the eternal deep ?

Shall it be of the grand old ocean,
    And its bright isles far away,
With life all free as th' unbounded sea,
    A subtle and golden day ?

Shall I tell of the glory of sunset,
  And the twilight soft on the lea,
The murmuring winds, through foliage and vines,
  And the moon that silvers the sea?

Shall it be a lay of the seasons,
  That fade like a dream away?
The spring so fair, and the perfumed air,
  And the songsters that trill so gay?
And the summer robed in splendor,
  Serene as a spirit dream,
Her throbs and sighs and cerulean skies
  Would I make my soul's bright theme?

Shall 't be of the autumn's fading,
  And the winds that sob and sigh,
And the leaves of gold, drifting fold on fold,
  And the flowers that droop and die;
The birds that trill us a last farewell,
  Tenderly, sorrowfully sweet,
Saddening the heart, doomed ever to part,
  And life's work so incomplete?

Shall I tell of the white-robed winter
  Sweeping down from icy zones,
And the frozen streams, and the pale, cold gleams,
  And its desolate sobs and moans?
Ah! shall it be of home and mother,
  And the years that have flown away,
And the loved of old, like a tale that's told
  From childhood's dear happy day?

Shall 't be of the innocent children,
  Believing of such is heaven?
Their prattle and glee 's a joy unto me,
  And care from the heart is driven.

Shall I sing of our lovèd country,
  And these bright, fair homes of ours ?
So happy and free from sea unto sea,
  Guard well thy bulwarks and towers.

And the grand "Old Flag" floating o'er us,
  Proudly ruling the boundless sea,
Ever unfurled, encircling the world,
  Hath glory enough for me !
Shall I sing of man's joys and sorrows ?
  Of woman's undying love ?
Of the ransomed that wait at the "pearly gate"
  Of the "city of gold" above ?

I would sing of all things beautiful,
  The heroic and the true,
With a quenchless flame and a deathless fame
  To brighten the whole world through.
A resurrection and a rising
  To a grander, nobler life,
In brighter spheres, where the golden years
  Exclude all of storm and strife.

SPEAK NOW.

AH, me ! the words unspoken
    Might have saved a soul to-day—
And perhaps a heart was broken,
    And made hopeless by the way.
If we poor blundering creatures
    But in wisdom would speak now,
We should see more smiling features,
    And less gloom on many a brow.

There would be far less of doubting,
    And far less of weary pain ;
If we ceased our cruel scouting ;
    We should wider friendship gain.
Many a way-worn wanderer
    Would rejoice if he but knew
That absence maketh but fonder ;
    That our hearts are leal and true.

Why not speak the word of warning
    When we know that danger's nigh ?
Why stand ye in idle scorning
    Whilst the heedless ones pass by ?
Why not help thy fallen brother
    To regain his feet once more ?
Do thy duty, let no other
    For thy help in vain implore.

Why not spurn the demon slander
    That hath slain so many hearts ?
Should we listen e'en, or pander
    Whilst he hurls his venomed darts ?

Why not speak the words of kindness
　　To those whom we truly love?
Why should we in our dull blindness
　　Wait the summoning from above?

Why not do the deed that's noble,
　　That life may the better be;
And thus scorning the ignoble,
　　Live in blameless purity?
Such are fearless when the battle
　　Rages on a blood-red field;
Fearing not the cannon's rattle,
　　They but to grim death will yield.

Brave hearts like these have nobly died,
　　Fadeless crowns to such be given;
The good in heart, and purified
　　Shall wear more stars in heaven.
Rest not, nor sleep, be brave of soul,
　　Seek the lost to soothe and save;
For life is brief, so near the goal,
　　From our childhood to the grave.

THE BATTLE OF CHATEAUGUAY.

FOUGHT OCTOBER 26TH, 1813.   AMERICAN FORCE, 3,500; BRITISH, 400.

REDLY the October sun shone that day
O'er the golden landscape stretching away
To the Laurentian Hills, o'er vale and stream
As lovely as ever a poet's dream.
O'er the land of the Maple Leaf so fair
Stole the wandering breeze, caressing there
With light, soft fingers, and murmuring low
Through the fading foliage, dying slow.
'Twas the peace of nature, touchingly grand,
Brooding over this fair Canadian land.

But another scene draws our thoughts away
To the far-famed field of the Chateauguay.
There beside it War's trumpets fiercely blare ;
And marshalling foemen are forming there !
The invader dares to pollute our soil ;
But brave, true men will his purpose foil.
Noble de Salaberry, knowing no fear,
Dreads not the foe, who by thousands draw near.
Gallantly those Frenchmen stand by his side,
Sharpshooters, every one, true and tried ;
And they coolly wait the oncoming foe,
And the river goes by in gentle flow.

"They come! they come!   Voltigeurs, steady !
Aim low, aim low,—be calm now and ready ;
Ye fight for your homes, and country so fair—
Yield not an inch, nor ever despair."
Their rifles they raised, aimed steady and well,
Fired low, and hundreds before them fell !

The foe now open with thunderous roar ;
Shot and shell from their guns they hotly pour.
Unflinching, the Voltigeurs firmly stand,
Though storm'd at by masses on every hand.
Swift volleys they hurl on the assaulting foe,
Sure and deadly by the river's flow.

Checked in their advance by the Voltigeurs,
Who heroically the storm endure ;
Patiently, though suffering loss and pain,
Their position they proudly, sternly maintain.

By sheer numbers being nearly surrounded,
Though the foe are stunned and confounded,
'Tis a critical time at Chateauguay.
Will de Salaberry in despair give way ?
No ! in sterner mould is the hero cast,
And will bar the way of the foe to the last.
Ah ! a clever ruse he's adopting now,
And a smile flits over his noble brow.

He extends his buglers widely in rear,
To sound the charge and lustily cheer.
'Twas a clever thought, and a master-stroke ;
On the startled ear of the foe it broke,
And, frightened, they everywhere give way—
Lost is the field, and lost is the day.
Breaking into instant, headlong retreat,
From humiliating and sore defeat,
Over the border they swiftly fly,
And the "Red Cross Banner" still floats on high.

All hail, de Salaberry ! hail, Voltigeurs !
Thy fame still lives, it forever endures ;
Ye sternly barred there the foe that day,
By the far-famed stream of the Chateauguay.

And redly the October sun sank low,
Flooding the world with its crimsoning glow ;
And the shadows fell on the golden scene
As beautiful as e'er a poet's dream.
And the pale, dead faces were laid away
By the murmuring stream of the Chateauguay !
And white-winged peace hovered there once more
In the fading light by the river's shore.

THE DEEP MINES.

DELVE down in the deep mines, O restless man !
   Wrest from the deep mines the red, red gold ;
Seize the diamonds and the precious gems ;
   In the deep, vast mines lies wealth untold.
Win from the deep sea, from the uttermost sea,
   The hoarded treasures of Neptune's realm.
Command thou thine own staunch, dauntless barque ;
   Hold the chart, and thyself guide the helm.

Quaff thou from the deep things of life, O man,
   The things that make life more broad and great.
Revere the good, the noble, and true ;
   Grasp destiny from the hand of fate ;
Chain the elements to thy chariot wheels ;
   Count all things subservient to thy will—
The things that ennoble assimilate,
   Pure as the cool, sparkling mountain rill.

Drink thou of the deep wells of love, O man !
   For life is empty without its sway ;
The love of friends, and e'en our fellowman,
   Make darkest night seem bright as the day.

Be kind, considerate of thy brother ;
  Smooth somewhat if thou canst his rugged way ;
Bear each other's burdens, battle side by side—
  United ye shall surely win the day.

Delve deep in thine own bosom, O man !
  Pluck gems of thought that dormant lie ;
Let thy fiery energy and deathless zeal
  Move the hearts of men, lift their souls on high.
If thou canst not o'er the mountain go,
  Penetrate it to the vale beyond ;
Look upward and onward, brave, pure soul,
  And Fortune may touch thee with her wand.

But if o'ertaken by an adverse fate,
  And thy dreams of greatness fade away,
Front thou the storm and battle's fiery rage ;
  Yield but to death—death's lurid, fatal day !
If all thy years should lead by lowly ways,
  Where wealth and fame ne'er ope their shining
      wings,
Be comforted, do thy humble duty well,
  In heaven thou mayst be honored more than kings.

LAURA SECORD; OR, THE BATTLE OF BEAVER DAMS.

FOUGHT JUNE 24TH, 1813. BRITISH, 47 REGULARS AND 200 INDIANS
AMERICANS, 570, WITH 50 CAVALRY AND 2 GUNS.

SHE knew, and her heart beat faster,
  The foe would march that day;
And resolved, though only a woman,
  To silently steal away
And warn the outpost at Beaver Dams;
  Alone, and on foot, to go
Through the dim and awesome forest,
  To evade the vigilant foe.

No one thought of a woman,
  And she gained a path she knew
In the lonesome, stately forest,
  And over the dark way flew.
On and on with a beating heart,
  And never a pause for rest;
Twenty miles of dim and distance,
  And the sun low down the west.

Startled sometimes to terror
  By the blood-curdling cry
Of wolves from the faint far distance,
  And sometimes nearer by;
And hollow sounds and whispers
  That rose from the forest deep;
Ghostly and phantom voices
  That caused her nerves to creep.

But she pauses not, nor falters,
    But presses along the way ;
Noiselessly through the distance,
    Through the shadows weird and gray.
In time must the warning be given,
    She must not, must not fail ;
Though rough is the path and toilsome,
    Her courage must prevail.

"To arms ! to arms, FitzGibbon ! "
    Came a woman's thrilling cry ;
"Lose not a precious moment—
    The foe ! the foe is nigh ! "
And a woman pale and weary
    Burst on the startled sight ;
Out from the dark awesome forest,
    Out of the shadowy night.

" They come ! they come, six hundred strong,
    Stealing upon you here !
But I, a weak woman, tell you,
    Prepare and have no fear."
The handful of British heroes
    Resolve the outpost to save,
With the aid of two hundred Indians,
    Allies cunning and brave.

Still as death the line is waiting
    The onset of the foe ;
And the summer winds make whisper
    In the foliage soft and low.
" Ready !" and each heart beat faster ;
    " Fire low, and without fear."
And they fired a crashing volley,
    And gave a defiant cheer.

Staggered by the deadly missiles,
    That like a mighty blow,
Fell swift on the line advancing,
    Fell on the astonished foe.
And for two long, desperate hours
    The furious fight raged there ;
Till the foemen, foiled and beaten,
    Surrendered in despair.

Well done, gallant FitzGibbon !
    Thy name shall live in story ;
Thy daring feat of arms that day
    Is wreathed with fadeless glory.
One other name my song would praise,
    A patriot soul so brave,
That dared the forest's lonely wilds
    FitzGibbon's post to save.

Noble woman ! heroic soul !
    We would honor thee to-day ;
Thou canst not, shall not be forgot.
    More lustrous is the ray
Time reflects upon thy deed.
    Thy talismanic name—
Canadians, sound it through the land,
    Perpetuate her fadeless fame !

THE SEA AND THE SOUL.

Oh, the sea! the sea! how it stirs my soul,
As its bright bounding billows onward roll;
Unfettered they toss their crests on high,
As if to assault the far vaulted sky.

Oh, the sea! the sea! when it murmurs sweet,
And its silver waves fall down at my feet;
And it flashes and ripples in sunny smiles,
Far away by a thousand happy isles.

Oh, the sea! the sea! when the wild winds roar,
And its thunderous waves rush on the shore;
And the dread tempest sweeps the storm-torn sky,
And the world is drown'd in its madden'd cry.

Oh, the sea! the sea! when the stars' pale light
Twinkle afar through the realms of night:
And the silver moon looks down on the tide,
O'er its undulating bosom far and wide.

Oh, the sea! the sea! unchained and free;
A limitless, typical mystery
Of eternity; how it rolls, it rolls,
And its awesome voice is warning men's souls!

Oh, the sea! the sea! what of the lone graves
Of the lov'd and lost in thy unknown caves?
Where are the ships of a thousand stern years?
Man's buried hopes, and his million tears?

But the sea ! the sea ! 'tis my glowing theme,
And I love to ponder beside it and dream,
With the lights and shadows falling between,
The weird phantom land of the might have been.

Oh, the sea ! the sea ! when I yearn for rest,
And the sun falls down in the purple west,
I seek thy shadowed and wave-worn shore,
And restful repose my bosom steals o'er.

THE BATTLE OF LUNDY'S LANE.

FOUGHT JULY 25TH, 1814. AMERICAN FORCE, 5,000 ; BRITISH
AND CANADIANS, 2,800.

THE summer sun down the sky fell low,
And soft, cool winds more gently did blow,
And the stream swept by with resistless flow
On that July eve of the long ago,—
A lovely landscape as ever was seen,
And nature's serenity crowned the scene.
A gold light shimmered o'er hill and stream,
And the shadows lengthened softly between.
Thus o'er this beautiful Canadian land
Fell the hush of nature, soothing and bland.

But hark ! on the startled ear there comes
The blare of trumpets and roll of drums,
And war's dread panoply bursts on the scene,
With its rumbling roar and thunder between,
As the bannered foe draws proudly nigh,
And the outposts before them quickly fly.
But Drummond draws up on the famous plain,
On the undulations of Lundy's Lane.

On a rise in the centre his guns he placed,
Deployed his infantry, and sternly faced
The menacing foe in battle-array,
As the shades crept out on the dying day.
Sixteen hundred dauntless, determined souls
The heroic Drummond proudly controls.

In contiguous lines the foe now comes,
To the blare of trumpet and beat of drums,
With supporting columns to reinforce
And cheer the lines on their onward course.
Drummond's batteries open with deafening roar,
Shaking the trembling river and shore ;
And hundreds go down in the deadly storm :
Torn are their ranks, but again they re-form,
Move forward once more with a rush and cry,
Confident that Drummond will turn and fly.
But he stands fast, and his battery flashes,
And his sturdy infantry volleys and crashes
On the brave advancing lines of the foe
Rushing up from the slope below.
Brown's infantry charged to the battery's side,
But to capture the guns in vain they tried.
They were met with the steel by Drummond's men
And hurled confused down the slope again.
They tried it again—rushed forward once more,
But broke like a wave on a rock-bound shore !

Brown's supports were brought up, and his cannon
        roared,
All along the lines the infantry poured
A withering, ceaseless and consuming fire :
And the rage of battle grew wilder, higher.
The enemy charged and charged again
Till their life-blood crimsoned the emerald plain,

And the awful din and the carnage there
Filled wives' and mothers' hearts with despair.

At length the long twilight closed around
The smoking cannon and death-strewn ground,
And the pitying night drew o'er the scene
Of horror a mournful and sable screen.
Still amid the darkness they fighting fell,
And the surging ranks bore a fire of hell !
Muzzle to muzzle the hot guns stormed,
Rending the ranks that again re-formed,
And rushed to the charge again and again
Through the infantry's fire and batteries' flame.
The guns were won, and retaken again
In the revel of death, at Lundy's Lane.

Here Riall came up with twelve hundred more,
To the help of Drummond, bleeding and sore :
Twelve hundred Canadians and regulars to stand
To the death for this proud Canadian land.
The brave foe brought up reinforcements, too,
Determined Drummond's lines to pierce through ;
And they close in a mad, mad rush again,
And the roar of the hot guns shake the plain.
Lurid, red flashes illumine the night,
Revealing a moment the dreadful sight
Of the lines struggling there in the gloom,
Where hundreds go down to a gory doom.

But Drummond the foemen foiled everywhere,
And disheartened, on the verge of despair,
At the midnight hour they fled from the field,—
Broken and beaten, they were forced to yield.
Throwing their baggage in the stream, in fright
They fled away in a desperate plight.

The moon had risen o'er the pitiful scene,
Her lovely face, all mild and serene,
Lighting up the horror of carnage there,
Revealing the ghastly and upward stare
Of pale, dead faces peering out of the gloom,
Just touched by the silvery midnight moon.
Lay them away on the hard-fought field
Where the musketry volleyed and cannon pealed !
War's tumult shall rouse them again no more,
The heroic dead by the river's shore.
Slumber on, brave hearts ! ye do battle no more
Near Niagara's awesome, eternal roar !

Oh, land of the Maple Leaf so fair,
Breathe even to-day a fervent prayer
For those intrepid souls who, fighting, fell
For home and country they loved so well.
Canadians ! tell it—repeat it again—
How our fathers stood there at Lundy's Lane,
With the regulars fearlessly side by side—
Stood there as heroes, conquered and died.
To rescue this land from the invader's tread
That field was piled with immortal dead.

MY WIFE.

I WANT her woman's kisses,
　I want her love and truth
And e'er as kind and gentle
　As in the days of youth.
I want her e'er beside me,
　Not enslaved, but free;
A help in time of trouble,
　And a comfort unto me.

We'd share life's joys together,
　Of its ills bear equal part;
In storm, or sunny weather,
　Trust each other's faithful heart.
I'd have her loving counsel
　When perplexed with care;
When the clouds are lowering,
　And threatening everywhere.

I'd hear her happy laughter
　Rippling light and gay;
And list her sweet voice singing
　Tender songs, that drive away
The petty irritations
　That fret life's every day,
And if not quickly banished
　Turn the bluest skies to gray.

I want her with the children
　To guard their tender feet;
To soothe and ever bless them
　With her presence fair and sweet.

'Tis mother's subtle influence
  That makes or mars us all :
By her early lessons given
  We either rise or fall.

And when the skies are smiling
  O'er all the summer land,
And nature is enraptured,
  I'd clasp her gentle hand,   .
And list the songs that greet us,
  Hear the wind's plaint and sigh,
Wooing the summer's beauty
  As it softly treadeth by.

I'd look when twilight falleth
  On the world in dreamy rest,
And golden rays still linger
  In glory in the west.
In that rapt quiet hour
  We'd watch the pale moon rise,
And in the tender silence
  Dream of fadeless Paradise.

When the shadow-land I enter,
  And fails life's fleeting breath,
I'd cross the stream beside her,
  The stream that we call death.
Life's years of light and shadow,
  Passed in sweet felicity,
Should be but the beginning
  Of our day, eternity.

NIAGARA.

I WAS rapt in unutterable amaze
As I looked upon its awful front,
And saw the terrific roll of waters
As down the deadly mesmeric gorge they fell
In power irresistible, tremendous,
As if the wrath of God would rend the world asunder
For the sin and wrong that man hath done !
And the earth trembled as one in fear—
And the thunderous roar of its awesome voice
Made all else seem silent as the dead !

Yet, majestic and supremely beautiful art thou
When the god of day pours o'er thy front his wondrous
        light,
Or when the golden stars and dreaming, silvery moon
Lighteth up the slumb'rous shadows of the night.
Aye, thou art sublime, though terrible, Niagara !
How diminutive are man's works compared to thee !
Thou awe-inspiring, terrific world-wide wonder—
Marvellous work of the Deity !

And thou hast rolled and rolled, Niagara ;
Adown the ages of the dim, mysterious past
Thou hast thundered in derision of the flight of time,
And mocked when nations to the grave were cast !
But the Creator holds thee in the hollow of His hand,
And when the sea shall render up its ghastly dead
Thou shalt be shorn of thy stupendous power,
And bow thy cruel and imperious head.

THE OJIBWAYS.

ALONG the shores of Point Pelee,
  Three hundred years ago,
The summer sun in rapture shone,
  And pure winds soft did blow.
The laughing waters rose and fell
  In soft caressing lave ;
And flashing sea-birds dipt their wings,
  And white gulls skimmed the wave.

The mallard ducks in thousands flew
  Along the rippling tide,
And eagles soared in heaven's blue
  In freedom far and wide ;
And gay kingfishers watched the surf,
  And divers cleaved the deep.
Across the waters far away
  Stole murmurs strange and sweet.

The finny tribes in schools did glide
  Along the sandy bars ;
The splendor of their jewelled sides
  Flashed up like silver stars.
The sturgeon floundered in their glee,
  Mud pouts and cats at play—
A subtle gladness brooded there
  Throughout the fair sweet day.

The warm south winds stole o'er the lake
  Along the shifting bars ;
The bright waves met in dashing foam,
  Flashing like crystal stars.

And skies serene, divinely blue,
  Met the enraptured gaze ;
On the horizon far away
  Hung a delicious haze.

Ashore ! ashore ! let's leap ashore,
  And glide 'neath cedar shade,
Where pine trees raise their fronded crests
  O'er many a sylvan glade ;
Where juniper in clusters grow,
  And twining vines wreathe o'er
The nooks and winding velvet ways
  That reach from shore to shore.

The walnut and the oak tree, too,
  Their sturdy forms uprear ;
The haunts of squirrel and raccoon,
  Wild-cat and savage bear,
And mink and otter haunt these shades.
  Their wants are all supplied ;
Sleek creatures, how they frisk and play
  In all their graceful pride !

Oft, too, is heard the howl of wolf,
  When night-time closes down ;
The sylvan glades, lost in the shades,
  With their fierce cries resound.
The bounding deer and graceful fawn
  Here, too, have made their home ;
Untamed, unfettered, and all free,
  These lovely haunts they roam.

Hark to that wave of melody,
  That here so sweetly thrills ;
It flows from all the nooks and glens,
  And from the sunlit hills !

O wrens, and redbirds fair and sweet,
  Jays, robins, join the song,
And bluebirds with the azure wing,
  A blithe and happy throng!

The whippoorwill, and catbird, too,
  Whose song steals on the night,
The chatter of the festive owl
  That shouts in weird delight!
A thousand voices join the lay,
  And rhythmic fluttering wings
Of every hue play interlude
  To the hymn that nature sings.

See, the flowers of every hue—
  Wild roses like a dream—
Breathe out their incense on the air,
  Odorous and serene!
The lily and the violet sweet
  Peep up on every side,
And buttercups and wild bluebells
  In all their native pride.

CHAPTER II.

Ah! Nature with a lavish hand
  Hath here her treasures strewn,
All undisturbed by ruthless man
  That scathes and mars too soon.
Back o'er the silent phantom past,
  Three hundred years ago,
Fair Point Pelee in rapture lay
  Where laughing waters flow.

'Twas here the red man made his home,
  Beneath the cedar shade;
The wigwams rose so quaint and queer
  By quiet nook and glade.

This, the home of the Ojibways,
    Fierce, untamed, and free ;
They dwelt in peace and plenteousness
    Beside this inland sea.

And Manitou had blest them so
    With fish and luscious game ;
The hunting grounds were so replete
    Before the white man came !
Where now are termed the " Indian fields "
    They grew the Indian corn,
And laugh and song with sweet content
    Roused up the summer morn.

Far on the north the marshlands lay,
    And pond, and wide lagoon ;
The home of snipe and mallard ducks,
    Geese, teal, and lonely loon.
Among the reeds, and rushes, too,
    The muskrats built their homes ;
They dotted o'er the wide expanse
    With quaint, ingenious domes.

And Willow Island far away,
    Stirred by the toying breeze
That makes the rice and grass fields wave
    Like tossing emerald seas.
From east to west, from shore to shore,
    The teeming marshlands lay ;
The Narrows, by the western shore,
    A picturesque causeway.

The pass that leads by Sturgeon Creek,
    And circles Pigeon Bay,
By which are reached fair Seacliff Heights,
    And regions far away ;

And looking southward, where the sun
  In golden splendor smiles
On Pelee Island, fitly crowned
  The queen of Erie's isles.

Aye, here it was, the red man's home,
  Three hundred years ago ;
And peace and plenty blest his lot
  By the bright water's flow.
He had the teeming forest glades
  For every kind of game ;
And Erie's fulness rendered up
  Fine fish of every name.

He drew on all the wide marshlands
  For furs both soft and warm ;
The bear and wild wolf tribute gave;
  And when the winter's storm
Whitened upon the sleeping hills,
  Prepared, and safe from harm,
The wigwams all with plenty stored,
  He knew no fell alarm.

Ah ! oft these shores resounded
  To his children's sport so gay,
And the songs of Indian maidens,
  Graceful as fawns at play ;
And the shout and free, wild laughter
  Of youths at game by day ;
Or as o'er the laughing waters
  In canoes they bore away.

Sometimes to the distant islands,
  Or over Pigeon Bay,
They went in bold adventure
  By sun, or star's pale ray.

But the chiefs and older huntsmen
　　Smoked in serene content;
Many moons had taught them wisdom,
　　Calmness they with pleasure blent.

Thus in the summer's rapture
　　Life was a peaceful dream;
And when winter fell upon them
　　The wigwams were serene
With warmth, good cheer and comfort:
　　The red man loved his home;
From his kindred and his nation
　　His heart would never roam.

He believed in the Great Spirit;
　　His subtle soul would thrill
To the voices heard in nature,
　　That taught the Great Spirit's will.
Strange, mysterious people!
　　Who can thy origin trace?
Are ye one of the lost ten tribes
　　Of Israel's wandering race?

CHAPTER III.

Awake! awake, Ojibways!
　　To dream in peace no more,
For there comes a bold invader
　　From eastward by the shore.
Rowing in swift, strong bateaux,
　　With strokes both strong and long,
To the cadence of fearless voices
　　In a gay boatman's song,

Come full two hundred singers,
　　In boats, a score or more,
Far o'er the laughing waters,
　　Skirting the eastern shore.

Who are they, these fearless strangers,
  Armed with sword and lance,
With arquebuse and musketoon?
  They are fiery sons of France,

Exploring the boundless forests,
  Locating rivers and seas;
Ignoring the red man's title,
  Coming his rights to seize.
Ha! they spy the eastern outlet
  That leads to the lagoon,
Far across the teeming marshlands,
  The domain of teal and loon.

They enter with eager spirits
  This strange tract to explore;
And halting not, they discover
  Point Pelee's western shore.
A causeway of cedar and hillock,
  From lagoon to lake they trace;
And their bateaux quickly transport
  By way of the Carrying Place.

And they gaze on the expansion,
  And cheerily launch away,
And disappear in the distance,
  Across wide Pigeon Bay.
The Ojibways in amazement
  Saw this strange concourse pass by;
A foreboding premonition
  Whispered of danger nigh.

Mitwaos in council assembled
  His chiefs and warriors brave;
Many scores of fiery stalwarts,
  Of countenance stern and brave.

And calmly they deliberated,
  Counselling for peace or war ;
Should they allow these daring strangers
  Their sacred rights to mar ?

After the chiefs had spoken
  Of the pending dangers nigh,
It was finally decided
  The strangers might pass by
In peace, and unmolested,
  If they did not interfere
With the vast teeming hunting grounds
  Of the nation, far and near.

When three moons had waxed and waned,
  The voyageurs, returning, came
From over the western waters,
  Lit by the sunset's flame.
And they drew up at the Narrows,
  The Carrying Place again,
A "cut" in the cedar hillocks
  Aglow with autumn's flame.

De Orville, their gallant leader,
  And Pontgravé and Le Jeune,
Knew their followers were weary,
  And made decision soon
To bivouac near the marshlands
  For a day of needed rest,
And to replenish their commissariat
  With fish and game the best.

The camp-fires were all alighted
  At the eve's afterglow,
And the pines and cedars quivered,
  And the waves made murmur low.

The scene was worthy a Rembrandt,
  So rich the light and shade,
And the starry vault above them,
  And the winds that whisper made.

" A song ! a song ! " de Orville cried,
  " The night is rife with glory.
Let 's while a merry hour away
  In singing and in story."
" A song ! a song ! " as one they cry,
  " Life hath enough of sorrow ;
Sing while we may with hearts so gay,
  Care cometh with the morrow."

" Le Jeune ! Le Jeune ! lead on, lead on,
  The stars are laughing o'er us ;
Give us thy latest and thy best,
  And we will join the chorus."
Le Jeune had a poetic soul,
  And voice of wondrous sweetness ;
He reached men's better, nobler part,
  And won them to completeness.

And the groups about the camp-fires,
  A picturesque, gay throng,
Heard many a quaint old story,
  Pun, laugh, and ringing song ;
And thus 'mid the wilds of nature
  Passed the joyous hours away.
Light-hearted, merry Voyageurs,
  Ever gallant and gay,

Beside the deep glowing embers,
  Passed the night in calm repose,
And in the soft early dawning
  Refreshened they uprose ;

And with arquebuse and musketoon,
   Spear, trap, and fishing-line,
They scattered o'er the marshlands
   And 'neath the haunts of pine.

And from the Narrows and the shore,
   Marshlands and wide lagoons,
There burst the crash of arquebuse
   And roar of musketoons.
And all day long the sport went on ;
   At eve they counted o'er
A tempting hoard of luscious game,
   Right welcome to their store.

CHAPTER IV.

The Ojibways from a distance
   Marked the slaughter of their game,
And their untamed fiery spirits
   With revenge were all aflame.
And Mitwaos, their brave leader,
   Summoned his chiefs once more ;
Their souls were fiercely chafing,
   And their savage hearts were sore.

And as bursts a pent-up torrent
   They pronounce for instant war
Not one dissenting chieftain
   The unity to mar.
The runners go swiftly forward
   The braves to summon now ;
And there's hurried preparation,
   And sternness on each brow.

The young and fearless warriors
   Meet in the cedar shade
The tender Indian maiden,
   And farewells are quickly made.

And the stern, unbending chieftain
　Clasps his true-hearted wife,
And kisses his dear papooses,
　And girds him for the strife.

Their dauntless leader, Mitwaos,
　Who to death will do his part,
Seeks his wife, the Singing Redbird,
　And folds her to his heart.
Ah ! those heathen souls are tender
　For children, wife, or mother,
Their nation, and a father's love,
　For sister and for brother.

To the south of the Indian Fields
　Their rendezvous is made,
Where the vines and the cedars cluster,
　And deeper glooms the shade.
Here gather fast the Ojibways,
　Just at the twilight's close,
To await the dawn's pale glimmer
　To fall upon their foes.

Now all girted up with wampum,
　With scalping-knife and spear,
With tomahawk, bow and arrows,
　The foe they do not fear.
And each chief hath his allotment
　Of braves to do his will ;
And well they know how to attack
　With cunning and with skill.

Directed all by Mitwaos,
　Whose plans are now complete,
Each one his post of duty knows,
　And how the foe to meet.

Then at the lonesome midnight hour,
    When the world 's wrapped in sleep,
The Ojibways form for battle,
    And on the foeman creep.

Proud Mitwaos in the centre,
    The whole at his command ;
Leaping Panther with the right wing,
    Who like a rock will stand;
And Lone Wolf with the left wing,
    The red men love him well,
And many an act of daring
    His nation of him tell.

The signal, an owl hoot, given,
    And stealthily through the gloom
They move forward in position
    To victory or their doom.
Aye, noiselessly gliding onward
    Through darkness dense and still,
By the signal of the hooting owl
    Or the cry of whippoorwill.

CHAPTER V.

Thus gain they the dark hillocks
    By the Carrying Place,
And like phantoms take position
    The waiting foe to face.
Aye, waiting were the Voyageurs,
    In silence, but prepared ;
Not as Mitwaos expected,
    To be surprised and snared.

De Orville became suspicious
    Of the distant, sullen mood
Of the Ojibways, and took counsel
    And the usual course pursued ;

Facing the impending danger,
  Placed sentries on the rounds,
Alert to the slightest movement,
  Awake to the faintest sounds.

The fires were allowed to smoulder,
  And, fearing no alarms,
Their appointments in good order,
  In ranks they lay on their arms.
But Le Jeune, whose tour of duty
  Was at the midnight drear,
Was disturbed by sounds peculiar
  That fell weirdly on the ear.

The hoot of the owl repeated,
  The cry of whippoorwill,
Nearer, and ever nearer,
  Through darkness dense and still.
Then swiftly rousing de Orville,
  They learn the foe is nigh,
And quietly rouse the voyageurs,
  Prepared to win or die.

So coolly they wait the onset,
  And just at the dawn's pale light
Comes a flight of hissing arrows,
  And on the fading night
Bursts a yell all fierce and hideous,
  As, opening the affray,
By a wild rush to overwhelm
  They hope to win the day.

But bursts the crash of arquebuse
  And roar of musketoon,
And the fatal stroke of halberd,
  And swords that deal death's doom.

And the Ojibways reel backward
   With many a brave laid low,
Close beside the silver waters,
   With their gentle ebb and flow.

But the Ojibways, though repellèd,
   Are firm and undismayed ;
And fiercely they rush down again
   From the dense cedar shade.
Preceded by a hail of arrows,
   With tomahawk, spear, and knife,
They spring to deadly encounter,
   Hand to hand, and life for life !

But again out-crash the arquebuse,
   And roar the musketoons ;
Delivered is the scathing fire
   By sections and platoons.
The brave Ojibways are falling fast,
   But they fiercely press the foe,
And shouts and cries are ringing
   As they stagger to and fro.

And stern Mitwaos, unflinching,
   A lofty soul so brave,
Calmly and proudly directing,
   Death-dealing strokes he gave.
And on the right, Leaping Panther,
   Gallantly leading the way,
By example to his warriors
   Must surely win the day.

Lone Wolf on the left is foremost,
   An avalanche in the storm
Of battle, sternly raging there
   On that September morn !

Again they are driven backward,
  With ranks bloody and torn ;
But they rally, and charge again,
  'Though of many red braves shorn.

Once more for their homes and nation—
  They'll leap on the foe once more,
And wrest from him the victory,
  Or die by Pelee's shore.
Again rose their shout of defiance,
  Their bosoms were aflame ;
And those fearless, dusky heroes
  Rushed to the carnage again.

De Orville had not been idle,
  But detached the brave Le Jeune
To turn their flank by the marshlands,
  And, in the onset, soon
To fall on the rear of Mitwaos
  With the deadly musketoons—
Two score of valiant Frenchmen,
  With volleys by platoons.

The shouts of the enraged combatants,
  As on each other they fell,
And the roar of the musketoons
  Seemed as a blast from hell !
The air was hissing with arrows,
  As they closed in the strife ;
Spear, tomahawk, knife, and warclub
  Drank many a Frenchman's life.

But the lance, the sword, and halberd
  Do well their deadly work ;
Not once do those gallant Frenchmen
  The fiery ordeal shirk.

THE OJIBWAYS.

Ha ! see, where the fight grows deadly,
  Meet de Orville and Mitwaos—
Proudly seeking each other,
  Their deadly weapons cross.

And as the red lightning's flash
  They come to the fierce assault,
And mighty blows fall fast like hail ;
  They spring like panthers, and vault,
To thrust, to guard, and to ward
  The crushing blow of the brands,
Followed swift by skilful strokes
  Delivered by master hands.

De Orville is cool and collected,
  With sinews strong as steel ;
Mitwaos he hath sorely wounded—
  Ah ! see the totter and reel
Of the unyielding chieftain,
  Who sinks, aye, sinks and dies!
And the Ojibways' hearts are broken ;
  List to their mournful cries !

Just then from the south came crashing
  The fire of brave Le Jeune ;
And the red men fell thick and fast
  To the roar of musketoon.
Assailed from the front and the rear,
  And their brave chieftain dead,
A panic seized upon them,
  And they turned by the shore and fled !

Fled southward, beyond the hillocks,
  Leaving their wounded and slain—
Never again to know freedom,
  But degradation and pain !

There was mourning in the wigwams
　For the braves that came no more—
Gone to be with Manitou—
　And the nation's heart is sore.

And many an Indian maiden
　Pined in the cedar shade,
And the tender Singing Redbird
　Soon in her grave was laid ;
And many an Indian mother,
　Once joyous as the day,
Mourned for her sons death-silenced,
　And forever hid away.

And the old men sit in silence
　Beside the sobbing shore ;
Hushed is the song and laughter,
　It resoundeth nevermore
Through cedar and pine glades ever
　Rustling to and fro,
Just as the winds caressed them
　Three hundred years ago !

CHAPTER VI.

The stern victors, too, are mourning
　Over their dauntless slain ;
Full twoscore of death-stilled heroes,
　Relieved of life's care and pain,
After the battle was over,
　Lone Wolf and good Pontgravé
Were found in the grasp of each other,
　And were laid in one grave away.

Then in the cut through the Narrows
　The slain were buried deep,
And a requiem mass sung o'er them,
　And forever there they sleep.

The Frenchmen then turned eastward,
　　Over the wide lagoon,
By the domes of busy muskrat
　　And affrighted mallard and loon,

And disappeared in the distance,
　　By the eastern shore afar ;
While a truce for a space is given
　　To exterminating war.
But a hundred years of despoiling
　　Ruined the Ojibways,
And dwindled away the nation,
　　And miserable grew their days.

Their rights were all unregarded
　　When the dominant white man came ;
Then the red man grew degenerate,
　　And his sun went down in shame.
To-day by the Narrows dreaming,
　　No vestige or relic we trace
Of the once proud Indian nation,
　　Save their bones at the Carrying Place.*

Uncovered by the storms of centuries,
　　That drift the sands away,
White and ghastly they are mouldering
　　Remorselessly to decay.
But beyond the northern marshlands,
　　In regions far away,
Wander two quaint, lonely relics,
　　Poor Joe and Bill Ohippewa.

---

* Indian tradition goes to show that a fierce battle occurred at the Carrying Place between the Ojibways and Voyageurs. Proof of this seems to be furnished in the fact that the "cut" there is full of human bones.

To-day, where the south winds murmur
   By Pelee's lovely shores,
I pause in sad meditation,
   And the mind in fancy soars
Backward through time's dim corridors;
   Dreamily thoughts will flow
To the palmy days of the Ojibways
   Three hundred years ago.

WRECKED.

ALL along the sea-lines dreary,
   Dark and threatening the storm arose;
And shadows appalling crept o'er us,
   Disturbed was the ocean's repose!
And madly it leaped upon us,
   Engulfed in a deadly gloom,
As the sea's tumultuous fury
   Hurled our ship on to certain doom!

Wrecked on the vastness of ocean,
   Cast up on an isle remote,
Storm-worn by the roll of centuries,
   By the billows savagely smote—
An interminable expansion
   Of stern dreariness all around,
Indescribable desolation,
   And a weird solitude profound!

And this forever before me,
   Wearing my spirit away;
God's hand seems heavy upon me,
   And I'm very weary to-day.

And ever a fair face haunts me,
    White hands that put coldly away —
Are ye beckoning over the ocean?
    Is regret in thy bosom to-day?

And through the weirdness of night-time
    I hear the moaning, incessant roar
Of the waves, that ever repeateth,
    Sobbingly, "Lanore, nevermore!"
Thus through my feverish dreaming
    It evermore seemeth to me
That her name forever is murmured
    By the lonesome voice of the sea.

And thus I'm wearily waiting
    The rescue, that never comes,
Alone on this desolate islet
    The mariner distantly shuns;
Straining my worn eyes out ever
    O'er the dreary wastes of the sea;
But no ship—no ship e'er cometh,
    And pleading hope dieth in me.

Aye, nothing but sky and ocean,
    Encircling me everywhere,
And the boom and swash of the billows,
    And the sun's incessant glare!
This only by day and by day,
    This for the years on years,
Alone, in the wilds of the ocean,
    Worn out with despair and tears.

THE BATTLE OF CHRYSLER'S FARM.

FOUGHT NOVEMBER 11TH, 1813. AMERICAN FORCE, 2,000; BRITISH
AND CANADIANS, 800.

WITH his right resting on the St. Lawrence,
  His left by a sheltering wood,
Morrison deployed his eight hundred
  And in the clear field firmly stood ;
Eight hundred firm British and Canadians,
  Determinedly biding there,
With the Red Cross Banner above them,
  Flaunting proudly in the crisp, cool air.

Well they knew that Boyd was advancing
  With two thousand to crush their line ;
But they stood like a wall, and as silent,
  In that trying, momentous time.
Aye, for the moment before the battle
  Far more dreadfully tries men's souls
Than when thousands are falling about them,
  And its madd'ning din round them rolls !

Then, too, it was an event momentous
  For this fair Canada of ours—
So much on the stern issue depended,
  So much on two desperate hours.
Nigh and nigher, wilder and higher,
  To blaring trump and rolling drum,
Covering their front with a skirmish line,
  On in war's wild clamor they come !

" Fire not a shot till the word is given!
  Let the proud foe draw very near ;
Then, like an avalanche, sweep their blue ranks—
  Remain steady, and have no fear ! "

4

Thus Morrison cried to his thin red line,
    Silently awaiting the word ;
Though the foe had opened with clamorous roar,
    Not a man in that firm line stirred.

At last the British the signal receive,
    And a mighty blow is given ;
A devastating rush of iron hail
    Through the foeman's ranks is driven.
And, oh ! how that red line volleyed and flamed
    Cool and steady, they fired low,
And crash after crash, in tumultuous din,
    Fell on the suffering foe !

And for two consuming and fatal hours,
    They struggled 'mid smoke and flame,
Till the earth was strewn with the gallant dead,
    Where Boyd hurled his thousands in vain.
Then ruined and beaten, and punished sore,
    He fled from defeat away ;
Victory perched on our banners once more
    On that ever-remembered day.

Canadian and British valor prevailed,
    And down through the annals of time
Their heroic deeds we commemorate,
    In hist'ry as jewels to shine.
O sunny land of the dear Maple Leaf,
    In union abiding and free
Under the Old Flag of a thousand years,
    Floating o'er us from sea to sea !

SUMMER TWILIGHT.

I SIT at the dear twilight hour
    Where the lilies and roses sleep,
And the thoughts that come unto me
    Are oh ! so calm and so sweet.
I list the sound of a footfall
    I know will come unto me
At the golden glow of sunset,
    When shadows steal o'er the sea,

All restful and soul refreshing
    As dew to the drooping flower,
Inwardly invigorating,
    Imparting new life and power.
And thus, removed from the turmoil
    Of day, with its din and strife,
I listen in calm contentment
    To the hum of insect life.

The songs I hear in the branches,
    Just stirred by the wandering breeze,
A concert of matchless music,
    Fill my heart with gladsome ease.
The silvery, mystic moonlight
    Enfoldeth the earth and the sea,
And the summer night is throbbing
    In nature's full harmony.

O sun, and sea, and shadow !
    O eve with thy dreamy light !
I revel amid thy splendor,
    Enrapt in a subtle delight !
Aleene ! I await thy coming,
    And the clasp of thy gentle hand,
To wander in blissful dreaming
    Near heaven's own borderland !

CANADIAN HOMES.

CANADIAN homes ! Canadian homes !
  Ye dot this wide Dominion o'er,
From the Atlantic's ebb and flow
  To the far, far Pacific's shore !
Nestling by a thousand streams,
  Crowning a thousand lofty hills,
A thousand valleys own thy sway,
  The patriot e'er with rapture thrills.

A hundred rivers wend their way
  By fertile plains toward the sea,
Bearing rich products of the soil
  In undisturbed security ;
And the great chain of inland seas,
  Teeming with commerce and with trade—
The land is proud of her true sons,
  And the real progress they have made.

Thy mountains tower to the skies,
  And free, wild winds roam o'er thy plains ;
And he who seeks this great, broad land
  His freedom and a good home gains.
Thy mountain sides and wide foothills
  Yield up rich ores of every name ;
Exhaustless is thy hidden store,
  Millions of wealth the seekers gain.

The matchless fisheries on our coasts,
  Our seas and rivers, lakes and streams,
Assure to all a rich reward—
  They so plenteously do teem.

Our railroads span the continent,
    A vast expanse from shore to shore ;
From north to south, from east to west,
    They stretch this grand Dominion o'er.

A system of canals have we
    Unequalled—search the world so wide—
Connecting all our waterways
    By lake and stream to ocean's side.
They come and go, the white-winged ships,
    Bearing rich burdens to and fro ;
We have enough, aye and to spare ;
    Our hearts with gratitude do glow.

Our kine are on a thousand hills ;
    Our wheat and corn lands, rich and rare,
Yield golden grain abundantly ;
    With the whole world do we compare.
The luscious grape here is produced,
    The vines are purple with its glow ;
The apple, peach, and pear, and plum,
    In plenty and perfection grow.

Invigorating our atmosphere—
    With skies of the intensest blue—
Producing an indomitable race,
    With brave, true hearts to dare and do.
Here woman is as beautiful
    As e'er this great wide world hath seen,
And in her dear Canadian home
    She reigns an honored queen.

Our famous schools dot o'er the land,
    Free as the winds that roam our plains,
And ignorance doth flee away ;
    Happily, intelligence reigns.

Noble colleges and institutes
　　Throughout this goodly land abound;
Within the easy reach of all
　　Is education to be found.

Thus blest, the Canadian lifts his head,
　　And all things dares in manly pride,
For man to man, the wide world o'er,
　　He's equal, proved and tried.
Remember it, doubting cynic,
　　History proves his sterling worth,
And in arms he is co-equal
　　With the bravest ones of earth.

And in the world's wide, busy marts,
　　In science, trade, and cultured art,
In the front rank he e'er is found,
　　Bearing no menial second part.
Contending with the bravest there,
　　He holds the fierce, disputed way—
Persistence and efficiency
　　Are sure to win the sternest day.

Religious tolerance have we,
　　A people chaste by Christian love;
Thousands of church-spires point the way
　　To the celestial courts above.
Thus blest, we dwell in freedom's light,
　　Defenders of our country's cause,
Loving our dear Canadian homes,
　　Respecting and keeping her laws.

These free and fair Canadian homes
　　Acadia's vales do beautify;
Her cities gleam like diadems,
　　Her towers mount upward to the sky.

And where New Brunswick lifts her head
In vigorous, friendly rivalry,
They shine like jewels in a crown,
An anchor to our unity.

Prince Edward's Island by the sea
Is safely, sternly girded round,
Taught by all nature to be free ;
Influenced by her voice profound
They build, secure in freedom's light,
A fabric safe, enduring, grand,
Proud of their dear island home,
And of this fair Dominion land.

Our provinces beside the sea
Send out their ships to every land ;
Alert to every enterprise,
The world's esteem they do command.
Aye, they are known on every sea ;
In every clime, and isle remote,
The Maple Leaf, our emblem dear,
Protectingly o'er them doth float.

Quebec ! Quebec ! thou dowered queen
Of beauty ! for thee nature smiles ;
A vista wide of hill and vale,
A river with a thousand isles,
Above whose calm, majestic breast
Frowns an impregnable citadel,
A safeguard to our entrance-gate,
Where Wolfe and Montcalm fearless fell.

Historic and heroic days
Those stern defiant cliffs have known,
The thunder of the battle strife,
Wild cheer, defeat, and dying moan.

Beautiful and historic stream,
　　Flow on, flow on, toward the sea—
The outlet to our wide domain—
　　Flow on in calm tranquillity !

Heroes of old ascended thee,
　　Brave men that would not be denied ;
They pierced the wilds beyond the flood,
　　And death and danger they defied.
From Saguenay to Ottawa,
　　Across the blue Laurentian hills,
Are homes of the French *habitant*,
　　And love for thee his warm heart thrills.

With habits all so queer and quaint,
　　Their social life we plainly trace ;
E'er faithful to their usages,
　　A happy and contented race.
And they have stood by Britain's side
　　When war was rife on every hand—
De Salaberry at Chateauguay
　　Dealt a good blow for this fair land.

Ontario speaketh to our heart—
　　More blest, and more diversified
Are the rich blessings of her soil—
　　We greet her e'er with love and pride.
Numerous cities dot her o'er,
　　Hamlets and town by hundreds rise,
A vigorous and enduring growth,
　　Throbbing with trade and enterprise.

Pastoral scenes so fair and sweet
　　Meet the glad, enraptured gaze ;
By verdured hill and lovely vale,
　　And a thousand broad highways,

By lake and stream and riverside,
   The children's laugh and mothers' song
Float out along the summer air,—
   A busy, bright, and happy throng.

O happy homes and loving hearts,
   By rural scenes, or city's ways !
Pinched not by poverty and wrong,
   Blest in the fulness of your days!
The busy days pass swiftly by,
   The evening brings good cheer along ;
Canadian homes are bright and gay,
   And purified by love and song.

Manitoba bursts on our view,
   The prairies stretching far away,
Where thousands make their happy homes,
   Blessing the auspicious day
They sought and found this "great lone land."
   And still they come from every shore,
Seeking out free Canadian homes,—
   And there is room for millions more.

Here towns are rising everywhere,
   A vigorous growth on every hand ;
Industry's ceaseless, cheerful din
   Is heard throughout this goodly land.
Then, Manitobans, thrice three cheers
   Ring out ! ring out, in swelling tones,
A shout for this Dominion wide,
   And for these new Canadian homes !

The prairie province opes the way
   To these far vast and fertile plains ;
The wheatlands of the world lie here—
   This Canada to all proclaims.

And on and on we wend our way,
  O'er areas vast our steps are drawn ;
We flit by hill and lake and stream,
  Beyond the great Saskatchewan.

We gain Alberta's grazing lands,
  Lovely with vales and streams and hills—
And countless kine are herded here.
  Stretching away to the foothills
Are undulations, emerald sweeps
  Of sunny plains in beauty drest,
With mountains towering to view—
  This is Canada's "great wild west."

We pierce the Rockies in our flight ;
  The steely way is swift and sure,
Our land's necessity and pride,
  Long as our union shall endure.
But on and on we safely glide,
  By mountains vast and stern and hoary ;
Our pen but faintly can portray
  The scenes of panoramic glory.

Here lovely valleys meet the eye,
  All rife with summer's winsome gladness ;
The summits of those gray cold peaks
  Are wrapt in winter's sternest sadness,
Defying the elements' rage
  Through mystic and untold ages.
God's hand hath builded them in might
  To commemorate His pages.

Below is verdant leaf and flower,
  Flora and fauna everywhere ;
The peaks are wrapt in perpetual snow
  And lit by the sun's fierce glare.

Below is the sigh of soft winds
　And the ripple of cooling streams ;
Aloft is the bitterest air,
　Where the frost eternally gleams.

The sides of the mountains ever
　Are great waves of emerald green ;
While the streams, from summits falling
　White as snow, are foaming between ;
The cedar and pine trees ever
　Tossing aloft their fronded plumes,
Where the winds forever whisper
　Nature's subtle and mournful runes.

And through and beyond the Selkirks,
　Down the Fraser we calmly glide—
All hail, fair British Columbia,
　Thou rich gem by the ocean's side !
Lovely land of mountain and stream,
　We greet thee with bosom aflame ;
A crown of laurel awaits thee,
　We sing of thy greatness and fame.

The fleets of the world come to thee ;
　Thy cities are growing apace ;
Thou art vigorously gaining,
　And everywhere we may trace
Prosperity and refinement
　In those far west Canadian homes ;
The field and the mine contribute,
　And we hail thee in heartiest tones.

Out o'er a measure of ocean,
　Of ripple and bright sunny smile,
The sea accords us a welcome
　To Vancouver's fair sea-girt isle—

Last link in the chain of our union,
　　A bright gem in the Western sea,
Imbued with loyal devotion,
　　Prosperous and happy and free.

We breathe the ozone of ocean,
　　Where our mammoth ships sail away
To the land of the Celestials,
　　And the Japs, at the break of day.
And southward unto Australia,
　　And the distant isles of the sea,
Our commerce is fast extending,
　　Reaching out vigorously.

Northward, by Behring and Polar seas,
　　E'er fearlessly our good ships go,
Undeterred by storms of the deep,
　　Or perpetual frost and snow ;
Seeking and finding seal and whale,
　　Faithful hearts that know no fear,
Venturing all in the enterprise
　　For their home and loved ones dear.

Returning by our "golden north,"
　　Penetrating the Arctic zone,
Bordering on the frozen deep,
　　All so desolate and so lone ;
Flitting by Great Slave and Bear Lakes,
　　"The fur country," winning our way
By Rupert's Land, lonesome and strange,
　　Leading downward by Hudson Bay.

Gaining the stormy Atlantic,
　　And wafted, by headland and shore,
Past the homes of our brave fishers
　　On e'er desolate Labrador,

Thus we have circled the Dominion,
 A vast and wonderful domain ;
Exhaustless in her resources,
 The world shall yet ring with her fame.

Then up in your might, Canadians !
 No matter what your creed may be,
And stand for country and the right,
 E'er steadfast in our unity.
The half a continent is ours,
 Then let our hearts be all aflame ;
The field 's sufficient for us all,
 Where all may win both wealth and fame.

We love this fair Canadian land,
 O'erstrewn with mountain, plain and lake ;
And we would even dare to die
 For our dear homes and country's sake.
Remember it ?   Aye, remember—
 They burn within our thoughts to-day—
Queenston Heights, famed Lundy's Lane,
 Stony Creek, Quebec, Chateauguay.

There, side by side with the regulars,
 Our fathers faced the invading foe,
And swept them from our sacred shores
 By stern-delivered blow on blow.
And should they dare to come again
 Where the old flag in freedom waves,
We'll meet them firm, unyielding still,
 And strew these peaceful shores with graves.

Hurrah ! hurrah for Canada !
 For the land that is great and free ;
" The flag that's braved a thousand years,"
 Ever that grand old flag for me.

Touch not its daring crimson folds—
  It bears no cringing coward stain;
No traitor hand shall pull it down,
  Nor mar its glorious fame.

It floats to-day o'er every sea;
  In every clime, in every zone,
That daring flag defiantly
  Is to the free wild winds out-thrown.
The sun may rise and set again,
  But not on Britain's grand domain—
The Empire dots the wide world o'er,
  And Britain's heart is all aflame.

Hurrah! hurrah for Canada!
  And the Empire that rules the sea!
In union with the Motherland
  We are ever safe and free.
Thus, moving on from year to year,
  All time shall sing our brave story—
A united empire rolling on
  To an immortal glory.

THINK OF ME.

List when the wind in summertime is sighing,
And a wealth of verdant bloom is on the lea;
Seek the path our feet together used to wander,
      And think of me.

Watch when the sunset's tender glow of evening
Fades into twilight's dreamy ecstasy,
And thy soul is soothed by nature's subtle fulness,
      And think of me.

And when the shadowy arms of night enfoldeth
The hills, and darken o'er the throbbing sea;
Steal tenderly out beneath the stars' pale beaming,
      And think of me.

Go when the autumn leaves are sadly falling,
And the melancholy winds appeal to thee,
And stillness broods where grass and flowers are dying,
      And think of me.

And when thy soul to music's touch is thrilling,
And thy voice repeats in tenderest melody
The songs we loved when you and I were dreaming,
      And think of me.

Weep when the dreary autumn rain is falling,
And sobbing winds are strewing o'er the lea
A wealth of golden leaves and pale dead flowers,
      And think of me.

And when thy day of life is slowly waning
Into the mystic light of the eternity,
Call back the dreamy years of life's glad morning,
      And think of me.

DULAC DES ORMEAUX ; OR, THE THER-
MOPYLÆ OF CANADA.

DESTRUCTION menaced fair Mount Royal,
   And the bravest cheek grew pale
When from the shadowy, awesome forest
   Came the blood-curdling tale
That the unsparing, ferocious Iroquois
   Would encompass them once more ;
Twelve hundred plumed and painted warriors
   Would in fury on them pour.

Palisaded around and bastioned,
   But war-worn and wasted so,
With the pale shadow of doom upon them,
   How shall they foil the dread foe ?
Often, when life and its cares seem darkest,
   Doth aid and guidance appear,
And the storm and the threatened danger
   On the horizon disappear.

Thus saved was the lovely Mount Royal
   By as heroic a deed
As e'er blazon'd the page of history ;
   And it came in their sore need.
Noble, self-sacrificing des Ormeaux,
   And sixteen fair youths so brave,
Resolved on a desperate rescue,
   Their homes and country to save.

Aye, resolved though to a man they perish,
   The rescue should be complete ;
And prepared for the awful issue—
   'Twas death, but never defeat.

Making their wills, and solemn confession,
   In war's panoply arrayed
They received the holy sacrament,
   And solemnly knelt and prayed.

And bidding their well-beloved friends farewell,
   As men who to death march away—
(Aye, and so were they, for all, all were slain
   In the merciless affray).
And stemming the current of swift St. Anne,
   They fearlessly launch away
O'er the sparkling Lake of Two Mountains,
   Onward, by night and by day.

And by the pass of the Long Sault Rapid,
   In a redoubt deserted, old—
A mere breastwork of logs and abatis,
   Covered by moss and mould—
There, with forty Hurons and Algonquins,
   They took their intrepid stand,
And waited the approach of the Iroquois,
   Who were very near at hand.

The French and their red allies strengthened
   Their frail post with earth and sod,
Leaving twenty loopholes for musketoons ;
   And, commending all to God,
They took post, prepared now and watchful
   Under the All-seeing Eye,
To fight heroically for their homes,
   And, if need, for them to die.

"Hist ! hist !" Dulac des Ormeaux whispered,
   "Make ready the musketoons ;
Hear the signal hoot of the boding owl,
   And the cry of lonely loons !

'Tis the stealthy approach of the Iroquois,
   Signaling their reptile advance ;
Mon braves, let's teach them what Frenchmen can do
   For love and glory of France !

" Let them come, let them come, now, very near,
   Then level the musketoons ;
Answer thus the hoot of the boding owl,
   And the cry of the lonely loons !
Hand to hand, use the halberd, sword and lance,
   Make these reptiles bite the grass,
And strike as the Spartans did of old,
   When Leonidas kept the pass !

" See ! through the dim and shadowy forests,
   They like deadly serpents creep—
Mark the cruel light in their devilish eyes,
   As our frail defence they sweep !
Steady, brothers ; comrades, aim low and sure,
   Let every good missile tell !
Rain sure on the malignant Iroquois
   A consuming fire of hell !"

And they opened then with crash and flame,
   And wild, savage cries of pain
Pierced through the roar of the musketoons ;
   Swift again, and yet again,
Sure volleys burst, hurling death, dismay,
   The old gray redoubt around,
And the withering fire from that brave band
   Struck many a red fiend down.

For five long days the Iroquois
   Swarmed around that frail redoubt,
Repulsed again, aye, and yet again.
   Worn by hunger, thirst and doubt,

And want of sleep, the Frenchmen prayed,
  And fought with valiant might
Through long, frightful days of carnage
  And the horrors of the night.

Iroquois reinforcements now arrived
  And the Hurons, in dismay
At the dreadful, inevitable result,
  In desertion fled away.
For three days longer seven hundred foes
  Beleaguered that frail redoubt,
Defied by the score of dauntless youths,
  Still barring the red fiends out

By a ceaseless fire of the musketoons ;
  Keeping their post night and day
With the unyielding courage of despair,
  Holding the red scourge at bay.
And, reeling in uttermost weariness,
  Realizing their doom is sealed,
They can but die in the unequal strife,
  But must not—no, must not yield !

The Iroquois, covered by wooden shields,
  Rushed up to the palisades ;
Up swift from the river's concealing banks,
  And sheltering forest glades.
Crouching below the fire of musketoons,
  They furiously cut away
Post after post of the frail palisades
  That held them so long at bay.

Firing through the loops on their pent-up foes,
  Tearing a breach in the walls,
They swarm within with ferocious joy ;
  But many a red fiend falls

By desperate sweep of the Frenchmen's steel,
   Deliv'ring lightning blows ;
Asking no quarter, and receiving none,
   From cruel, insatiate foes.

Thus selling their lives in a noble cause,
   Not one of the French are spared ;
But hundreds of unsparing Iroquois
   Their gory death-bed shared.
Thus checked was the advance of the Iroquois
   And Canada was saved
By as heroic an act of devotion
   As war's annals ever gave.

And the defence of the Long Sault passage
   Shall nevermore fade away ;
All time shall honor the heroic defence—
   Canada's Thermopylæ !
Pause, Canadians ! pause by this spot—
   Seek the Long Sault's rapid flow—
Call back the famed scene enacted here
   Two hundred long years ago.

GOLDEN HAIR.

A HEAD of golden hair,
  With many a silken fold ;
A face as beautiful as e'er
  Was wrought in human mould ;
An eye as blue as ever
  Italia's skies can be,
That shone as stars of heaven
  In soul-lit purity ;

A form that tranced the vision ;
  A matchless, perfect grace
Of a life all pure and God-like
  Lighting the sweet, fair face ;
A voice as low and silv'ry
  As flutes at eventime,
Or trill of harps Æolian,
  Tender and so divine ;

A head of golden hair,
  Haunting my soul alway,
In the silent hours of dreamland,
  Or blaze of noontide day.
Yet vain are all thy dreamings,
  O heart ! A year ago
We laid that head so golden
  Under the daisies low.

THE CONVICT.

FRENZIED by the destroying curse of drink,
  In fury uncontrolled I struck him down ;
The insult was bitter, and I went mad—insane—
  And with one fell blow slew him, and fled the town.
In a moment I was sobered, and realized
  The awful deed my savage hand had done,
And a dreadful terror on my senses fell ;
  Before arrest, stern punishment had begun.

Oh ! the horror of that moment when I realized
  That I my fellowman, once friend, had slain ;
That I was lost forever and for evermore,
  And my brow burned deep by the damning brand of
    Cain.
"Lost ! lost !" I cried in agony to heaven.
  Demoniac laughter on my pained ear fell—
The answer to my prayer came not from heaven ;
  It seemed to rise from lurid voids of hell.

Pursued, arrested, and for life condemned—
  Caged as a wild beast behind bolts and bars—
The iron door closed out the world so fair,
  The panoply of heaven, sun, moon, and stars ;
Closed out home, mother, father, sister, brother,
  And one that was so fair, and loved me so ;
Broken are their hearts, because I was so dear
  In the sinless happy days of long ago.

Once only was I lured by the red wine,
  And joined the revel in the maddening bowl.

'Twas fatal! In that appalling direful hour
    Lost was all the world, and ruined was my soul ;
Forgotten was my mother's warning, and
    I saw not the pit made for unwary feet,
But past the portal and the dividing line,
    My awful ruin was complete.

Stunned, and almost crazed by agony
    And remorse, I wept such bitter burning tears
As come from those, all lost to earth and heaven,
    Who, hopeless, brood o'er past and following years.
I prayed with awful fervency to heaven
    To forgive and heal my weary, broken heart,
Appealing for the lowliest place in paradise,
    That I might with the angels bear some humble part.

I know not, but sometimes it seems to me
    A pitying God will my fell deed forgive ;
Will lift the grievous burden from my weary soul,
    And let the suffering, forsaken sinner live.
And thus I wait behind the bars and iron door,
    In gloomy corridor or stifling cell,
Suffering the nameless horrors of the damned
    In this relentless, dreary, earthly hell.

THE BATTLE OF LACOLLE MILLS.

FOUGHT MARCH 30TH, 1814. AMERICAN FORCE, 4,000; BRITISH
AND CANADIAN, 340.

TEN miles inland they ventured
  To the "Stone Mills" at Lacolle;
Four thousand rough invaders,
  Our country to control.
Canadians e'er rally quickly
  When dangers thicken round,
And to duty's call immediate
  Give no uncertain sound.

The call was swiftly given,
  And the "Stone Mills" occupied,
Loopholed and greatly strengthened,
  And the enemy defied.
Of stern British and Canadians
  The little force formed round;
Resolved at every hazard
  To hold their vantage ground.

The foe moved up on every side,
  And made their grand attack;
The old walls blazed in fierce return,
  And drove the proud foe back.
Three guns were now brought forward
  The mill to batter down;
The "Old Stone Mill," the good old mill,
  In defiance still did frown.

The gunners fell beside their guns,
   So hot, so fierce the fire
The British poured upon them
   To prevent them drawing nigher.
For two long hours the cannonade
   Stormed at the old mill walls—
The good old mill, the brave old mill,
   That totters not nor falls.

" Ho, Voltigeurs, and brave regulars !
   Form quickly side by side,
And charge the foe's battering guns,"
   The gallant Handcock cried.
And they swept across the open
   Up to the cannon's side—
Those grand soldiers' hearts were burning,
   As an army they defied.

Swiftly through the infantry's fire,
   Up to the cannon's flame,
So fearlessly they struggled,
   Charged and charged again.
Those gallant men could do no more,
   And they fell back fighting still,
Gaining once again the safety
   Of the sheltering mill.

The fire was now redoubled,
   The old mill blazed and roared ;
A deadly hail from all the loops
   Upon the foe was poured.
'Twas all too hot for Wilkinson
   At Lacolle Mills that day,
And he turned about in utter rout
   And swiftly fled away.

Heroic Handcock! heroic men!
   Thy mem'ry shall not die—
Canadians, join with me to-day,
   And shout it to the sky!
Weave, then, a fadeless laurel wreath
   For those who nobly gave
E'en life for British liberty,
   And this fair land to save.

THE NINETEENTH CENTURY MAIDEN.

O RADIANT maiden! thou art so fair,
With thy azure eyes and thy golden hair;
The bloom of the lily and rose on thy face,
Thy sunny smile and thy exquisite grace,
The joyous light of thy innocent eyes,
Deep wells of the soul and clear as the skies;
And pure as the snow the sheen on thy brow—
O mayst thou e'er be as stainless as now.
Thy voice is as soft as the summer wind,
Thrilling, pathetic, a music divine;
And wonderful is thy power to-day,
And thy influence and thy gentle sway.
The world does homage to-day at thy feet,
A captive at will to slavery sweet.

Man battles amain the vast wide world o'er;
He delves in the mines for their precious store;
For the gems of the sea, searches far and wide,
Through the rage of the storm and the rushing tide.
Aye, in every clime, and in every zone,
He struggles with might for thee and home;

Stepping bravely to battle to win thy smiles,
Fearlessly leading where the foremost files
Charge to the battery's flash and thunder—
A hero for thee, to the world a wonder.
With the battle o'er, the victory won,
And hope beaming brightly to cheer him on ;
With riches and honors and fame replete,
He seeks but to lay them down at thy feet,
E'er trusting and honoring thee, his pride,
Asking only the bliss to be at thy side.

There are to-day many wandering feet,
Reckless, despairing, and ruined complete ;
Driven from the light of thy witching eyes,
They are drifting away 'neath sunless skies.
Oh, nineteenth century maiden, fair !
With thy azure eyes and thy golden hair,
Of thy subtle power beware, beware !
Drive not unheeding to ruin, despair,
Hearts that are noble, unselfish, and true,
That would all things dare, even death, for you.
Let all thy ways be e'er kindly and good ;
Thus crowning thy pure gentle womanhood
With graciousness, love, and truth most wise,
Guiding men e'er safely toward the skies.

MUSIC.

CELESTIAL concord of divinest sounds,
  Music has solaced all the years,
Smoothed the rough road for worn and tired feet,
  And lulled the grievous pain, too deep for tears.
All my days it's been a comfort unto me,
  A subtle influence, chastening all life,
Lifting up despairing hope and trust once more,
  Guiding past the hidden shoals of sin and strife.

As a boy, I heard it flooding all the fields,—
  Nature's songs appealing ever unto me—
Bird lays, and the soothing winds that steal away,
  And the deep, eternal murmur of the sea.
I hear it in the harmony of the night,
  When stars glow in the unfathomable deep,
And when the foliage and the nodding flowers,
  Alike with all the world, are wrapt in sleep.

I hear it in the patter of the summer rain
  That freshens all and cools the thirsty ground ;
And in the thunder's reverberating roar
  I hear a harmony majestic and profound.
I hear it in the tiniest rivulet
  That winds its laughing way by mead and lea,
Kissing the feet of sunny emerald hills,
  And the glide of mighty rivers to the sea.

O voices! voices! singing, ever singing
　　In joyful, tender notes from day to day ;
I hear the songs I love forever ringing—
　　Their echo and re-echo never dies away.
A thousand instruments seem ever playing—
　　Stringed instruments, reeds, lutes of sweetest tone—
Martial bands, and trumpets swelling ever,
　　Stir the hero, and the king upon his throne!

Play on! play on! all instruments of music,
　　Join all your voices in the ecstasy of song,
And the deep harmony of nature blending
　　Will elevate and purify the world's vast throng.
If I should march to battle, play for me
　　The strains that lift the shrinking, doubting soul ;
And when I cross the dark and fatal current,
　　Sing, and the Lethean waters shall not o'er me roll.

WATERLOO.

CHAPTER I.

NEAR Belgium's gay capital, the long night through,
Paced the alert sentinel of Waterloo,
And through the lonesome watches beat the dreary rain,
While wandering winds sobbed o'er the darkened plain.
Through the chilling, dismal gloom of the boding night
Beat shadowy wings in a weird, phantom flight.
Two mighty rival hosts lay along the dank hills,
And the bosom of Europe anxiously thrills.
Dread moment uncertain, the stern fate of a day
To crown and uncrown, and sweep thousands away
To doom ; impetuous youth and veteran gray
Must go down in the morrow's desperate fray.

Sleep well, gallant hearts ! Britain's hope and stern pride,
Imperial France, ye have dared and defied.
The invincible clans of Old Scotia are there,
And the manhood of Erin, so gallant and fair ;
England's noblest and best, in quiet repose,
Resistless in battle, the dread of their foes.
Slumber on, brave, true hearts ! rapt in tenderest dreams
Of Scotland's grand highlands, and lowlands, and streams ;
Of Erin's green isle, and her rivers and rills,
Her lakes that reflect back the sunny-clad hills ;
Of old England's green lanes by meadow and vale—
Heroic, fair land ! rich in romance and tale.
Noble trinity ! indissoluble, beautiful, brave,
The morrow brings victory, or death and the grave.

Aye, sleep on, then, sleep on, for never again
May ye reach the old homestead !   And alas, all in vain
The loved ones may anxiously wait there for you—
Their warm hearts were breaking when they bade you adieu.
But ye're here in true manhood to guard England's glory,
And all time shall ring with the immortal story.

Hark ! 'tis the bugle and the slogan's fierce cry,
Piercing the dawn e'er its gray shadows fly.
Repeat it again ! how it wakens and thrills !
Ha ! 'tis answered defiantly from those southern hills,
And a marshalling host in the pale dawn uprose,
The divisions of France, most gallant of foes.

But the Duke is alert, and draws up for the storm
Two lines of foot ; and at intervals forms
The horse in the rear in a stern, stately array,
To calmly abide the coming affray.
The guns of the Duke frown down from the hills,
And his intrepid soul with sure confidence thrills.
His reserves are formed up near Mont St. Jean,
His centre the Brussels road is lying between ;
And thus, with his grand dispositions complete,
He dares e'en the genius of Napoleon to meet.

And grand dispositions the Emperor, too, made,
And his lines of hills were sternly arrayed
With masses of infantry in contiguous lines ;
And supporting columns with skill he combines
With his famous cavalry at intervals in rear,
Divisions of uhlan, dragoon, and cuirassier.
His splendid artillery crown the heights everywhere,
And for the pending struggle they coolly prepare.
With his right on Planchenoit, his left lapping Merc Braine,
An imposing front is presented.   And there plain,

Near La Belle Alliance, his reserves can be seen ;
The " Old Guard " and the " Young Guard " in column
     between
Divisions of horse, and steel-clad cuirassiers,
And the Emperor they greet with *vives* and cheers.
On the Charleroi road he now takes his post,
From the centre to direct this magnificent host.
A brilliant staff is there grouped by his side,
And the " soldier of destiny " beams on them in pride.

Thus with two lines of heights, with death's valley between,
And the calmness of summer, of meadow and stream,
Napoleon is there where his proud eagles wave,
The genius of France seeks her glory to save.
But Wellington waits where the red banners stream :
The Lion is roused by the Eagle's fierce scream,
And like eagles they hover to fall on their prey,
Poised for the swoop, for a dread moment at bay.

CHAPTER II.

Dread moment ! there waiting the burst of the storm ;
And the bravest of hearts are anxiously torn.
Yet o'er the fierce grandeur of that famous scene
Shone the peaceful June sunlight mild and serene.
Ha ! from the left of the French, in splendid array,
Comes the opening attack of the fateful day !
Downward and onward, gaily, steadily before
The batteries' fierce flashing and opening roar !
Prince Jerome, their great leader, shouts " Forward !
     Avaunt ! "
And presses sternly the attack on stout Hougomont.
But the position is held by intrepid souls ;
Though the valor of France upon them rolls
In fiery masses, assaulting on every side,
The Guards stand firm there in unconquerable pride.

All through the red carnage of that dreadful day,
They held the divisions of France at bay.
Though thundered and stormed at, and torn by balls,
They hold Hougomont with its blood-stained walls ;
Though heaped and pent with Ponsonby's gallant slain,
The gory sacrifice there hath not been in vain.

Now tremble the hills by the bellowing thunder
Of the raging batteries, rending asunder
The grand advancing lines, or the devoted square,
And the charging squadrons, that so sorely fare
By the storms of fierce shot that around them fell,
Withering as the consuming red jaws of hell !

The British right wing had been fiercely assailed,
But the desp'rate assault had signally failed.
The Emperor's favorite move 's now brought to play,
To pierce the Duke's centre and hold Blucher at bay.
For this four gallant columns of infantry form,
With Kellermann's squadrons in support of the storm,
And seventy-four field guns to rend the Duke's squares.
None there of success or of vict'ry despairs !
Three resounding cheers for the Emperor they gave,
And for their leader Ney, " the bravest of the brave,"
And majestically descend the southern hills,
While admiration the lines of Britain thrills.

Onward, right onward, with firm measured gait,
Gaily and confidently to their impending fate.
But the British guns thunder down on them once more,
Tearing and rending to their incessant roar.
But Ney gains the ridge, and the cowed Belgians fly
Disgracefully before his column's loud cry.
But men more worthy of the name are found near,
Grim and determined, and devoid of all fear.

6

Picton ! the dauntless, immortal, grand fiery soul,
Will here bar the way to the gallant, onward roll
Of Ney.   He deploys two brigades into line two deep,
And prepares the swift advancing columns to sweep.
Then a deadly volley on the grand foe they pour,
Rending their proud ranks as through them it tore.
"Forward with the bayonet, charge home without fear!"
Shouts the hero, Picton, and there bursts a wild cheer
From the British line as it falls fierce on the foe,
That, confused, reels back to the valley below.

Now the Duke hurls on them a cavalry brigade ;
And, oh, the result of the wild charge they made!
Cutting down whole battalions of dismayed Gauls ;
And to Picton's proud prowess there instantly falls
Two thousand prisoners.   Then charge forward once more!
To the guns, to the guns that bellow and roar !
And they reach them, and sabre the French gunners
        there—
And Ney's mighty columns are filled with despair.
His supporting guns are made useless for the day,
And those valiant troopers ride proudly away.
But they ventured too far 'mid elation and cheers,
And are charged in return by Milhaud's cuirassiers.
Blown by the desperate work they had done,
'Twas wise to decline, and the encounter to shun.
Thus Ney's splendid attack completely failed,
Though four to one to the stern foe he assailed.
But in repelling this great attack Picton fell,
The intrepid commander all loved so well.
And Britain will hold him in remembrance dear—
Noble soldier ! Britain's hero ! a soul without fear !

CHAPTER III.

Now far on the horizon the Prussians appear ;
The Emperor cries, "Grouchy is coming, is near."

This to reanimate his divisions once more,
By repeated reverses grown doubtful and sore.
The cuirassiers are advancing with Milhaud again,
And columns on the left of the Duke fall in vain.
All along the vast lines falls fast the iron rain,
And the pale dead by thousands encumber the plain.
Grand cavalry charges sweep "death's valley" between—
Like fatal whirlwinds of wrath they glitter and gleam.
Crashing volleys from the steadfast infantry pour,
And from both lines of torn hills the guns madly roar.
Vast clouds of sulphurous smoke shroud the scene,
And the wounded by thousands in agony scream!

Ha! the Household Brigade meet the French Cuirassiers;
Like an avalanche they charge with three ringing cheers;
Like eagles they swoop down on that steel-clad brigade—
Oh, the flash of their sabres, and the havoc they made!
Crushed and bleeding the cuirassiers turn and fly,
Leaving squadrons of slain, and their wounded to die.
Fresh masses now attack La Haye Sainte once more;
Hougomont still resounds to the murderous roar
Of attacking lines, sacrificing thousands in vain,
For the bloodstained chateau they never shall gain.

The Emperor now seeks to hurl a crushing blow,
And flings his cavalry *en masse* on the foe;
Hoping still the Duke's grand centre to penetrate,
On the verge and vast ruin of impending fate.
The famous Kellermann directs this splendid array,
Trusting the result will decide the fate of the day.
But the Duke comprehends.   See his flashing gray eyes!
From line and from columns the command swiftly flies,
"Into square! into square! across the valley again
Comes the cavalry *en masse* to charge us amain!
To the guns! to the guns! rend their columns asunder;
Shake the earth once again; let Napoleon wonder

What manner of men he hath met here to-day.
Keep your ranks, hold your squares in invincible array!"
Steady the clans of Scotia sound the slogan once more.
Let it stir ye as never it stirred ye before.
Let Erin's hurrah through the storm fiercely break ;
Gallant souls, whose courage even death cannot shake.
Art still calm, Britain's sons, proudly waiting the shock ?
Aye, calm and cool, though the earth doth tremble and
    rock ;
Though rent your firm squares, and thinned your red lines,
Ye are dauntless still ; on your grim faces shines
An unconquerable light, flashing everywhere,
Firm as the abiding hills, shaken not by despair.

Steady now, fearless hearts !   See, the foe proudly comes,
Rolling on in huge masses where thunder the guns
That leap from the very earth in maddening roar.
And grape, shot and shell devastatingly tore
Through Kellermann's vast squadrons of horse, coming on
Steadily and gallantly, though thousands had gone
Down in the awful struggle, mangled and torn,
Since the opening glory of the summer morn.
They come, they come, in magnificent array !
And the gunners from their guns are driven away.
Like a whirlwind they charge on the devoted squares
Which Kellermann hoped to have caught unawares.
But they are ready; and before their bristling steel
The imperial squadrons now stagger and reel !

Round and round those stern squares they sweep madly in
    vain,
Falling there thick and fast in the withering rain
Of incessant volleys, that on them ruthlessly pour
From the heroic squares that are bleeding and sore.
And those famous steel-clad warriors of France fall fast,
Smitten and riven by the hot devouring blast.

They fall back—charge forward—and repeat it again,
Till the reddened earth is pent with their gallant slain.
But at last they fly from their ruinous sore defeat,
All mangled and broken and ruined complete.
From the firm squares the gunners rush forward once more,
And again the hot guns madly thunder and roar.
Thus all Napoleon's heavy horse at Waterloo
Was destroyed in attempts those squares to break through.
As the sea waves that rush on an iron-bound shore,
They rolled on the Duke, broke, and fled back once more.

CHAPTER IV.

But La Haye Sainte to Donzelot's infantry fell—
The heroic Frenchman fought there nobly and well—
Thus securing the Emperor a lodgment sought,
A strategic point for a decisive onslaught
On Wellington's centre, that he still seeks to gain,
Where his best troops were broken, and broken in vain.

Blucher is coming! hear his guns' opening roar,
Pressing the right of the French, now in peril sore.
The Emperor detaches Lobau's corps complete
And Dumont's horse this fatal new danger to meet.
But Bulow turns Lobau's left, and Planchenoit is won
Near to the going down of the red summer's sun.
But the Emperor checks Bulow with his Young Guard,
And for a time they gallantly keep watch and ward
O'er the right of the French, fighting desperately there—
Still hopeful, though desperately assailed everywhere.

Will the Emperor's star of destiny go down to-day,
And his vast fabric be swept forever away?
His sun of victory set now to rise no more,
And the splendor of his dreams die on War's stern shore?

Avalanches of attack he still hurls on the foe;
Ceaselessly and recklessly they surge to and fro
All along the Duke's firm lines, but surging in vain.
The bright valor of Britain those stern lines maintain
Unbroken by the desperate destroying strife,
Though to maintain them thousands are bereft of life.
The stratagems of a lifetime could not prevail;
His hitherto decisive moves were of no avail.
He might hurl his raging storms of grapeshot and shell,
He might thunder as the ravening maw of hell,
Hurl his cavalry *en masse* on the devoted squares,
Rush his infantry forward, and lay his deep snares,
Which must have ruined any other army complete,
Slaughtered, dismembered, and put to retreat;
But the Britons stood steadfast in undaunted pride,
And the legions of France they dared and defied.
And they cumbered death's valley with the enemy slain,
Like sheaves in the ripe harvest of winnow and wain.
And thus sorely assailed near the set of the sun,
The Iron Duke exclaims, "Would that night or Blucher
    might come!"

The hour of seven o'clock had now been told,
Still the rage of the battle uncertain rolled.
Like gladiators of old they tugged and tore,
And gory thousands have fallen to rise no more.
The burning issues of the day are deep and wide—
Shall Europe have liberty from the despotic pride
Of Imperial France, waged by a single mind,
A genius of war, to human sufferings blind?
But his fate is approaching in the lurid gleam
Of the loud raging cannon, and the living stream
Of Britain's deathless valor, that will never yield,
And they'll win it or perish, this desperate field.

A dark mass near La Belle Alliance is seen to form
Into gigantic columns, to drive like a storm

In irresistible fury o'er the death-strewn plain,
To o'erwhelm the Duke's centre and cut him in twain.
They are the Old Guard and Young, twelve thousand and
    more,
Veterans of a hundred battles, who o'er and o'er
Had grasped victory from defeat on many a field.
Surely Britain's array to these powers must yield.
The Emperor reserved them for a *coup de main,*
And he sent them forward assured they would gain
For him the victory.   And their triumphant cheer
Of " *Vive l'Empereur !* " rose from souls void of fear.
Majestically they descend the slope of the hill,—
'Tis a sight the most stony of natures to thrill,
The *elite* of the French army, as onward they go,
The heroes of Austerlitz, Wagram, and Marengo.
Between Hougomont and La Haye Sainte lies their way,
Where the British await them there, sternly at bay.

Now with redoubled vigor their batteries thunder
On the allied lines, firmly waiting yonder,
Where the devastating missiles ruthlessly pour
'Mid the horrible din and the deafening roar
Of the deadly conflict raging frightfully there,
And the moans of the dying and cries of despair.
The drooping spirits of his lines he must reanimate,
And sends an *aide-de-camp* at a lightning rate
To announce that Grouchy is coming—is near—
And his divisions lift up their voices and cheer.

Now from La Haye Sainte Donzelot pushes again
An avalanche of attack, like withering flame.
On the left centre of the allies, bruised and sore,
Are the stern German brigades, firm as rocks ; and o'er
The din and tumult the French legions might hear
The shout of defiance and the Germans' grand cheer.

"They're coming! the attack will be the centre, my lord,"
Said Lord Fitzroy Somerset, waving his good sword,
And directing, as he spoke, his glass on the foe,
The advancing columns in the red vale below.
"I see it," was Wellington's unmoved reply,
As he ordered Maitland's brigade to deploy, and lie
Down behind the ridge of the torn sheltering hill,
For a few moments longer restraining their will.
In front of them are formed in a firm red line
A brigade of infantry abiding their time.
On the right of the Guards is Adams's brigade,
Waiting the dread shock as though on parade.
Stationed above, and partly upon the road,
The grim guns form up, and quickly, silently load
With grape, and await the signal there to open—
Though all hearts are aflame, not a word is spoken.

It is an awful moment, one to try men's souls,
And the horrible din all about them rolls.
On the far left the Prussians are pounding away,
But the brave French fight sternly and hold them at bay.
All along our grand lines the French batter in vain,
Though the dead strew the hills and encumber the plain.

Dark masses of Guards climb the slope of the hill,
Stately columns coming on with confidence still ;
Their guns cease fire as above the ridge they now show,
Tipped with the gleam of the sunset's red glow.
Then began that cheer those who heard never could forget—
From those famed Belgian hills doth it echo yet.
From Hougomont, near the right, with its blood-stained
        walls,
To Papalotte on the left, it thunders and falls
In long-restrained, pent-up vengeance ; and through
The true instinct that valor teaches well they knew

The hour of trial had come, when that wild cry flew
From rank to rank, as it echoed and thundered anew.
"They come! they come!" repeat it, and shout it again;
And "*Vive l'Empereur!*" rolls up from the plain.

Preceded by a tempest of grapeshot and shell,
And a charge of cavalry that fought nobly and well,
Ney's column fired its volley and advanced again
With the bayonet, and was met by roar and flame
Of our raging guns that now rent him through and
    through.
The dark columns of the Guards, as near us they drew,
Moved obliquely to the right, then on they came—
A desperate movement in a desperate game.
Adams' brigade on their left flank's deployed four deep,
And the dark ranks of the Old Guard they rend and sweep
By successive volleys.   Hot and scathing they fell;
And the blows they delivered told nobly and well.
But though scathed and mangled, still on they came,—
A noble chivalry, to preserve a stainless fame.
All Europe acknowledges a devotion sublime
That shall live for ever in the annals of time.
Ney, himself on foot, at their fearless head is found;
Twice his leading divisions are turned around
As the destroying fire wastes and consumes him there;
But his dauntless soul knoweth no craven despair!

By the prestige of a hundred battles sustained,
The crest of the hill they have already gained.
The artillery close up; the flanking fire from the guns
On the road dismembers, slaughters, shrivels and stuns
The famous Old Guard; and with their front blown away
Can they still crush the British and thus win the day?
The Duke seized the moment and instantly cried,
"Up, Guards, and at them!"   And they uprose in stern
    pride,

As stately as ever, aye, as ever was seen ;
And the sun's setting glory threw o'er them its sheen.

The hour of fierce triumph and vengeance had come
At the going down of the warm, peaceful June sun.
One deadly volley on the coming French they pour,
And three hundred are death-stricken to rise no more.
Then with the bayonet they charge, knowing no fear ;
On the French foe they rush with a wild British cheer.
Then came the most dreadful struggle all war can present—
Crashing columns of heroes, blood-stained and rent.
Foot to foot, and eye to eye, they stagger and reel
By the furious crash of the ringing cold steel.
Long restrained, the British are furious now,
And passionate valor burns on each stern brow.

And the French generals fall fast on every side :
Michel, Jamier, and Mallet have heroically died,
And Friant is sore wounded and helplessly falls ;
Ney, his dress pierced and ragged and torn by balls,
Shouts to his wavering legions still to advance
Once more for the Emperor and Imperial France !
But his leading files now waver and hesitate
On the brink and the ruin of impending fate.
The British press down upon them sternly and well ;
The cavalry gallop up, and at last pell mell,
Overwhelmed and beaten, the torn French fall back
O'er the winnows of slain that encumber their track.
The decisive moment of the awful day had come,
And a thrill through the grand allied ranks did run.

CHAPTER V.

"The field is won ! Order the whole line to advance.
Roll *en masse* on the wavering legions of France."
Thus ordered the Duke, and a responsive cry
Of joy and glad triumph pealed up to the sky.

On they came four deep, and like a torrent poured
From the heights; and our hot guns boomed and roared.
A fiery wave of valor they rolled on the foe,
And irresistibly swept them to the valley below.
All along our lines, from Papelotte to Merc Braine,
Rose that thund'rous cheer of great triumph again.

" Let the Life Guards charge them," here the Iron Duke
    said ;
And a grand brigade of horse, by Lord Uxbridge led,
Rode down on the French centre, sabreing them there.
Broken and dispirited, they waver in despair.
Incessantly our cavalry charge on the foe,
Flashing and flaming in the lurid sunset's glow ;
Piercing and dismembering the French everywhere,
While the infantry press forward the laurels to share.
With the bayonet the foe they sweep from their path,
A Nemesis of fate in o'erpowering wrath.
The Prussian guns play on their right flank and their rear ;
The British bayonet in front ; while a panic of fear
Spreads through their wavering ranks, and the hopeless cry
Of "*Sauve qui peut !*" resounds from their ranks reeling by.
All in vain Marshal Ney, " the bravest of the brave,"
Soult, Bertrand, Gourgand, and Labedoyer, to save
The day, burst from the disorganiz'd mass, and on them call
To stand firm, to conquer, or heroically fall !
" For the Emperor and sunny Imperial France.
Steady the lines and re-form, and again advance."
A battalion of the Old Guard alone obey.
With brave Cambronne at their head, between the prey
And their pursuers they form into square and stand,
A sacrifice offering 'mid the ruin at hand—
An offering to the tarnished honor of their arms
Irretrievably ruined and fleeing in swarms
Of disorganized masses before that oncoming wave
Of British valor.   No earthly power can save

The lost day ! Ruin'd and beaten, and drifting away
Before that magnificent advance and array
Of chivalry, worthy of " the brave days of old."
Glorified in the sunset, onward it rolled !
Through the " valley of the shadow of death " they go,
Devastatingly rolling upon the lost foe ?

Meanwhile, near La Belle Alliance, the Emperor still
Had some regiments in reserve, biding his will ;
And was rapidly rallying his beaten Old Guard,
Hitherto invincible—the watch and the ward
Of his army—the last card in the desperate play
Of the game of war, hitherto winning the day.
The remnants of his cavalry he'd collected, too,
Still hoping the British to pierce and break through.

But the Duke's eagle eye fathoms his useless game,
And his valiant soul is now grandly aflame
As he launches Vivian's cavalry brigade
Against him.   And oh, the immortal charge they made !
Through the " valley of the shadow of death " they tore,
And on La Belle Alliance like a torrent pour,
Sweeping all before them—cavalry, Old Guard, and all ;
And like destroying angels on his reserves they fall.
Completely successful, they rode calmly back again
Proudly over the lurid, ensanguined plain !
O gallant hussars of a famous brigade,
All time shall echo the destroying charge ye made !

The Emperor strives his disasters to repair,
And with lightning speed rides thither, everywhere,
Commanding, ordering, imploring, but in vain.
Broken and confused, they only exclaim,
"*Mon Dieu ! Mon Dieu !*" and fly swift from the frightful
     field,
Despairing masses that stagger and reel

In inextricable confusion of headlong flight,
Into the gloom and darkness of the falling night.
The Emperor by his staff was now borne away,
And disappeared in the shadows dim and gray—
Disappeared, and his sun will rise nevermore ;
Gone down on the "soldier of destiny" for evermore ;
But on freed Europe the sun of peace doth rise,
And the acclaims of freedom peal up to the skies.

British valor all Europe never can forget ;
On that "field of fields" it is flaming grandly yet,
And Wellington's fame to posterity is given,
Through storm and tempest unsullied, unriven.

Who can forget the close of that eventful day ?
And the meeting there in the fading twilight gray
Of Wellington and Blucher, clasping hands again
Mutely over the heaps of wounded and slain ?
Clasping hands as brothers, with hearts too full to speak,
While tears wash the battle stain from the soldier's cheek !
Aye, that was a meeting the world cannot forget,
And the effect is lasting, it endureth yet.

EXULTATION.

All hail, old Scotia's invincible clans,
    And the gallant sons of Erin's green isle,
And Britain's indomitable men-at-arms !
    The genius of fair fame doth on them smile.
United, ye are e'er invincible,
    A trinity that will not be denied,
The fate of imperial France at Waterloo,
    The humbler of Napoleon's despotic pride.

THE LAMENT FOR THE DEAD.

But, oh, the sight of that pent red field,
    Weird and terrible for evermore !

'Mid the awful silence of the slain,
   Britain's generous heart is sore.
Though the laurels of fame crown her brow,
   She mourns for her immortal slain ;
Though famous fore'er and signalized,
   She bows her illustrious head in pain.

Thousands marshalled there that sweet June morn,
   Strong and beautiful, side by side ;
Eve saw them in eternal repose—
   Fearless in heart they dared and died.
Play solemn dirges and bear them away,
   Play them tenderly, soft and low ;
Let the drum's muffled tone fall on the ear,
   Steadily, mournfully, and slow.

Reverently in the valley of death
   Lay them away to final sleep ;
Fit place to crown the immortal dead,
   Where brave, true comrades o'er them weep.
Oh, soldier hearts ! grand, intrepid souls !
   The years thy laurels shall renew ;
Britain thy devotion ne'er can forget,
   On that field of fields—Waterloo.

THE DOVE'S SONG.

LISTEN ! for I hear the dove's sweet song,
   So tender and mournfully sad,
Up from the vale where the maples bloom,
   And the springtime e'er maketh glad.
Hast wandered afar from a fairer clime ?
   Was thy home in Southern bowers ?
Is life more fair, and more fragrant the air,
   Than in this grand Northland of ours ?

Tell me, sweet dove; for thy mournful voice
   Hath wakened old memories to-day
That have only slept through the weary years
   That have silently flown away.
Art thou mateless and all alone, sweet dove,
   That thy dear song is never gay ?
Art thou calling down the emerald glades
   In vain, pleadingly, day by day ?

Thy plaintive voice stirs a tenderness
   Called up from the shadowed deeps,
Where a pale light flickers o'er hidden graves,
   And a dream-world forever sleeps.
Surely 'tis lovely enough, sweet dove,
   O'er the hills that are sunny and sweet ;
And the lilies bloom in the vale below—
   Nature's sweetness lies at thy feet.

The sun and the wind are caressing thee,
   And all other songsters are gay ;
Canst thou not forget, and joyously sing
   As the bright hours pass away ?

'Tis ever the same, and 'twill ever be
   A mysterious, subtle regret;
There are losses that sadden evermore,
   And they cling to the worn heart yet.

BLINDED EYES.

THE silver band was playing divinely
   At the close of a perfect summer day;
And my heart in unison was throbbing,
   As I brushed a tender tear away.
In the soft glow of the golden sunset
   I saw two poor blinded eyes upturned
To the purpling skies, so fair and deep,
   And my soul with sympathy yearned.

He had caught the tender, passionate strains,
   Swelling and dreamily dying away,
As wave after wave sweetly rose and fell,
   The soul welling up in immortal lay.
The light softly fell on his blinded eyes,
   And over his speaking and careworn face
Stole a holy light unutterable;
   A glow of ecstasy there I could trace.

His soul was attuned to melodious strains.
   What he saw through his weary sightless eyes
I never may know; but surely it was
   A glimpse of the heavenly paradise.
For surely God's pity is reaching down
   To the help of the poor and sightless here;
And He takes the poor groping toil-worn hands,
   And points the way to the heavenly sphere.

The sun went down, and the sad shadows came
   Merging into the dreamy, soft twilight ;
The music ceased, and we stole away
   Into the deepening gloom of night.
And in the dream and mystery of life
   We move along on our separate ways ;
But the pleading look of those sightless eyes
   Will follow me all my allotted days.

Ah, me ! we, too, are oft blindly groping
   In the weird darkness and danger alone ;
We see not the dread pitfalls before us,
   And oft are defeated and overthrown.
Sometimes, through the cold mist and the dimness,
   We catch a glimpse of resplendent day,
And a strain of sweetest music supernal,
   The refrain of a distant celestial lay.

THE VETERANS' REUNION.

AFTER the flight of thirty long years
   They came at the welcome call ;
Someone had suggested a reunion
   Of the "old corps," one and all.
They came from the village and crossroads,
   The town, the shop, and the farm ;
Just as they did thirty years ago,
   When their hearts were young and warm.

They met at the "campfire" of reunion,
   Clasped hands as comrades once more,
Recalled the deeds of the dauntless past,
   And their campaigns recounted o'er.

7

"Fall in!" the old commander shouted,
　　"Fall in—after thirty years!"
With the same old ring, save a tremble,
　　And his eyes were misty with tears.

And they formed in column by the left,
　　"Proved" in sections and in fours,
Just as they did thirty years ago,
　　Guarding our frontier shores.
But not with the same quick precision
　　As when young and strong and gay;
But they did it, and with kindling eyes,
　　Though old and worn and gray.

"Call the roll!" the old major ordered,
　　"Call the living and the dead!"
And a solemn hush fell along the line,
　　And bowed was each veteran head.
The orderly stepped to the centre,
　　In front of the grand "old corps,"
And called the names that were dimmed by time,
　　As he had thirty years before.

And the "Tommy A's" along the line
　　Answered, "Here, sir!" or "Dead! dead!"
The sections were thinned by the march of time,
　　Where all youthfulness had fled.
A route march through the town was taken
　　And the people *en masse* turned out,
And greeted the flag and the grand "old corps"
　　With welcome and loyal shout.

Then they deploy from column to line,
　　And turn to the right in fours;
And the band and the colors anon "take post,"
　　And the loyal heart upsoars.

They "squared" their shoulders, and looked to the
    front,
  And the air was rent with cheers ;
The band struck up, and they marched away
  To the "British Grenadiers."

But not as they did thirty years ago,
  For time mars the soldier's form ;
Not so erect or steady the pace,
  But to-day their old hearts are warm.
And, if need be, for the Union Jack
  E'en yet they would take their stand,
To fight for the flag all love so well,
  And our fair Canadian land.

Their ranks are formed for the last grand march
  Down to a strange riverside—
The wonderful river all must reach,
  That is deep and dark and wide.
They soon will have gained its margin—
  God grant them safe transport o'er,
And a campfire and grand reunion,
  A bivouac on the other shore.

DISCREDITED.

FORGOTTEN? aye, cruelly forgotten !
  Passed by with looks of disdain
By the world, whose thin friendship is rotten,
  That honors but riches and gain.
The poor are looked down upon coldly,
  Though grand men in poverty have died ;
And I assert, with just indignation,
  They were slain by the world's cold pride.

They struggled alone in the valley
  To win up the far heights of fame ;
And they pleaded but kind recognition,
  But you thrust them down coldly again.
And you sneered at the lines they had written—
  Lines that shall live till time is no more— .
Fiery songs that light like a beacon
  Along many a soul's dark shore.

And their thoughts were deep and uplifted ;
  They soared like eagles on high,
Or delved in the depths of the ocean
  Of knowledge that borders the sky.
They stood on the loftiest mountains,
  And gazed on the circling spheres
Of starry realms, the mystery of space,
  In ecstasy, rapture, and fears.

They read from the grand book of nature,
  And traced there the finger of God,
In starry ways of the fathomless deeps
  That lead to man's future abode.

They communed with the mystery of ocean,
    Heard its billows sing grand and free,
As they rose in the storm or sank to repose
    In murmuring tranquillity.

And over the landscape that rolls away
    Saw mountain, and river, and stream;
The undulations of emerald plains,
    In the lights and shadows that dream.
And they heard the voice of murmuring winds,
    And the bird songs free and wild,
Till their souls were filled with subtle sweets,
    As nature upon them smiled.

Great souls were theirs, and all things daring
    To uplift their weak fellowman,
Bringing light and freedom to the nations
    By the searchlights of Justice to scan
The wrong and oppression by tyrants wrought,
    The weak and the helpless enslaved;
Counting it gain if but freedom's cause
    Was uplifted and fallen man saved.

THE BATTLE OF STONY CREEK.

FOUGHT JUNE 6TH, 1813. AMERICAN FORCE, 3,000; BRITISH, 700.
CAPTURED 4 GUNS, 100 PRISONERS, AND BOTH THE AMERI-
CAN GENERALS, CHANDLER AND WINDER.

FORWARD, into the midnight,
 Silently, stealthily go,—
Forward, noble "seven hundred,"
 Like a storm burst on the foe !
Not theirs to falter or murmur,
 But silently to obey ;
And they move like phantoms forward
 Through the shadows dim and gray.

Only the signal 's given,
 Never a spoken word ;
But their dauntless hearts are burning,
 By passionate valor stirred.
Onward, steadily onward,
 Moves that heroic line ;
Softly the night winds murmur,
 And dimly the pale stars shine.

Pauses now the "seven hundred,"
 Suppressed is even the breath—
A pause on the brink of midnight,
 The fateful hour of death !
"Fire !" cried the hero Harvey,
 "On them a dread volley pour ; "
And a flash leaped bright and blinding,
 And burst a deafening roar.

Whole ranks were stricken by it
   Before that withering rain ;
Then through the tumult ringing
   Burst Harvey's cry again :
"Forward now the 'seven hundred';
   Close up firm your lines of steel ;
Sweep the field with the bayonet ;
   Let the foe your fury feel."

Though the guns rained upon them
   A tempest of shot and shell,
And musketry fiercely volleyed,
   And many a hero fell,
They charged with a ringing cheer
   Through the batteries' fierce flame,
And fell on the reeling ranks
   Of the foe, who all in vain

Attempted to stay the sweep
   Of that line of deadly steel.
With their torn and bloody ranks
   They stagger, and they reel
Backward in broken fragments,
   Back into headlong retreat.
All hail "noble seven hundred"!
   Your victory was complete.

Honor the men of "Stony Creek,"
   The dauntless, brave "seven hundred";
Long we'll remember the noble slain.
   A rescued country wondered
At the famous charge they made
   Under the dome of night,
Heroically storming an army,
   And putting the foe to flight.

VOICES.

O VOICES ! voices ! mysterious voices !
　　Why are ye haunting me evermore ?
Thrilling my soul with your ceaseless murmurs,
　　Like phantom waves on a ghostly shore ?
And whether by day, toilstained and weary,
　　Or when eve fades into lonesome night,
Still in dreams ye haunt me like a vision,
　　Hovering near at the dawn's pale light.

Some are soothing and laden with sweetness,
　　And others are weary all their days.
Ah, how the voices of children move me !
　　God bless their tender, innocent ways !
And the voices of old float around me,
　　Though silenced by time's faded years ;
Their feet have passed o'er the dark river
　　That winds through the dim vale of tears.

And the voice of the seasons, ever flowing
　　Outward and into the void of time,
Sadden my heart with their pain and losses,
　　And the few sweet days that were divine.
The voice of winds at the solemn midnight,
　　Through realms of space as they soar on high,
Chanting wild dirges o'er land and ocean,
　　'Neath a dreary moonless, starless sky.

Or caressing the beautiful summer,
　　Sweetly asleep 'neath the silver moon ;
Or lightly playing o'er mead and moorland,
　　And hills asleep in the golden noon.

And the voice of the sea, the strange blue sea,
   As 't restlessly ripples on the shore ;
Or when tempests sweep o'er its heaving bosom
   And mighty billows in anger roar.

And the voice of the sphere's silent glory,
   Forever sweeping the vast unknown ;
Revolving around some wonderful centre—
   O celestial centre !—Alcyone !
Listen, my soul (for 'tis not finite),
   To a song that comes from the infinite shore,
Stealing down through the far starry spaces,
   Repeating its rapture o'er and o'er.

Sometimes 'tis as of a thousand harpers,
   And a thousand voices blending sweet—
Can it be, my soul, that 'tis an echo
   Of the angels' song at the Saviour's feet ?
Sing on ! sing on, ye mysterious voices !
   Though I can't tell all your song would say,
We may know the way of the starry spaces
   When night-time fades into endless day.

DIVIDED.

Hope died to-day, and I'm thinking
   Of a time that never can be ;
And my thoughts grow strangely tender
   In asking and praying for thee.

Thou'st turned away from my pleading
   The light of thy starry eyes,
That rival the purest beaming
   Of the bluest of summer skies.

Sweet eyes, that sometimes kindled
   With love-light when I was nigh—
A wistful and tender yearning
   That mem'ry recalls with a sigh.

Thy voice, so low and so thrilling,
   And soft as the summer wind
That plays o'er the sunlit fountains,
   Entrancing both heart and mind.

Thy face, as pure as an angel's,
   Half veiled by thy golden hair,
Star-gemmed with God-like meekness,
   So kindly, so wondrous fair !

In vain, oh, heart, are thy dreamings !
   The flowers lie dead on the lea ;
The sun 's gone down in the shadows
   That darken the dreary sea.

The winds moan low o'er the hilltops,
   The waves sob along the dim shore ;
And night gathers fast in the valley—
   Will the day return nevermore ?

THE HURONS.

CHAPTER I.

BACKWARD, backward, through time's vast
    chambers,
  In a dreamful reverie go;
Flitting down the vanishing ages,
  Fifty and two hundred years ago.
Between Lake Simcoe and Lake Huron,
  In the radius of Ontario,
Waved a grand primeval forest
  In the sunlight's ebb and flow.

A great wide stretch of wooded landscape,
  Interspersed by stream and rill;
With gentle swells and undulations,
  And sylvan glade and shrouded hill.
And all this great wide reach was teeming
  With all kind of luscious game;
The moose and red deer roamed by thousands,
  In nature's freedom went and came.

The savage bear and wild wolf haunted
  This wide expanse in quest of prey;
The lynx and wildcat, too, were prowling
  The dim aisles by night and day.
The crafty fox here thickly burrowed,
  Mink, otter, and the festive coon;
The cunning beaver by the streamlet
  Built under cover of night's gloom.

The wild fowl covered all the streamlets—
　　Geese, ducks, and teal, and lonely loon;
Their ceaseless babble and their chatter
　　Enlivened all the forest's gloom.
And song birds covered all the branches,
　　Sweet birds of every shade and hue;
And waves of melody they uttered,
　　As down the forest aisles they flew.

The night-bird, too, the night made vocal,
　　The cat-bird, owl, and whippoorwill;
They wakened up the dim recesses,
　　When summer nights were warm and still.
And through the awesome, stately forest,
　　Mysterious voices ebb and flow;
And weird, fantastic, ghostly shadows
　　Through faint, far distance palely go.

And Lake Simcoe and grand Lake Huron
　　Swarmed with fish in countless store;
All the warm bays and sunny inlets,
　　The streams and rivers round the shore.
And over all this wide expansion
　　The sweet wild winds in rapture blew,
Rustling through the dim old forest,
　　And o'er the lake's wide bosom blue.

There sun and shadow alternating,
　　And skies of cloud or sapphire hue
Domed o'er the loveliness of nature—
　　The far, far past this picture knew.
Here was the home of the proud Hurons,
　　Fifty and two hundred years ago;
Thirty thousand happy Indians
　　By the bright water's laughing flow.

Herein they dwelt for unknown ages,
　By the Iroquois tribes hated so;
A fragment of some long lost nation,
　Prehistoric, but who may know?
Aye, here they builded quaint, queer wigwams,
　Indian towns by shore and stream,
Palisaded round and bastioned,
　Double-rowed, and looped between.

Thus, to guard 'gainst outer foemen,
　They builded strong, and to endure
The siege, or onslaught, or surprises,
　They sought and labored to secure.
Within were store-rooms wide and ample,
　With food to last at least a year,
From the Indian maize and cornfields—
　Of famine they need have no fear.

And all the tepees and warm wigwams
　Were blest with comfort and good cheer;
Stored with fish and game in plenty,
　The winter had for them no fear.
Fine robes and mantles of warm bearskin,
　Wolf and lynx and the festive coon,
Otter, mink, the fox and sly beaver,
　As soft and warm as summer's noon.

This great wide reach of lake and forest,
　River and stream and flowing rill,
Rendered up their richest fulness
　To the hunter's unerring skill.
Laws and customs they established
　In some far-off, unknown age—
Who shall penetrate the mystery
　That enshrouds their history's page?

And those barbaric laws and customs
  Were respected and obeyed ;
Sure death it was to the transgressor
  Who the nation's cause betrayed.
And they believed in the Great Spirit ;
  Manitou they worshipped there ;
A future state of peace and comfort,
  The happy hunting-grounds so fair.

Within those palisaded hamlets
  Strange rites and festivals were seen ;
The weird, blood-curdling pagan war-dance,
  A frightful and barbaric scene.
And the great council of the nation,
  Many grand war chiefs, stern and brave,
Deliberated all great questions,
  And cunningly decision gave.

And those red children of the forest
  Had their queer games, their social hour,
A relaxation from all turmoil,
  A rest from war's relentless power.
Then the great chiefs and older warriors
  Smoked in peace, and stories told
Of their strange lives and great adventures,
  Heroic deeds and ventures bold.

And the younger braves and maidens
  Enacted what to youth belongs,
And told their tales of love and rapture,
  Danced and sang their tribal songs.
Wandering by the shore or river,
  Life to them was fair and sweet,
Many a dusky Indian beauty
  Had her lover at her feet.

Oft in their light canoes they glided
    O'er the waters' sparkling blue,
Lingering in the dreamy sunset
    'Neath fading skies of sapphire hue.
Ah! those heathen souls were happy,
    Communing there with nature's heart;
Beneath the wide-domed arch of heaven
    They had of life a tender part.

And the lithe children of the nation
    Played in wild, ecstatic glee,
Nimble in untrammelled nature,
    As squirrel leaping from tree to tree.
And marriages were celebrated,
    Funeral rites were quaint and queer;
Believing Manitou was near them
    The mourner's troubled heart to cheer.

Like us they had their hopes and passions,
    Ambition stirred their pagan souls;
Strange fear and awe and superstition
    An almighty hand controls.
And in the wind's low sob and whisper,
    The waves that murmur on the shore,
The phantom voices of the forest,
    And in the storm king's mighty roar.

CHAPTER II.

And thus it was with the proud Hurons
    In that far-off and happy time;
Those strange children of the lone forest,
    Reared where nature reigns sublime.
And thus it was the Jesuit fathers
    Found this strange people by the shores
Of Lake Simcoe and wide Lake Huron
    In palisaded towns by scores.

There with infinite care and kindness
   They labored on through blood and tears,
Suffering torture and privation
   For many long and weary years.
But the grand light at last is dawning,
   Their work at last is signalized ;
O'ercome at last, the Huron nation
   Receives, is won, and Christianized.

And the dense wilderness resounded
   With song and praise to God above ;
Those savage hearts grew meek and tender
   When purified by Christian love.
And they followed the Great Spirit,
   And with never-failing zeal
Taught the lost from tribes far distant
   Of the Saviour's love to heal.

And for war no more they thirsted,
   But prayed that peace might e'er prevail,
And tore the warpost from its socket—
   No more they would their foes assail.
Now they worked among the maize fields,
   Hunted, fished, and stored away,
Wisely, industriously preparing
   For winter's tempestuous day.

Suddenly the sky grew threatening,
   Shadowy forms seemed in the air ;
A ghostly moan swept down the forest,
   A weird, hush'd wailing of despair.
Was 't to warn of danger pending
   Those phantom shapes and mournful cries
Came from across the faint, far distance
   Along the dismal, startled skies.

And those frightened forest children
  Gazed in awe upon the scene,
And they appealed to the Great Spirit
  That he would save, and intervene
To avert impending danger,
  And clear the sinister skies again,
To assuage the fear that fell upon them,
  Relieve their hearts from anxious pain.

Suddenly the war-whoop sounded
  From the ferocious Iroquois,
And from the dense concealing forest
  They burst with fierce and hideous noise.
And they fell upon the Hurons,
  Stunned by fright and unprepared ;
There was no preconcerted action,
  Cunningly they were caught and snared.

In vain the Huron warriors struggled,
  In vain they nobly fought and died—
They could not stem that whirlwind onset,
  And hundreds fell on every side.
The old and young alike were butchered,
  Not e'en the little child was spared ;
In vain the cry for life and mercy,
  All, all that hideous slaughter shared.

Hundreds, too, of pleading prisoners
  To the torture post were tied,
Burned and mangled and insulted,
  When on God for help they cried.
Aye, like wolves compelled by hunger,
  They thirsted for the Hurons' blood ;
And remorselessly they slaughtered,
  Revelling in the crimson flood.

8

And when sated, like the wild wolf,
  They glide like serpents swift away,
And gain the dense concealing forest,
  Disappearing 'neath the shadows gray.
Then was mourning in the wigwams,
  O'er their kin in hundreds slain ;
Burned and rifled habitations
  Make sore the heart by loss and pain.

CHAPTER III.

Thus commenced those dread incursions
  Of the relentless Iroquois ;
Unceasing in their deadly hatred,
  They burst with frightful cruelty,
At hours or moments unexpected,
  On the despairing Hurons there,
Slaying, burning, and desolating
  The Huron Nation everywhere.

All their good towns were laid in ashes,
  And thousands slain in bloody strife ;
Hunted and pursued forever,
  Their certain doom the scalping knife.
Amid it all they prayed unceasing,
  Through dire distress and fell despair—
Pled for mercy and deliverance,
  And for Divine protecting care.

Driven at last to desperation,
  They left their homes and stole away,
And gained the Island of St. Joseph,
  In the lovely Georgian Bay.
Here they built a fortressed mission,
  And by thousands huddled round,
With the stern winter time upon them,
  A storm-swept region, iron-bound.

There with suffering and privation,
　　And their dread foemen lurking near,
With pestilence in thousands slaying,
　　And tortured by consuming fear,
They prayed for peace and preservation,
　　Sustained in that dread anxious hour
By the assurance of the Great Spirit,
　　Trusting still His mighty power.

All through that direful time malignant,
　　Of persecution, blood, and flame,
The intrepid Jesuits preached unceasing,
　　Absolved and blessed in Jesus' name.
Driven by want and sheer starvation,
　　O'erwhelmed now and desolate,
They leave their lone bleak island fortress
　　In desperate, appalling state.

Hell only hath a rage co-equal
　　To the ferocious Iroquois.
Again they fell upon the Hurons,
　　Gloating like fiends, with hideous glee ;
Torturing, exterminating, burning,
　　Glutting their diabolic hate,
Red demons of incarnate fury,
　　A hideous and satanic state.

In vain the Huron braves did rally,
　　Fighting all desperately there,
Only to fall in the dread *melee ;*
　　Beaten, massacred everywhere,
They fled now through the awesome forest,
　　Fled by river, and stream, and rill,
Seeking all vainly for concealment
　　By lonely vale and towering hill.

For an implacable foe pursues,
    And o'er this wide expanse so fair
Was a reign of woe unutterable,
    With grim death revelling everywhere.
And it ceased not for a moment,
    That frightful carnage, by night nor day,
Till *en masse* the Hurons perished,
    Swept from their mother earth away.

No more Lake Simcoe and Lake Huron,
    Nor all that great wide reach between,
Shall echo to the Huron's war song.
    A weird strange life, which like a dream
Hath floated out by mystic spaces,
    Down the silence of ceaseless flow,
Lost and mouldering with the ages,
    Fifty and two hundred years ago.

And I pause in reverie dreamful
    By Lake Huron's liquid tide,
But no primeval forest greets me.
    O'er the expansion far and wide
Are dotted homes, reposing peaceful,
    Gemmed by river, hill and stream,
Crowned by the sunlight's golden glory,
    Where pagan wigwams once were seen.

ON THE HEADLAND.

It stood on a lonely headland,
    Pointing far out to sea,
Braving the storms of centuries,
    A venerable giant tree.
No other ones grew near it,
    It towered there alone,
As if forever listening
    To the ocean's weary moan.

And phantom, mysterious voices
    In its topmost boughs were heard
When the wind sobbed o'er the ocean,
    And its giant form was stirred.
It crooned perhaps of a thousand years,
    Of a thousand years ago,
When all life was summerladen,
    A tender and golden glow.

It stands no more on the headland,
    Pointing far out to sea ;
It welcomes no more my coming,
    It complains no more to me.
It yielded at last to the tempest,
    'Twas forever swept away ;
Alas, for the vacant places,
    Time ever winneth the day.

I stand to-day on the headland,
    Looking far out to sea,
Tired of life and the burden
    Forever resting on me.

And over the lonely ocean,
    The cold clouds roll stern and gray,
Obscuring a tender vision
    Of a fair land far away.

ONLY A VISION.

IN my vision I stood on a loftier mount
    Than this wonderful world hath seen,
And gazed down a valley deep and dark,
    Where so strangely rolled between
Lone shores that were weird and unearthly,
    A river as black as death's doom,
When a hopeless soul is departing,
    And night comes in horror and gloom.

And the old and young there assembled,
    With burdens too grievous to bear ;
And their deep moans and lamentations
    Rose up anguished from everywhere.
I saw by a light dim and waning
    A river of deep, dark despair,
And a voice, as of God, sternly warning—
    Up on high it floated somewhere.

And I raised my eyes toward heaven—
    Not a ray of sunlight was there ;
Fierce clouds swept along, as if driven
    By fiends through the desolate air.
I listened in awe as that warning
    Came in tones stern, yet tender as love,
Reaching down in that sorrowful valley
    Saying, "Hopeless souls, look above."

And up from those depths dark and dreary
   Rose a prayer such as earth never heard,
So full of unutterable pleadings,
   The very hills and mountains were stirred.
Suddenly the clouds rent asunder,
   Rolled back, and the light of the spheres
Burst forth in intenseness and glory,
   Lighting up that lone valley of tears.

I heard songs of praise and rejoicing,
   Such music as earth never heard,
Entrancing my soul with its rapture,
   Such immeasurable joy it conferred.
And quickly that vale, late so barren,
   Bloomed with fruits and the fairest of flowers,
And music and laughter came rippling
   From hillsides, sweet vales, and green bowers.

And the river flowed on in its beauty,
   By mansions so fair on the lea ;
On and on, flashing in the sunlight,
   Gliding peacefully to the sea.
I knew there was rapture in heaven
   When the wanderers returned to the fold,
For I heard the songs of the angels,
   Attuned to their sweet harps of gold.

I, too, would have joined in rejoicing
   With the friends of the long ago :
One fair as the angels awaiteth
   Where the sunset gates are aglow.
But suddenly the thought came to me
   That I was forsaken and lone,
On a desolate far mountain height,
   Cast out ever from friends and home.

For there was no way from the mountain,
  And I sank with a bitter cry
On the bleached and tempest-swept rocks,
  O'erwhelmed and alone to die.
Many years have passed since that vision
  Rapt my soul on that fatal day,
And still I am lost on the mountain,
  And heaven seems far away.

THE WORLD WANTS A SMILING FACE.

THE world wants a smiling face, my boy,
  The world wants a bright smiling face ;
'Tis the passport to favor on sea or land,
  In every profession and place.
The world cares little, my darling boy,
  And heeds not the lonely and sad ;
But caresses ever the smiling face,
  And whatever maketh it glad.

Besides, 'tis a duty, my noble boy ;
  God gave man the instinct to smile,
To lighten the burden his brother bears
  For many a lone, weary mile.
Then keep your heart pure, my darling boy,
  Doing ever the Father's will ;
And whatever your station in life may be,
  Rich blessings thy years all shall fill.

Remove the obstacles from your path,
  Though your hands be bleeding, my boy ;
The brave and the pure that fight to the last
  No evil can ever destroy.

Smile, though your heart be breaking, my boy;
   To the world say never a word;
Go fearlessly on, and you'll win at the last
   The victory, though long deferred.

Smile on the children, my darling boy,
   " Of such are the kingdom of heaven ";
From the loved of home withhold it not,
   'Tis a potent and sunny leaven,
Raising the despondent to strength again,
   Removing the gloom from the day;
It crowns all life with a nameless grace,
   Putting sorrow and care away.

Your brother needs your bright smile, my boy,
   And the clasp of your strong right hand;
His pathway may be with danger beset,
   In many a strange, far land.
Pass not the sin-stained of earth, my boy,
   Raise the fallen again if you can;
A purified soul, forgiven and blest,
   Rejoiceth the Saviour of man.

Smile on the unfortunate, my boy,
   Take the hand of the poor and old;
Sympathy warmeth the desolate—
   'Tis better than silver and gold.
It leadeth up to the starry heights,
   'Twas divinely, wisely given;
Soothing and blessing all the long way,
   It surely entereth heaven.

THE VOICE OF TEARS.

'Twas only the voice of a stranger,
    But never through all the years
Have I heard a tone so pleading,
    So unutterably full of tears.
I looked, and I never have seen
    A face so touchingly sad ;
Surely all hope had flown away,
    Never again to be glad.

His eye had a far-away look,
    And a shadow of nameless pain ;
A patient, pathetic gaze,
    That never would smile again.
What was it, oh, thou tearful voice ?
    Was fortune against thee arrayed ?
Did all hope and trust flee away ?
    Was thy love and friendship betrayed ?

'Twas only a meek, worn stranger,
    All alone on life's highway,
So patiently moving onward
    To the close of a weary day.
Ah, me ! but my eyes were blinded,
    And never through all the years
Was my heart so moved for another.,
    Oh, desolate voice of tears !

THE GARDEN.

'Twas an Eden of bloom and beauty,
  At the dawning sweet and fair,
And the incense of sunny bowers
  Perfumed the summer air.
The azure sky domed above it,
  And the wind that softly sighed,
And the song of nature, subtly sweet,
  I heard there on every side.

The car of time, with its worn-out years,
  Moves sadly along the way ;
The lonesome voice of the autumn winds
  Sobs low with the dying day.
And once again in the dimming light
  I stand in the garden gate,
But I start—and the tears suffuse my eyes,
  'Tis so faded and desolate.

THE BATTLE OF QUEENSTON HEIGHTS.

FOUGHT OCTOBER 13TH, 1812.

THEY crossed in the gray of the morning,
  Stole o'er from the other shore,
To invade the land of the Maple Leaf,
  Two thousand proud foes, or more.
A detachment of the old Forty-Ninth
  And Dennis's brave volunteers
Opposed their landing determinedly,
  Opening on them with cheers.

The roar of the guns from the battery
  Rolled down Niagara's gorge,
Awakening Brock and his fearless men
  From their rest at old Fort George.
And in hot haste Brock and his *aides-de-camp*
  Rode fast through the pale, cold light,
Bidding Sheaffe and his men to follow on
  To aid in the coming fight.

Meanwhile the Americans won the heights,
  And the guns half way below ;
Their loss was a serious menace, too,
  In the hands of the haughty foe.
Swift as the fleet wind Brock gained the vale
  And lifted his flashing eye,
Measuring the foe on the cold, gray steeps,
  And the battery nearer by.

"The guns must be won !" Brock quickly cried,
  And came an answering cheer
From the intrepid, ready Forty-Ninth—
  Brave souls devoid of all fear !
" Forward ! charge home to the battery's side !"
  And dauntless he led the way,
Driving the foe from the smoking guns
  By the cold steel's deadly play.

Heroically leading, he drew their fire,
  And fearlessly fighting fell,
Pierced through the breast by a mortal shot,
  The leader all loved so well.
" Don't mind me," he thoughtfully cried ;
  " Push on, brave York volunteers !"
Sent a message to his sister over the sea,
  His eyes suffused with tears.

Thus perished war's genius gloriously,
    A great leader young in years ;
So loved and mourned for, brave, pure soul,
    Thy name we bedew with tears.
Gallantly Sheaffe by St. David's moves up,
    Turning their flank by the way,
Gaining the heights by an impetuous rush,
    Not a moment held at bay.

Consuming volleys they hurl on the foe,
    Then charge with their deadly steel,
And hundreds are slain in the mad *melee*—
    See the foe in panic reel !
The British line sweeps resistlessly down ;
    The proud foe must surely yield.
Ha ! they break—they break into headlong flight
    In defeat from that blood-red field !

Over the heights in mad flight now leaping,
    Some were impaled on the trees,
Where mockingly their garments fluttered
    For years in the storm and breeze.
Some plunged in the cold rushing river
    To gain safely the other shore,
But were lost in the swirl of its waters,
    And were heard of nevermore.

Nine hundred men surrendered to Sheaffe,
    A force greater than his own.
Ah ! 'twas a gallant day, and nobly won ;
    Signally the enemy were overthrown.
And, standing there on the glorious Heights,
    They cheered for country and king ;
They unfurled the " flag of a thousand years " ;
    Their shouts o'er the scene did ring.

'Twas a far-famed day for our lovèd land,
　　Ring it over the world so wide ;
Like veterans Canadians fought that day,
　　With the regulars side by side.
Dearly the victory was won for us
　　In the death of beloved Brock.
Immortal hero ! thy irreparable loss
　　Was to all a grievous shock.

They muffled their drums and reversed their arms,
　　And marshalled around his bier,
And solemnly bowed their war-worn heads,
　　And silently dropped a tear.
E'en the painted savages loved him well,
　　And o'er each stoical face
Stole a shadow of pain and tenderness,
　　Hallowing that sacred place.

A grateful country has planted there
　　A monument tow'ring high,
His memory e'er to perpetuate,
　　Pointing ever to the sky.
The hero and his *aide*, parted not by death,
　　Secure their relics rest there,
In the lovely land of the Maple Leaf
　　Ever so loyal and fair.

Aye, a grateful country placed it there—
　　On earth there's no grander scene—
And we sing with a grateful, fervent heart
　　To our country and our Queen.
Revere, then, the dead, and honor them still,
　　They died our freedom to save ;
God bless the flag of a thousand years
　　May it long o'er us proudly wave.

A FOREST DREAM.

BARE and gaunt the forest standeth,
  Reaching out so wide and high,
As if mutely supplicating
  Mercy of an angry sky.
Oh ! such hollow and weird voices
  Issue from its solemn aisles,
As if lonely forest phantoms
  Mourn the loss of summer's smiles.

I have sought the dim old forest
  And its old familiar ways :
Frozen streams, dark glens and bowers,
  Dear to me in childhood's days.
All is silent and forsaken,
  Leaf and flower lie cold and dead,
Mute appealing to the memory,
  Telling of a day that's fled.

I have known when summer's mantle,
  Fair and sweet as poet's dream,
Covered in a wild profusion
  These old haunts with rustling green.
Then the forest aisles were merry
  With the glee the song-birds made,
And their gentle echoes followed
  Every stream and fragrant glade.

Then I sung with boyhood's rapture,
  Leaped and shouted in the dell,
Till the golden hush of sunset,
  With its silent shadows, fell

O'er the hills that, rapt in dreaming,
    Watched the moonrise on the sea,
Where the wavelets danced and murmured
    Low voiced and mysteriously.

Life was one long dream of gladness—
    All unknown the future lay;
Ah! the years have brought deep sadness—
    Summer's merged in winter's gray.
And I wander, bowed and weary,
    Grieving o'er the faded past,
As the snowflakes flit around me,
    Borne upon the winter's blast.

WOMAN.

O June, thou art beautiful as ever!
    Nature's wrought in her wondrous way
A dream reverie of lilies and roses
    Wherever we wander to-day.
Breathing up so tenderly everywhere
    A fragrance subtly sweet,
Where the soft, low winds kiss the sunny hills,
    And the waves fall down at our feet.

But woman is fairer and sweeter still,
    And divine as a spirit dream;
And claiming all homage and tenderness,
    And to reign in man's heart supreme.
Thus, crowned in her perfect loveliness,
    All alight are her witching eyes;
And peeping therein we dream, aye, we dream,
    Of the angels in paradise.

O winsome woman! this lovely June day
    More fair than the roses in bloom,
Or lilies that ope by the purling stream,
    That fade from our life's way too soon,
We pay thee court, we acknowledge thy sway,
    We lay all we have at thy feet;
The cottage is home, and the mansion 's alight,
    When blest by thy presence so sweet.

When the heart would faint in the battle of life,
    And our strength and our courage would fail,
We are roused by thee to a nobler strife,
    And again the foe we assail.
And if thou art true and point us the way,
    We face all opposing powers;
Though the fight be grievous and sorely long,
    The vict'ry will surely be ours.

THE JESUIT.

CONSECRATED to a lonely life of celibacy,
Seeing only a vain delusion and a fallacy
In terrestrial unions—man's uncertainty of bliss,
Suspended in the balance o'er an infinite abyss—
Appalled by sin and its delusive elements everywhere:
The cry of a lost world—an intonation of despair
Rising up from the depths of impenetrability;
The infinite to the finite, out from dread eternity,
Breathing subtly to the spiritual, the list'ning soul
Answereth "deep unto deep."

And responsive to the irresistible communion
(Wond'rous affinity! mysterious, inscrutable union!)

9

Impelled to consecrate all of life, and all that life e'er gave,
To the cause of Christ, and by field and flood a world to save.
Moved by pity for man's fallen and suffering state,
O'erwhelm'd in the vortex of a direful, impending fate,
Man must be lifted up and placed upon the narrow way,
More in the divine radiance and pure celestial ray
Of God's own light. And thus the Jesuit is impelled;
By an undying enthusiasm of religious zeal
He goes forth to the rescue, to alleviate and heal.

And deeply learned and skilled in every earthly lore,
He gleans the gems of thought from the deep mines of
     every shore;
Searches for knowledge down the long vistas of the past,
Surmounting all impediments, winning the field at last.

Thus equipped, a diplomat, he is found near thrones of
     kings,
In palaces and parliaments; his subtle influence brings
Nations to the Church's imperious, predominant feet:
In her insatiable interest all things must bend and meet.
With black cassock, the cross and rosary at his girdled side,
He goes forth, the Church's consecrated champion and her
     pride.

No distance is too great to stay his eager, tireless feet;
Nor heat, nor biting cold, nor raging tempest, rain and
     sleet,
Can deter him from his purpose. On his devoted head
The elements beat in vain. Unsheltered and unfed,
He is found in the lonely wilds of every land and zone,
Fearless of every danger, oft suffering and alone.
Braving disease, pestilence, and the martyr's tragic death;
Having no home, no wife, no country, only heaven in
     view,
And the redemption of the heathen, a weary work to do;

Sacrificing all desires of the weak and mortal frame,
Sustained through hard years of toil by heaven's quench-
    less flame.

Such was Jean de Brébœuf, the Ajax of the Huron tribe,
A martyred hero, who all impediments, e'en death, defied
In the pursuit of duty, the lost lonely wilds to save,
Winning a crown of victory, and at last a martyr's grave.

Over the far ocean the impassioned zealot came,
Hot in the pursuit of duty, with heart and soul aflame ;
Stemming swift rivers along the rough and tortuous way,
Pressing forward through the dense lone wilderness day
    by day,
With soiled and tattered garments, and naked, bleeding
    feet,
Bearing a weary burden, his necessities to meet.
He sought, and found by Lake Huron's vast and majestic
    side,
The pagan Huron nation in all its savagery and pride—
A vast tract stretching from Lake Simcoe to the Georgian
    Bay,
A scene of rustic loveliness in that strange time far away.
Thirty thousand Hurons, in palisaded towns by scores,
Built within the shadowy forest and along the shores ;
A strange people, the red Hurons, of some far, forgotten
    age ;
An unsolved mystery, a blank on history's page !

Boldly entering the towns and wigwams, undismayed
By barbaric savagery in threatening form arrayed ;
Through lines of spears and warclubs, tomahawks and
    flashing knives,
Stained by the blood of foemen, red with a thousand lives !

Aye, he went with but the cross of the Saviour at his side,
Raised a prayer to the Father, and to the red men cried,
"Peace! our mission's peace; we come in the Great Mani-
    tou's name,
To bid our red brothers war no more, but to enkindle a
    flame
Of peace and friendship; for 'tis the Great Spirit's loving
    will
That his red children should war no more, that hate no
    more should fill
Their hearts, and as brothers to abide in a lasting peace—
In seeking the "happy hunting grounds" strife and war
    must cease.

With Père Daniel, Lalemant, Raguenean, Garnier, and
    Davost,
He built a mission house and chapel, watched by friend
    and foe,
Thus raising a Christian altar where pagan orgies reigned,
Upheld by a lofty purpose, by power divine sustained.
Unwonted sounds and echoes woke the lonely forest aisles,
The chant of ancient litanies down the weird, dim defiles;
The pleading passionate prayer rose, swelled, and died
    away
Down the vast corridors of the wilderness weird and gray.

Thus besought were savage tribes to espouse the sacred
    cause,
To abandon their pagan usages and barbaric laws.
The story of the Cross and God's infinite love was told
By the fearless Jesuits, and passionately unrolled.
But it fell on stolid ears, and the dark, benighted mind
Of the Huron nation. A stoic heathenism, all blind,
Repelled the Cross, and in derision turned away
With muttered imprecations; and threatenings day by day

Fell on the unswerving servants of the altar and Cross,
Counting all suffering but gain, and even life no loss,
If the cause of Christ with the Huron nation should prevail.
Then let evil, every danger, e'en hell itself assail,
They would lay their lives, their all, at the Saviour's sacred
    feet :
For their red brothers' redemption they would all torture
    meet.

For years they met with but discouragement, grief, and
    care,
Scowls and menaces, distrust, and persecution everywhere ;
Fierce jealousies, stirred up by the tribal " medicine men ";
A subtle pagan power, cunningly concealed, and when
Their ascendancy was threatened, stirred the dark, be-
    nighted mind
To acts of cruel violence—a superstition blind.
Thus suffering hunger, thirst, cold, heat, almost in despair,
And the powers of darkness combined ; the spirit of the air
Echoed demon laughter ; up from the deeps it rose and
    fell :
Up in derision from the very maw and counterscarp of hell ;
And the wolf howled down the phantom corridors of the
    night,
And lost spirits shrieked, and all of good seemed put to
    flight.

But 'mid it all those devotees toiled on incessantly ;
As one they sought God's help in prayer and pleading unity.
Though scoffed and mocked, they importuned the Huron
    warriors still
To espouse the Saviour's cause and obey His loving will.
And when the deadly pestilence subdued the nation's pride,
And pale death stalked among the sad wigwams far and
    wide,

And a thousand braves were stricken in this disastrous
    hour,
And a thousand maidens perished by its fell, destroying
    power.
The aged and the children, too, were in hundreds swept
    away,
And the Huron hearts were breaking 'mid the horrors of
    the day ;
And pitiful distress and helplessness reigned everywhere,
And the nation bowed in mourning in the frenzy of despair.

'Twas then the Hurons realized the Jesuits' noble worth,
Learned to love their pale-faced brothers in that time of
    death and dearth ;
For moving 'mid the dying and the stricken night and day,
Nursing, soothing, absolving, and bearing the dead away,
Won they the Hurons, and the Saviour's story they receive,
Taught in their adversity to repent and to believe.
Thus was that strange people redeemed and Christianized,
And God's cause established, and the Jesuits signalized.
The Hurons sought war no more—'mid blessings of peace
    and love,
Longed for Manitou, and "the happy hunting grounds
    above."

But a scourge more dreadful now on the repentant nation
    fell :
The unsparing Iroquois, with the malignancy of hell,
Swept down upon the Hurons, caught by stealth, and
    unprepared.
All, all that hideous slaughter met—not one, not one was
    spared.
Though fighting sternly to the last, with the courage of
    despair,
They could not stem that fierce onslaught—pale death
    was rampant there.

Their palisaded towns were burned in rage by scores and
    scores,
And exterminating war reigned round Lake Huron's lovely
    shores.

Amid it all Brébœuf, of the Huron mission, stood
With the gentle Lalemant, a brother supremely good ;
And they absolved and blessed, fearless of their impending
    fate,
Caring for the wounded and dying, braving the foeman's
    hate ;
Amid the dreadful carnage, surrounded by flashing knives,
Red with the blood of the Hurons, red with a thousand
    lives !

Captives at last, by bloody hands borne to the torture post
With hundreds more, and surrounded by a gibing, fiendish
    host,
They met death by the most awful torture without a groan,
Blessing e'en the hands that mangled and seared to the
    very bone.
Aye, without a murmur, those steadfast souls bore the pain,
Exhorting all to look to God, that they should meet again
Where the cruel torture and life's dread sufferings are o'er,
Meet Manitou in endless life, where sorrow comes no more.

And thus perished those martyred, heroic, devoted souls
For the cause of Christ ; and as long as the grim ages roll
Shall their immortal deeds and imperishable fame be sung,
Till the last trump to waken the dead through all space
    be rung.

UNDER THE STARS.

I ARISE sometimes in the night-time,
   And go out 'neath the stars alone,
In the dim silence of night-time,
   When the skies are tender of tone.
In the holy silence of nature
   I calm my anxious soul,
Sometimes by the hard day grown weary,
   And beyond my will to control.

And I go where the waves' low murmur
   Soundeth ever along the dim shore,
And I'm soothed by the voice of the waters,
   And peace cometh unto me once more
When the winds are caressing the roses,
   And there stealeth an answering sigh
From the dew-bespangled foliage
   To the wanderer passing by.

I stand on the bridge of the streamlet,
   Where we met in the long ago ;
Where we met, and where we two parted
   In the twilight's silvery glow.
I listen again for her coming,
   Though 'tis only an empty dream ;
All I hear is the night wind sighing,
   And the rippling of the stream.

Then I pass where the vale is sleeping,
   O'er the emerald moonlit hill,
And gain the awesome shadows
   Of the forest deep and still.

And through the still gloom and the distance
  I hear the faint, far-off call
Of elfin and strange phantom voices—
  On my ear they dreamily fall.

O holy silence of nature!
  I am calmed with a pure delight.
Hush! for man's voice would but mar
  The harmony of the night.
All sinless the planets are glowing,
  Penetrating the vast, far voids
Of the mystery of creation
  Beyond the lone asteroids.

Subdued, and again submissive
  To whatever 's in store for me,
I strive to be uncomplaining,
  Though beset with adversity.
And thus, when the spirit is weary,
  My strength kindly nature restores;
Through her vast illimitable chamber
  My calm soul in ecstasy soars.

UNEXPLAINED.

THERE are many ways in this feverish life
  Where the rocks are grim and bare,
With no soil for tender plants and flowers,
  Nor rain nor dew is there;
Where the sterile rocks are bleak and bare,
  And the skies are shrouded and gray,
With sweeping winds from a desolate sea,
  Where there's never a summer day.

And a burning sun in a desert land,
   And the winter stern and cold,
And the wandering feet without a home,
   And weary and poor and old ;
And the poor in heart where all love hath died,
   And the dreary, haunting years,
And the friendship dead, and the broken home,
   And regret and pain and tears.

And the hopes that died, and the broken vows
   That severed far and wide,
And the toilworn hands, and the sad unrest,
   And the loss on every side ;
And the favored ones 'neath sunny skies
   That dream there the hours away,
And the struggling poor in barren lands,
   Where sad day follows day.

And the ships that sail over angry seas,
   And nevermore reach the shore ;
And the aching hearts, and the weary watch
   For the loved that come no more.
Ah ! I cannot still all these strange, sad thoughts,
   Nor stay these falling tears ;
The lonesome way is rough and long
   Through life's uncertain years.

And at times in the solemn night-time still
   I sink by the hard way alone,
With the voiceless silence around me,
   And my troubled rest a stone.
There comes to me a glad thought through the
     gloom,
   That rest will the sweeter be
When the weary burden is cast aside
   On the shores of eternity.

LIFE'S HIGHWAY.

CHAPTER I.

Life began in an old cottage,
　Near the margin of a stream,
Close beside a grand old forest,
　Where I saw the sunlight gleam
O'er the hills lit up with splendor
　By the radiance of its light,
Searching out the dim recesses
　Of the borders of the night.

Shimm'ring o'er the vales and woodlands
　Wak'ning all the birds and flowers;
Caressing breezes through the leaflets,
　Murmuring in fairy bowers.
Oh, the melody of song-birds,
　I can hear it, hear it still,
Flooding all the fields and woodlands,
　Rising o'er the rippling rill.

And I hear the tinkle, tinkle
　Of the bells and lowing kine,
Echo, echo, down the grasslands,
　Near the cornland's waving line.
And I hear my father singing
　Quaint old songs by field and fell;
Memory retains them fondly,
　Still I love on them to dwell.

And my school days were so happy ;
　All my tasks seemed light as air,
My companions kind and joyous,
　And the world was bright and fair.
How we tripped along the hilltops,
　Played beside the quiet stream,
Frolicked in the leafy woodlands,
　Where the lights and shadows dream.

There we planted in the springtime,
　Tilled in sultry summer weather ;
And the days went by so merry
　As we sung and wrought together.
And we reaped the harvest gaily,
　Sending many golden wains
From the wheatlands and the cornlands,
　Rich with summer's welcome gains.

And we stored in golden autumn
　'Gainst the white-robed winter time,
Food in plenty for the household,
　And the fowls and many kine.
And we laid away the apples,
　Hoards of russets, red and gold ;
Put the cider in the cellar,
　And defied the winter's cold.

Then when the gold leaves were falling
　In the mellow light and shade,
How we fought the frisky squirrels
　For the chestnuts in the glade.
We had many nooks and crannies
　In the old house by the stream,
Up among the dusty rafters,
　Where none but gay boys would dream.

And when winter's storm-king covered
  All the hills in white array,
And the legions of the northland
  Were assembled for the fray—
All the fierce and white-robed legions,
  Sweeping down from Arctic seas,
Flinging out their frosted banners
  In defiance to the breeze—

And when day was darkly closing
  In fierce storm, and sleet, and cold,
We secured the fowls in safety,
  Put the kine within the fold.
Then with evening's gathering darkness
  The warm lights were all agleam—
The bright, ruddy, dancing firelights
  In the old house by the stream.

And we boys went in a-romping
  With no ceremonial fear ;
All aglow with health and gladness
  To dear mother's welcome cheer.
Then we sought the nooks and crannies,
  Where the chestnuts could be found ;
Brought the cider from the cellar,
  Passed the ripened fruit around.

While with many a quaint old story
  Of weird legion, love and war,
We whiled away the hours so happy,
  Scarcely ever knew a jar.
And we joined with hearts o'erflowing
  In glad music and in song ;
Scarce dreaming of the world beyond us,
  With its mighty restless throng.

When the moon was brightly beaming,
  Silvering the icebound rill,
We skated on the frozen streamlet,
  Or toboggan'd down the hill.
Our light hearts were glad within us,
  And our blood was pure and warm,
As we fought the white-robed legions,
  And defied the fiercest storm.

There was brother Jack and Molly Dean,
  Sister Nell and Lawrence Dare;
And I and blue-eyed Minnie Lee,
  And scores of youths and maidens fair.
How we made the hillside echo
  With song, and jest, and laughter gay;
Frolicked to our hearts' contentment,
  Then homeward wound our merry way.

And 'twas thus in peace and plenty
  The years went too swiftly by;
We had never known a sorrow,
  Nor had scarcely felt a sigh.
Ah, thou generous, good old home,
  Thy dear circle was complete;
We had no absent ones to roam,
  "No weary wandering feet."

CHAPTER II.

'Tis well that childhood and youth should be bright,
All sunny with bloom, and the golden light
Of innocent days of love and fair hope,
Gathering strength with life's battles to cope.
Awake or asleep, a vision, a dream;
The real and unreal are floating between
Mysterious shores, as the stream glides away;
The mystery of life, and the grace of a day.

Ah, who can measure the fleetness of years?
The height of our joys, the depth of our tears?
The horizon bounds our dim vision here,
And our thoughts are vague as the boundless sphere
Bordering round us ; vast ethereal sea
On the awful confines of eternity !

Anxiously we peer into the abysmal gloom,
Striving to read there futurity's doom ;
And we walk with hope in its radiant light,
Or grope lone and lost through the realms of night.
'Tis either a season of bliss or pain,
Of grievous loss, or of welcome gain ;
The peace of love, soothing every care,
Or a barren waste and a grim despair.
A few there are that glide calmly between,
Leading sunny lives, knowing no extreme
Of love or of hate, of sorrow or pain.
Caring not for the world, its wealth nor its fame,
Serenely they glide like a summer day
Down the stream of time, flitting swift away.
What are thy works, thy wisdom, O man?
A little point in God's marvellous plan
Of creation ; a weak dependent, thou,
On help Divine ; doubt written on thy brow.
E'en the orb we inhabit, we dimly trace
Its spectral course through the realms of space,
As careening we sweep through voids unknown,
Round an infinite centre, Alcyone !

Aye, life 's a mystery, a fleeting breath,
Pursued by phantoms, o'ertaken by death.
'Tis merely a step from day into night,
From darkness into the marvellous light
Of a day of golden, supernal bloom
Beyond the confines of death and the tomb.

Our childhood 's a joyous and peaceful dream,
With no set purpose to darken between ;
To sing, and to shout, to frolic away
The bright, happy hours of the rosy day.
But youth will awaken, and hear afar
The muffled roar of the world's stern war.
Ambition will rise in their hearts of fire,
To fame and honors they too will aspire.
And thus it hath been, and ever 'twill be,
Till time dies out in eternity.

CHAPTER III.

We boys had hopefully crossed the Rubicon,
    And entered the arena, the battle of life ;
An ensanguined field, where millions of men
    Engage in the ruthless, pitiless strife.
Glowing pictures of the world beyond had reached us,
    Alluring our tender, untried feet to roam ;
And we grew ambitious and unsatisfied,
    And wandered away from the dear old home.

Out on the highway, the strange highway of life,
    We joined in the conflict, with hope beating high,
Heeding not the mutterings of the storm afar,
    As it darkened along the edge of the sky.
We saw not the foes that lurked by the wayside,
    We knew not the road was so dreary and long ;
We only were eager to join in the conflict
    For wealth and fair fame with the ravenous throng.

But our paths diverged, and my brother and I
    Parted, to meet in this life nevermore ;
And a lonesomeness and heartache came unto me,
    A poor wanderer ; and weird shadows stealing o'er
The way that I must go with pain and vague regret ;
    And haunting dreams of the loved ones and of home
Were ever with me in the conflict's surging tide,
    Where I strove for victory unsupported and alone.

And brother Jack went on the sea,
　　And sailed its blue depths far and wide,
In quest of wealth and tempting fame
　　To crown his patient waiting bride.
Many a day hath passed away
　　Since Molly Dean watched on the shore,
With fading face and weary eye,
　　For brother Jack will come no more.

Far, far away on southern seas
　　The wild typhoon in fury fell ;
Of Jack's good ship and gallant crew
　　Not one was spared the tale to tell.
They say 'twas at the eventime,
　　When sunset's glory crowns the lea,
They found poor stricken Molly Dean
　　In her last sleep beside the sea.

And when the summer time had faded
　　And bird songs no longer were gay,
Minnie Lee drooped low like the lilies
　　And peacefully passed away.
They laid her to rest where the roses
　　And lilies in summer may bloom ;
And the winds softly sigh to the daisies
　　That modestly mantle her tomb.

By the shores of a western sea
　　Dwelt sister Nell and Lawrence Dare ;
For them the skies were ever clear,
　　And all the world was kindly fair.
But in the old house by the stream,
　　The old folks mourned from day to day ;
In loss and loneliness they pined,
　　And faded swift from earth away.

10

And they are resting side by side,
   Near Minnie Lee and Molly Dean,
In the still city of repose,
   Near to the margin of the stream.
Sleep on ! sleep on ! oh, loved and lost,
   The lonesome winds around thee sigh ;
Sleep through the years we trust will bring
   A never-ending " by and by."

CHAPTER IV.

I'd sought the busy marts of men,
   The city's fev'rish, ceaseless din,
Where strife and vile rapaciousness
   Are steeped in crime and vaunted sin.
The rage of commerce and the clash
   Of steel and iron works that fill
The air with vibrant, rasping sound,
   And human voices harsh and shrill.

Machinery's fierce and grinding roar,
   The shouts of lab'rer and artizan,
As stroke on stroke with might and main
   They strive to lead the rushing van.
Remorseless as the hand of fate
   Stands capital with sword in hand,
To grind the toiling millions down
   To servile state through all the land.

A thousand vehicles that ply
   Along the hot and dusty ways ;
The rushing of a million feet ;
   A universal hungry craze
For wealth, and pomp, and pride, and power ;
   All heedless of the anguished cry
Of weaker fellows trampled down,
   Unheeded, helpless, and to die.

In the arena packed and pent,
  The speculative gambler's bower,
Where stocks are fiercely bought and sold,
  And men are ruined in an hour :
Hark ! the frenzied, madden'd shout,
  Exultant or despairing cry ;
Triumphant ones go proudly forth,
  Or, ruined, creep away to die.

A few there are that win the way
  Through battle's fierce and fiery flame ;
Their dauntless and intrepid souls
  Win up the dazzling heights of fame.
A few that dwell in palaces,
  Afar removed from toil and strife,
There idly dream the years away
  That bound their vain, luxurious life.

A few there are of noble heart
  That heed the orphan's pleading cry,
The widow's want and helplessness,
  And to the rescue gladly fly.
They come like sunshine from above,
  To light and cheer man's lonely way ;
Their mission is of charity,
  To help his darkest doubtful day.

'Tis theirs to soothe the broken heart,
  To see the wicked wrong redrest,
To lift the fallen up again,
  And give the homeless wanderers rest.
'Tis theirs to bear the dead away,
  To hear the last sad plaint and sigh,
To teach the mourner patience still,
  And tell the suffering how to die.

'Tis theirs to point the narrow way
   That leadeth where there are no tears,
No night, no sin, nor selfishness,
   Beyond life's disappointing years.
God sees and hears these noble souls
   That fight through every ill and pain ;
Giving their all, it shall be said,
   Their lives were not, were not in vain.

I mingled in the stern affray—
   Ah ! how I strove to win the prize
Of wealth, position, and a name,
   By bold, successful enterprise.
Oh, days of anxious thought and toil !
   Oh, nights of fev'rish restlessness !
Either elated or deprest
   By hope's uncertain, wearing stress.

And though I gained some stubborn days, .
   And won the smile success attains,
A cringing world I found would laud
   The potent power that wealth maintains.
Aye, though I crowned the stubborn heights,
   I could not hold the fateful field,
The combinations were too great ;
   When all was lost I could but yield.

I fled far out along the way
   Beyond the city's ceaseless din ;
I sought for nature's quietude,
   Beyond its cruel haunts of sin.
The arena knew my face no more ;
   I longed for quiet and for rest ;
A tender peace stole o'er my heart
   As light was fading in the west.

CHAPTER V.

And I was saddened and subdued ;
  No friendly smile would on me beam ;
I longed then for the olden days,
  And the old home beside the stream.
But destiny had made decree
  That I should nevermore return,
But on and onward go alone—
  Ah ! how these tears my eyes do burn.

Ambition stirred my soul no more,
  And I had very weary grown ;
A nameless sorrow filled my breast,
  Life's every hope was overthrown.
I stood alone on life's highway,
  With empty hands that wrought so long,
Alone, unheeded and forgot,
  As some lost dream or phantom song.

The summer sun was burning still,
  Though autumn days were drawing nigh ;
The song-birds sung in fading bowers,
  And sad-voiced winds went sobbing by.
But nature's song is dear to me,
  It searches out my every care ;
Its subtle voice brings peacefulness,
  As soothing as an angel's prayer.

And thus I move along the way
  That leads me toward the setting sun ;
I see the lengthening shadows grow,
  And leaves turn crimson one by one.
The harvest days are over now,
  The meadow-lands are safely mown,
And calmness broods where plenteousness
  Enriches many a happy home.

But from the fields all reaped and brown
  There comes a weird and haunting strain;
Where late was heard the reaper's song,
  Strange phantom voices plead in vain.
They seem to plead for some lost cause;
  An invisible, unknown power
Speaks through the shorn, deserted fields,
  And faded leaf and blighted flower.

And in the calm autumnal days
  A solemn gladness comes to me,
And though I go with empty hands
  Resignation hath set me free.
The mournful winds sob sadly now,
  The lengthening shadows grow apace,
The skies in sombre hues are dressed,
  And dead leaves flutter in my face.

And still I press along the way—
  'Tis growing rough for tired feet—
I hear the muttering of the storm,
  And watch the vivid lightning's leap.
Its blinding flashes rend the skies;
  The rain a torrent on me pours;
The mighty oak is rent in twain,
  And the dread tempest round me roars.

And thus I march along the road,
  Though blinded oft by sleet and rain;
I shiver in the chilling winds,
  And moan with weariness and pain.
And when the shadows gloom the way,
  The darkness of the lonesome night
Brings out the stars in cold array,
  And frost gleams in the ghastly light.

Then I upraise a pleading prayer,
   And sink exhausted to the ground ;
With but a crust my ev'ning meal,
   I fall into a rest profound.
And dreams of old come unto me,
   I climb again youth's shining hills,
And view the woodlands and the fields,
   And song of birds my glad heart thrills.

I hear again my father's voice,
   And brother Jack is by my side,
And sister Nell and Lawrence Dare,
   And Minnie Lee, the village pride ;
And all the friends that blest my youth
   On me their loving glances beam,
And life once more is blithe and gay
   In the old cottage by the stream.

My mother's hand is on my brow ;
   To me a perfect rest is given ;
I hear the songs of heavenly choirs,
   I dream, my soul, I dream of heaven.
I hear what mortals may not tell,
   A sacred greeting meets me there,
And ecstasy my being thrills,
   Heaven opes to me so wondrous fair.

The dawn's cold light falls on my face,
   I wake benumbed by frost and dew,
I pray for strength to bear me up—
   Again my journey I pursue.
My thoughts flow backward as I go,
   And yearning still for other days,
The shadows colder, denser grow,
   The skies now wear a shroud of haze.

CHAPTER VI.

Golden light of life's glad morning,
  Oh, so long, so long ago,
I am looking, looking backward
  From the hills all white with snow.
And it is so bleak and dreary,
  Oh, this long and toilsome way!
And my feet are worn and weary
  Marching onward day by day.

And the road is growing rougher,
  Desolate on every side,
The mountains tower higher, higher,
  And the storm sweeps far and wide;
And the skies are ever shrouded
  By the clouds, all stern and gray,
And the light grows dim and dimmer
  As night-time closes down the day.

And I scarce can trace the pathway
  That I tread with pain and moan,
And I have no place of refuge,
  And my rest is but a stone;
But I'm marching, ever marching
  Toward the far-off sunset shore,
And I sometimes catch the flashing
  Of its rays that glimmer o'er

The rugged, bleak, and lofty mountains
  That seem e'er to bar my way
Toward the "city of the sunset"
  That I'm nearing day by day.
Up and down the grim, dark mountains,
  Where the torrents leap and roar,
I am struggling onward, onward,
  Oft with heart so faint and sore.

Through the vales of desolation
　Where no living thing is seen,
Over crags and yawning chasms,
　Where dread dangers lurk between.
But I press on through all perils,
　While the days pass one by one;
Soon I'll reach the "City Golden,"
　Beyond the setting of the sun.

The light that glows above the mountains,
　Grows brighter, nearer every hour;
It sustains and cheers me onward,
　Renews my courage by its power.
And I'm trusting for a meeting
　Where the lights immortal beam,
With the friends that blest my childhood
　In the old cottage by the stream.

———

THE BATTLE OF ABRAHAM'S PLAINS.

WOLFE had gained the Plains of Abraham
　Ere the slumbering sun uprose,
Formed his lines, and calmly waited
　The onslaught of England's foes.
The September sun all golden
　Rose upon the glorious scene,
Lighting up the hills far distant,
　And the mighty murmuring stream;

Touching with peaceful, glowing fingers
　Wall and tower and citadel;
Toying along the smoking cannon,
　And ramparts torn by shot and shell.

It played along Wolfe's Highland clans,
   Those kilted, plaided, fearless men
From Scotland's heathery hills afar,
   And Lowland vale, and loch, and glen.

It burst on England's lines of scarlet—
   Those living walls glowed like a flame—
And flashed along their bristling steel,
   Resistless all in war's dread game.
Oh, it was a sight most glorious,
   Those silent lines abiding there
In the glad light of that fair morning,
   Terribly grand, and yet so fair.

Meanwhile, from Beauport and Point Lévis,
   Wolfe's besieging batteries roared ;
Shaking the doomed and tottering town,
   As on the citadel they poured
A storm of iron, like a torrent,
   Rending and smashing everywhere ;
Filling the heroic defenders
   With dread suffering and despair.

And their calamity but deepens—
   A breathless messenger appears,
And news of sudden, dreadful import
   Falls upon their startled ears,
As they learn with dread amazement
   Wolfe has climbed to Abraham's Plains,
And has made his dispositions
   With lightning strategy and pains.

But Montcalm, the heroic Montcalm,
   Though o'erwhelmèd by surprise,
Issues swift his ringing orders
   As from point to point he flies.

And there was blaring then of trumpets,
   And the roar of trampling feet,
And tumultuous preparations
   Their stern awaiting foes to meet.

Ha! they issue forth in swift, hot haste,
   And form upon the noble plain,
A chivalry worthy any cause,
   Their country's laurels to maintain.
Now they advance in swift array,
   Seven thousand Frenchmen side by side;
Rolling upon their intrepid foes,
   They come, they come in undaunted pride.

The issue is half a continent,
   But unmoved as if on parade,
Wolfe's valiant line awaiteth there,
   Invincible and undismayed.
Aye, tumultuously the French come on
   To sweep the British from the plain,
And all along their furious lines
   Burst sheets of blinding smoke and flame.

And as crash on crash of musketry
   Leaped in fierce incessant roar,
The French continued to advance,
   And a murderous fire to pour
On Wolfe's intrepid, impassive lines,
   That stood there awaiting the word;
And obeying, even unto death,
   Not a man there flinched or stirred.

What, still unmoved the British line?
   Though ghastly, gory gaps are torn
Through those gallant ranks unmovable,
   And of many a hero shorn?

Still, still unheeding, impassive still ?
  And no answering, no reply ?
And Montcalm's ceaseless volleying lines
  Are drawing very, very nigh.

All along those kilted, scarlet lines
  Wolfe had flown with swift, hot speed ;
" Fire not," he said, " without the command.
  Stand firm, brave hearts, and never heed
Montcalm's clamorous, advancing lines.
  Abide like rocks and never fear ;
Listen for the word, and be prepared
  When the fierce foe draws very near."

At last Wolfe's ringing voice cried, "Fire !"
  And thus the welcome order came ;
And instantly from that gallant line
  Leapt a withering sheet of flame.
The roar resounded through the hills,
  And when the dense smoke rolled away,
Revealed was the foe's torn, bloody ranks,
  Where hundreds of their brave dead lay.

Another volley is instantly poured
  On Montcalm's now shattered line ;
Then with a cheer that waked the hills,
  And a grand rush that was sublime,
They fell upon their struggling foes
  With the bayonet's deadly play,
And swept the French from that gory field
  In ruined, disorderly array.

" They run ! they run !" shouts an *aide-de-camp*.
  " Who run ?" brave Wolfe quick cried.
" The foe, sir," and then Wolfe exclaimed :
  " God be praised," and calmly died.

For sorely hurt by the first French fire,
   Heroically leading the way,
The beloved commander faltered not
   Until won was that great day.

And another of immortal fame
   Was on that great day laid low
On the red field of Abraham's Plains,
   By the great river's ebb and flow.
Montcalm, the e'er intrepid Montcalm,
   Beloved, revered, and honored so ;
A true patriot, with a great white soul,
   Gave his life there long years ago !

And 'tis fitting now in after years,
   That a united brotherhood
Should bedew their mem'ry with our tears,
   Those two who on that great day stood
Contending for their country's cause.
   Time the barriers hath swept away,
And a united people celebrate
   In true abiding peace to-day.

'Tis well that from that far-famed field
   A united monument should rise,
Upbearing two illustrious names
   Toward the glory of the skies.
There, towering o'er the famous scene,
   Keeping the watch of death evermore,
Fierce storms of time shall not dissolve
   The tribute by the river's shore.

MINNIE LEE.

I shall never see thee more, Minnie Lee,
  Minnie Lee with thy gold-brown hair,
And thy violet eyes, so sweet and pure,
  And thy face so wondrous fair.
I've loved thee long and well, Minnie Lee,
  But the dream was all, all in vain ;
And the busy years that drift slow away
  Have left but a ceaseless pain.

Do you remember a time, Minnie Lee,
  When we wandered hand in hand
By a silv'ry stream in the warm sunlight,
  That wound through a fair summerland ?
The world was all glad and bright, Minnie Lee,
  Mantled in wondrous bloom
Of beautiful foliage and flowers,
  And laden with rich perfume.

The emerald fields stretched far away
  In the mellow and rosy rays ;
And the crown of the distant hills was lost
  In a purple and golden haze.
And the soft south wind toyed with your hair,
  And sighed among the flowers,
And wandering o'er the billowy lea,
  Was lost in woodland bowers.

Sweetly and gladly the sweet songbirds sang,
  Aye, thrillingly glad, and so free ;
And gazing enrapt on thee, well I knew
  That time was a heaven to me.

But the summer passed and changes came
  O'er the face of the world so wide ;
And an iron hand prest cold on my heart,
  And banished me from thy side.

I shall never see thee more, Minnie Lee,
  And I'm tired and sad to-day ;
I am longing for rest, but finding none,
  As the years drift slowly away.
And I bow my head while the tears fall fast,
  And my soul is heavy with pain ;
I can only see the gathering gloom,
  My prayer was all, all in vain.

THE SOUL.

THE soul is like unto a mighty ocean
  In unfathomable sublimity ;
In calm, or storm, or wild commotion,
  And is measured but by eternity.

The body, its fitting earthly receptacle,
  Must perish and dissolve beneath the sod ;
It hath but a span to bloom and to fade,
  But the soul is co-existent with God.

THE PRODIGAL SON.

The prodigal son had wandered
  Far away in a foreign land,
And squandered the portion given him
  By a father's bountiful hand.
Alone, as the chill night was falling,
  And all through the black dreary day,
The damp wind swept cold from the mountains,
  And the sky was sodden and gray.

Famishing, weary, and forsaken,
  Poor wanderer, thy ruin 's complete ;
Thou fain wouldst have appeased thy hunger
  With the mere husks the swine did eat.
Where now are the friends that lured thee
  To scenes of mad folly and vice ?—
False friends that thy wealth had purchased
  At such grievous sacrifice.

Heavily the chill rain was beating
  On his poor defenceless head;
None but the Heavenly Father knew
  Of the repentant tears he shed.
" How many servants of my father
  Have bread enough and to spare,
And I perish here of fierce hunger ? "
  His cry rang out on the air.

But list ! he prays for deliv'rance
  In very throes of despair ;
His sobs pierce the night, and e'en heaven
  Is moved by that passionate prayer.

And a holy voice whispered " Peace !
  Thy sins are forgiven thee ;
Henceforth let thy life be stainless ;
  Rise up, go forth, and be free."

Then the rain ceased its dreary beating,
  The wind sank to a gentle sigh ;
The moon looked forth in her beauty,
  Silvering earth and the vault on high.
And blest was that son worn and weary
  As he sank to restful repose,
And in dreams his spirit wandered
  To the land of the vine and rose.

And just as the sun lit the mountains,
  And in glory shone on the lea,
He rose and returned to his father
  Far over the wide rolling sea.
And oh, there were hearts filled with rapture
  When that wayward son was forgiven ;
Voices in prayer and thanksgiving
  Ascended like incense to heaven.

———

AUTUMN RAIN.

ALL day I've sat and listened and watched
  The drearily falling rain,
Driven by wearily sounding winds
  Against my cold window pane.
The clouds drift low in the valley,
  Obscured is the lonely sea ;
Yet mournful tones from her bosom
  Are borne on the winds to me.

All nature seems dead or dying,
  Enshrouded as by a pall;
Mouldering leaves in eddies flying
  Patter dank against the wall.
And all the day on my sensitive ear,
  'Mid the sere grass and the flowers,
Beats the dreary rain like mourners' tears,
  Grieving sadly through the hours.

There are lonely graves on the hillside,
  And thoughts that are full of pain,
And dreams and regrets that are wakened
  To-day by the autumn rain.
I listen in vain for a footfall,
  And a voice that 's hushed and still,
Whose gentle, flute-like tones so tender
  Could all my poor being thrill.

There is silence upon the uplands,
  Save the sob of the wind and rain;
No dear note of the songbirds greet me
  From forest or vale or plain.
They 're flown with the beautiful summer
  To a clime by the south wind fanned,
With never a care nor a sorrow
  In that far-off southern land.

And I would go hence in the gloaming,
  Ere the light of the soul be dead;
I would rest where no earthly turmoil
  Could disturb my lowly bed.
Perhaps at the heavenly dawning,
  Far beyond the light of the spheres,
I may hear that voice and light footfall
  Through eternity's changeless years.

THE BATTLE OF THE CANARD RIVER.

FOUGHT JULY, 1812. AMERICAN FORCE UNDER GENERAL HULL, 2,500.
BRITISH AND INDIANS UNDER COLONEL PROCTOR, ABOUT 400.

HULL crossed the strait at Sandwich
　　With near three thousand of the foe,
Occupied the site of Windsor,
　　And prepared to strike a blow
He believed would prove fatal
　　To our southwestern borderland ;
Demanded instant full submission,
　　And the support of his command.

Ah ! he knew not how Canadians
　　Loved the brave old Union Jack,
But scouted at the dauntless souls
　　That drove the foeman back.
He, with o'er-confidence and pride,
　　Formed his invading force once more,
And marched away that summer day
　　By the noble river's shore ;

Marched downward by the river
　　With banners bedight and gay,
To subjugate the British post
　　That held him there at bay.
Swiftly out from old Fort Malden
　　Proctor led his valiant band,
Formed beside the Canard River,
　　Taking a bold, intrepid stand.

A handful of British heroes,
  With Indian allies fierce and brave,
Cunningly taking position
  Our southwestern border to save,
In silence grim awaited
  The clamorous march of the foe,
And the wind sighed in the foliage,
  And the river made murmur low.

As the dead the British were silent
  Till the American line drew near,
Then thundered on them a volley,
  And defied them with cheer on cheer.
The advancing foe was staggered,
  And confused by the deadly rain
That Proctor hurled from the Canard
  In volleys again and again.

And all in vain Hull struggled
  His wavering line to maintain ;
His men were falling around him,
  And the field he never could gain.
Proctor swept them from left to right
  In confusion ; Hull strove in vain,—
In sore defeat, and put to retreat,
  He fled by the river again.

THE TAKING OF DETROIT.

August 16th, 1812. American Force, 2,500. British and Canadians, 700, and 600 Indians. American Army surrendered to General Brock with Detroit and the whole State of Michigan.

'Twas summer, and over the lovely scene
The golden sun shone mild and serene.
Shimm'ring o'er the stream in murmuring flow,
And the whispering winds blew soft and low.
All nature at rest, peaceful, dreamful, bland,
Claspt tenderly our dear Canadian land.
But around o'er all is clamor and war;
Passion, destruction, are near and afar.
The murmuring stream, the foliage that stirred,
Nature's subtle pleading, never are heard.

Hull with his army had recrossed the stream.
Baffled and beaten, his ambitious dream
Of conquest had ended in sore defeat;
From Proctor's front he was forced to retreat.
Brock placed his guns by the riverside—
A gallant soldier with a soldier's pride—
Protected his front there sternly and well,
Demanding the surrender of Fort Springwell.

Refused, Brock opened with thunder's roar,
Shaking the trembling river and shore.
The *Queen Charlotte* and *Hunter* swept around,
And rent and ruined trench, moat and mound.

Covered by the guns, Brock crossed the stream,
And forming his little columns between
Flanks of Indians, moved forward once more
To storm the fort by the great river's shore.

Hull's courage failed, and his flag he hauled down,
Surrendering the State, fort, and the town ;
And his beaten forces, guns, stores and all
Were included in that momentous fall.
All Canada rang with Brock's deathless fame,
And every heart was all grandly aflame.
They raised the Old Flag o'er the conquered foe,
Where the stream goes by in murmuring flow.

THE DANDELION.

I was weary of toil and heartache,
  And the ways of selfish men,
And wandered away through the woodlands,
  By streamlet and lonely glen.
And soothing and sweet was the greeting
  The grand old woods gave to me ;
A whisper of angel voices,
  And a glimpse of eternity.

And out where the green hills were smiling
  In the sunlight's mellow beams,
I wandered all enraptured
  By subtly happy dreams.
The glad morning never was fairer,
  A gracious and perfect day,
And the wondrous bloom of springtime
  Had crowned the loveliest May.

And a thousand songsters warbled
  In melody sweet and clear ;
From nook and glade and wildwood bower
  It ravished the list'ning ear.
And the soft skies never were bluer,
  The breezes never more bland,
And a restful calm and peacefulness
  Brooded sweetly o'er the land.

I turned my eyes from the fair blue skies
  To the turf beneath my feet ;
And it mantled the rolling landscape
  In emerald waves complete.
I paused with a thrill of pure delight—
  A gleam as of sunset bars
Shone from innumerable dandelions,
  That twinkled like golden stars

By stream and mead and sun-crowned hills
  As far as the eye could trace ;
And the little busy honey bees
  Sipped the dew from each golden face.
Ah, little life of a few sweet days,
  Born when the world is in bloom,
Thou never wilt know the blight and chill
  Of the winter's dreary gloom.

Aye, a few sweet days to bloom and fade,
  And gently to pass away ;
Caressed by the sun and murmuring winds,
  And the songbirds' wild sweet lay.
Ah, spring and summer, ye fade too soon
  With all your beautiful days ;
Ye leave us in loneliness and tears,
  Along life's cold wintry ways.

THE DEATH OF SUMMER.

WHERE are now the gladsome summer,
　　Singing birds whose wild songs thrill,
Dark green foliaged waving wildwood,
　　Fragrant glade and rippling rill?
And the voice, as soft as angel's,
　　Of the low caressing wind,
As it kisses earth's warm beauties,
　　Wooing gently and so kind?

Where the whisper and the murmur
　　Of the sunlit, dancing sea?
The mysterious deep-toned music
　　Of the waves so grand and free?
Looking where the isles seem sleeping,
　　Gemmèd on the slumbering flood;
On and on through sunlit vistas
　　Fancy free our souls have trod.

And the hazy cloudlets floating
　　All the laughing sunlight through,
Mirrored on the glorious splendor
　　Of the sky's infinite blue?
Leading up the vaulted highway
　　Of the planets' centring spheres,
Till our souls are lost in wonder
　　'Mid ecstatic thoughts and fears.

Where the dreams we wooed at twilight?
　　Fairest time of all to me;
When the silver moon beams softly,
　　And the stars gem earth and sea.

Oh, the whispering, murmuring music!
  Oh, the songs of summer night!
Unseen harps in tones of rapture,
  Thrilling me with strange delight.

Ah, to die at close of even,
  With the heart so strangely glad—
Blissful as a dream of heaven—
  Death could not be drear or sad.
Fairest joys the soonest vanish;
  Summer died but yesterday;
Chill and blight of autumn banished
  All her loveliness away.

"BIG MIKE FOX."

A NOTED CHARACTER AND PIONEER IN THE EASTERN PART
OF ESSEX COUNTY, ONTARIO.

BIG MIKE was a giant Canadian
  Who never was known to do
A mean or unmanly action;
  His great heart was kind and true.
He loved with a steadfast devotion
  The friends of his early youth;
And he fearlessly did his duty,
  And as fearlessly spoke the truth.

He was a terror to evil-doers,
  But a friend to the poor and old:
Big Mike had a home of plenty,
  And a heart as good as gold.
He was one of nature's noblemen,
  One of Canada's pioneers;
A specimen grand of true manhood,
  Honored by fulness of years.

He hewed him a home from the forest—
    Who has heard not of Big Mike's fame
As an axeman and famous hunter
    Of the red deer and savage game?
Yet his was a kindly nature,
    Tender and void of guile;
His friends and neighbors all loved him,
    And sought his approving smile.

He loved "this Canada of ours,"
    And the grand old " Union Jack ; "
And traitors did well to keep shady
    When Big Mike located their track.
With an ever unswerving purpose,
    He never was known to fail;
In pursuit of a worthy object
    He never relinquished the trail.

When rebellion was in our borders,
    Prepared for the coming fray,
He shouldered his trusty rifle,
    And to the frontier marched away.
And bravely he did his duty
    With his manly breast to the foe;
He was every inch a soldier
    In those days that tried men so.

Big Mike heard voices in nature
    That appealed to his thoughtful soul—
The sounds of the winds in the night-time,
    And the thunder's mighty roll;
The drip of the rain, and the sunshine,
    And the shadows that fall between
The golden sunset and twilight hours,
    And the beauty of night serene.

The songs of birds, the humming of bees,
   The flowers that bloom by the way,
And the awesome tones of the forest,
   Through the distance dim and gray.
The rill, the streamlet, and river,
   That murmuringly onward flow ;
The hills, and the towering mountains,
   Cloud-capped in eternal snow.

The splendor of the starry ways,
   And the awful solitude,
The frightful voids and the spaces vast,
   The mystery of infinitude !
And all things that God hath created,
   From the sea to the tiniest flower,
Were a source of proof and assurance
   Of divine and mighty power.

Being wedded to one he loved dearly,
   Time's changes could never destroy
Their mutual love for each other ;
   And 'twas ever a source of joy.
But the years that are swiftly going
   Bear man's joys and sorrows away,
And his youth and his manhood's vigor,
   Remorselessly to decay.

The summer to autumn was merging
   When the wife took ill and died ;
As by a tempest he was shaken,
   Uncontrollably the strong man cried.
Somehow Big Mike was never the same
   From that irreparable day ;
And he strangely weary and silent grew,
   And his look was far away.

Over the fields, by the nooks and ways
    That had blest his early life so,
As in a dream with her so loved,
    He silently went to and fro.
Sometimes with his trusty rifle
    He sought for the lurking game ;
But, lost forever the incentive,
    The hunting was never the same.

And all aimlessly he wandered
    Through the forest gray and dim,
Through the stately and awesome forest,
    That was ever so dear to him.
The old friends, concerned for his welfare,
    Said, "Why don't you get wedded again ?"
But Big Mike raised his stately head,
    And a look as of nameless pain

Spread over his grand and honest face,
    As he said (with voice full of tears),
"I loved my wife when she was but a child—
    I have loved her all these years—
Aye, and I love her supremely still—
    And far more precious to me
Is the grass that grows on her quiet grave
    Than another can ever be.

"My heart is laid in her lonesome tomb,
    And there will be no change in me ;
Faithful in life and faithful in death,
    And through all eternity."
And there came a day when Big Mike sat
    By the shore of the soundless sea ;
There calmly waiting to launch away
    Into endless eternity.

Then they laid him by his dear one's side,
　　Where above them the grass doth grow ;
And the sighing winds, and the sobbing rain,
　　And the seasons that come and go
Are all unheeded by Big Mike now.
　　Ah ! 'tis seldom his like is seen ;
Put a fadeless wreath on his silent brow,
　　Keep his mem'ry ever green.

WINTER TIME.

I'm tired to-night of the winter time,
　　Its dreariness, moan, and woe,
The lonesome wind, the sleet and snow,
　　That continually come and go.
And the chill white robe that enfoldeth
　　The earth in a cold embrace—
Just as we shrouded the form we loved,
　　And covered the pale dead face.

The blast rolls down from an icy zone,
　　Where the lonely Arctic sea
Hath stormed and raged through infinite years
　　In terrible, desolate glee.
The trees are rocked and the hills are swept,
　　And the vales are pent with snow,
By the furious sweep of the icy winds,
　　That ceaselessly come and go.

The trees are bare and the hills are dead,
　　And the vales are shorn of their bloom ;
Where all was joy ere the summer died
　　Is now but a mocking tomb.

The stream is hushed, and the river stilled,
  And the sky is dark as doom,
And the merciless swirl of the driving snow
  Makes deeper the dismal gloom.

Relentless winter! thy iron clasp
  And withering icy breath
Earth's fragrant loveliness have slain—
  Thou art but a type of death.
And phantom hands seem beckoning me,
  And voices as from the dead—
Dear spirit voices of long ago—
  As I bow my stricken head.

My heart is full and the tears will fall,
  And my thoughts are heavy with pain;
I'm weary of loss and loneliness,
  And this wild, dark winter plain.
I long, so long, for the summer time,
  With its birds and fairest flowers,
The sun-crowned hills, the song of the sea,
  The meads and the greenwood bowers.

The murmuring rills and soft twilight,
  The sigh of the wandering breeze,
Caressing the sea, and dying away
  To a whisper among the trees.
But as I dream and the snow falls fast,
  Comes this thought with glad surprise:
There'll be no grievous loss nor death,
  No winter in paradise.

I SAW HER FACE TO-DAY.

I saw her fair face to-day,
   After the flight of years ;
I saw, and my eyes grew dim
   With a mist of weary tears.
Lost, when the summer faded
   Into sad autumn time,
And the winds grew melancholy—
   A tender and sad repine.

Sad and silent we lingered
   As the twilight crept away,
And the shadows nearer drew
   Through the stillness soft and gray.
We'd loved with a love as holy
   As mortal heart e'er knew,
But we severed the tie and parted,
   Into lonesome night withdrew.

Wandering, and never at rest,
   After the long flight of years,
To look on her face again
   Through a mist of weary tears.
The sun of life is falling
   Low down the pale, wan west ;
The twilight draweth nearer,
   The time for peace and rest.

THE FLIGHT OF TIME.

CHAPTER I.—THE CREATION.

The flight of Time! how strange, aye, how strange thy
    story!
Thou wast when vast creation's wondrous glory
Lighted up the weird inanimate universe,
And bade the intense darkness and the gloom disperse.
Aye, when the earth was shrouded in Plutonian gloom,
All without form, and void, and lifeless as the tomb,
'Twas then God said, " Let there be light, and there was
    light,"
Establishing divisions of the day and night;
'Twas then the boding shadow of thy mighty wing
Fell on the brooding sea and every earthly thing;
And when the lighted spheres stood forth sublime,
Commenced thy inexorable flight, O Time!

And wast thou amazed at that momentous hour?
Didst veil thy face to God's stupendous power?
Thou heardst the song the planetary systems sung,
As o'er the deeps and through the starry heights it rung.
And earth was glad with sunshine, and her lovely hills
Bloomed fair beside the rivers and the rills;
And waves of melody rolled down from hill and vale;
Sweet breath of flowers was borne upon the gale.
Created man rejoiced in Eden's innocence,
His every want supplied without recompense;
He dwelt with fair Eve in ever blooming bowers,
A man and woman, unconscious of their powers.

And thou wast there when lovely Eve, the tempted, fell,
And man was hurled from thence to verge of hell !
Then was vice and death and carnage ushered in,
And vile deceit, and cunning, by the scourge of sin.
Man became an outcast, with a curse upon his head,
Doomed to toil and drudgery for his daily bread.
Leaving lovely Eden and innocence behind,
With sore tempted and troubled heart, and all blind
With remorseful tears, and vague dread of the unknown,
Clasping the hand of Eve, they faced the world alone !

Wast thou moved to pity, O remorseless Time ?
For ne'er was scene more pitiful or more sublime.
Oh, momentous, measureless, sad, and direful fall !
A covert sin, an act, that sorely smote us all,
Making man's feverish life a battle all the way,
From earliest morn unto his latest day ;
Beset by every evil, no rest is given—
A lost and ruined soul, with scarce a hope of heaven !

But the world was peopled, and from every plain
Rose cities grand that gained an envious fame ;
And the ships of commerce whitened every sea,
And men and nations all strove for the mastery ;
And war and cruel bloodshed was the common lot
Of nations, who supremacy and conquest sought :
The centuries were marred by pomp and pride,
And servility and wrong was rife on every side.
And through the grinding cycles of corroded years
Thy tireless pinions swept through seas of blood and tears
Of nations, and of peoples, who rose up and fell—
Many nations, who unto death fought brave and well
For country and their loved country's deathless fame,
For tempting martial glory and a deathless name ;
Nations, who in pride and lust of power forgot
God and justice, and only aggrandizement sought.

12

CHAPTER II.—THE EXODUS.

Imperial Tanis in the setting sun did gleam,
Reflected in the gliding Nile's majestic stream,
Egypt's famed metropolis. In glory shone
Her palaces, vast temples, minaret and dome.
Proud Pharaoh strode perplexed his palace home.
His stern, unbending iron will had harder grown,
And would not bow to heaven's diviner will ;
The scourge must fall again, and Egypt suffer still.

And calm had grown soft evening's closing hour ;
The fading light fell weird on wall and tower,
And cooler winds breathed tender, soft and light,
And deeper, denser grew the lonesome shades of night.
Strange stillness brooded o'er the unhallowed place,
A look of awesome fear filled every face.

Stealthily the Hebrews withdrew to watch and pray
In their habitations unto the dawn of day ;
Listening intently through the boding night
For the destroying angel on his dreaded flight.
Stern warning had been given to Israel's watching host,
And sprinkled with lamb's blood was every entrance post.
Well knew they that their deliverance was at hand,
That they should turn their faces to the promised land.

Hark to that awful cry just at the dawn's pale day !
Up, Israel ! up ! and with the Lord's own help away !
Every first-born of Egypt that dreadful night was slain,
And lamentations rose from city, hill and plain.
On, Israel ! on ! seize this momentous hour ;
Have faith, and thou shalt see thy God's protecting power.

And out from Rameses they poured along the way,
Filled with thoughts of freedom through the anxious day.
Pharaoh was obdurate and with revenge embued,
And with his fiery hosts the Israelites pursued.

But God was with Israel, and set before their sight
A pillar of cloud by day, and one of fire by night—
A guide to lead them in their sore and troubled flight
By which they may escape Pharaoh and his might.

The sea is now before them, the enemy in rear,
Hemmed in on every side, their hearts are filled with fear.
But Moses is with them, they hearken to his word :
"Stand still," he said, "and see the salvation of the Lord :
The Egyptians ye shall see no more forever."
Look up to God and pray mightily together."
Then he stretched his mystic rod out o'er the sea,
And the waters were divided, and Israel was free.
And as they passed through safely to the other shore,
Joy beamed on every brow—they were slaves no more.

But the Egyptians pursued them with chariot and spear.
Beset by deadly danger, they grow pale with fear.
Ha! the waters are upon them—no hand can save ;
They sink! they sink to death in one pent, dreadful grave!

Didst thou hear it, O Time, that swelling, joyful song
Of great deliverance from Israel's grateful throng ?
Art thou glad when ravening tyrants meet their fall,
And freedom's cause is lifted up high over all ?

CHAPTER III.—BELSHAZZAR'S FEAST.

Stern Time, thou wast at proud Belshazzar's sumptuous
    feast,
When the pomp and splendor of the sensuous East,
Robed in gold and crimson, graced the banquet hall,
And 'mid revelry saw the hand write on the wall ;
Thou mark'st the look of horror on each frozen face,
And the deadly silence that fell upon the place
Of infamous lewdness, aflame with light and bloom ;
Thou knew'st the hand was writing Belshazzar's doom !

The vessels of the Lord had been ushered in,
And desecrated by debauchery and sin;
Stained by impious draughts to the gods of gold,
Of silver, brass, and iron, in defiance bold.

Hark! hark! What means that ominous and boding
    sound?
'Tis the march of a million feet that shake the ground.
'Tis the Medes and Persians thundering at the walls,
And before whose impetuous rush proud Babylon falls.
And ere the dawn's pale light falls soft o'er all again,
Her proud and impious king is like a wild wolf slain.

CHAPTER IV.—THE STAR OF BETHLEHEM.

And didst thou sing, then, with the mystic morning star
That shone o'er Bethlehem from heaven's gate ajar?
And didst thy grateful praises like a river flow
When Christ was born there nineteen hundred years ago?
And didst thou follow Him to soothe and bless His life,
Marking His neglect and care, agony and strife?
The meek and lowly Saviour who came a world to save:
For the fallen and sinful His life He freely gave.

All His precious days to man were gladly given
In teaching him the way that leadeth up to heaven,
In visiting the poor, and soothing grief and pain,
Healing every ill, and restoring life again.
And thou heardst His accusers when in rage and hate
They rudely pushed Him forward unto Pilate's gate,
Where Pilate pled His innocence, finding no just cause
Of complaint against Him to the state or laws.

But still they loudly clamored for His precious blood,
And shamefully crucified Him, the spotless Son of God.
O fatal sixth hour on Calvary's rugged hill!
When the sun withdrew, and in shuddering stood still,

And the temple veil in the midst was rent in twain,
And the earth trembled as if in throes of pain,
And all nature quaked with terror and amaze—
'Twas hard for the Lord's followers on it to gaze.
The world had never seen, nor ever will again,
So great a sacrifice, nor such suff'ring and pain.

And didst thou, O sleepless Time, shed a single tear?
For thou didst pause awhile benumbed with fear.
And didst thou when He rose to His Father's house on
    high
Hear the singing of the angels pealing through the sky?
And didst thou there rejoice that He so freely gave
His life man's poor and ruined soul from sin to save?

Thou knewest all the prophets and their checkered life
Of noble struggle—grand heroes in the strife
With sin and despotism. To save man's ruined soul
They endured every privation, and their goal
Was heaven and immortality. They would draw
All mankind after them by keeping God's just law.
With Paul, they counted suffering and loss but gain.
Avoiding earth's allurements and the bauble fame,
They went among the lowly to help, save, and cheer,
Facing death, every danger, undeterred by fear.
And from home and country they went at duty's call,
In the work of rescuing man from his sad fall.

CHAPTER V.—A NIGHT IN OLD ROME.

A night in old Rome! The sighing southwind blew
Down from the purple vine-clad hills, and stealing through
A thousand bowers, summer-laden and so fair,
In odorous bloom it revelled everywhere.
A million golden stars looked upon the night;
Over all the crescent moon cast a dreamy light;

And the witchery of music floated on the air
In sweet notes gay and tender.   Devoid of every care,
A million hearts were dreaming in that dreamful hour,
Tenderly enveloped by love's mystic power.
All Rome seemed wrapt in dreamful white-winged peace,
And from every weary care wooed sweet release.

But see ! the vast amphitheatre is all ablaze
With brilliant light, revealing the expectant gaze
Of a sea of eager faces packed and pent—
The fierce and gentle strangely in the weird light blent.
And tier on tier the immense radius circles round
The dread arena—fateful and most cruel ground,
Where many a brave life went out on thy red soil
Against sword and shield, or in the dread lion's toil.

All Rome was there—the proud, the poor and great,
Her chivalry and beauty, the Emperor in state.
And the expectant throng await with bated breath
The tragedy's beginning, the revelry of death !

Hark ! hark ! that blood-curdling, thund'rous, awful roar,
As opens wide the den's concealing iron door !
A majestic lion leaps forth with one great bound
Into the arena, with roar that shakes the ground.
All proudly he sweeps with stern, undaunted eye
That glittering throng.   But hushed is now his cry
That chills the very stoutest heart, and makes run cold
The blood of the most dauntless, and the strong and bold.

But opes another door, and like a flash of light
Another leaps within—and bursts upon the sight
A gallant gladiator, with bright spear and shield,
Of stern and lofty mien that will not bend nor yield.
And the dread beast attacks with hungry, savage roar,
And the gladiator falls lifeless to the floor.

But in sprang another of gigantic mould,
With visage all stern, unconquerable and cold ;
And he couches his great spear, and with fearless stride
Attacks the forest king, and wounds his tawny side.

Aroused to furious anger by the pain,
He rushes like a deadly avalanche again.
The dauntless foeman feels his fierce and scorching breath,
And is hurled a bleeding mass to instant death !
Another and another in pride of manhood came,
But the most horrible result was still the same ;
And a dreadful shudder moves that vast spellbound crowd,
And tender women sorrowfully are bowed.

But amid the horrors of that ensanguined scene
Another calmly enters with countenance serene :
A very Apollo, and of most kingly mien —
A more noble form grand old Rome hath never seen.
And, though young in years, he moves with stately
        grace,
And a soul devoid of fear looks from a perfect face.
His only weapons are his Roman sword and shield,
With which he hath made way on many a desp'rate field.
A murmur of admiration everywhere is heard,
And the coldest hearts to sympathy are stirred
As with a courtly wave that kings might imitate
The heroic gladiator advances to his fate.

The forest king awaits him with a fiery eye,
And again is repeated that most awful cry ;
And with a malignant, prodigious leap and bound
He hurls his deadly charge, but the foe is not found :
For the brave gladiator springs lightly aside,
And on his speaking face beams confidence and pride ;
And again he avoids the lion's ruthless might,
And like streaming lightning flashes in the light

His Roman sword, that stills that savage roar,
And the dread forest king sinks lifeless to the floor ;
And the gladiator bows 'mid thunders of applause.
But again is heard between the weird lull and pause
The gay heralds loud proclaiming Cæsar's will,
That the lists should now be opened to the skill
Of the most famed gladiators, four and four—
A battle unto death, to death and nothing more.

CHAPTER VI.—THE GLADIATORS.

The attendants quickly remove the ghastly slain,
And cover up with sand the gruesome crimson stain.
Again the heralds with trumpets loud proclaim
Permission to begin in cruel Cæsar's name.

And they came forth bedight in crimson and in gold,
And a tempest of applause round the arena rolled.
Oh, it was a sight ! those grand men all arrayed
For the conflict, all so calm and undismayed.
And fiery youth was there, and veteran middle age
With stern front all scarred by battle's ruthless rage ;
But the most imposing and kingly of them all
Was the lion slayer, responsive to the call.

And in that boding hour, there waiting for the fray,
Did sad thoughts steal backward along the toilsome way ?
And a glimpse of home did memory bring once more,
And the welcome smile of mother at the open door ;
The loved ones waiting for those that come no more ?
And do they play again beside the streams and rills,
And as boys again climb the vine-clad purple hills ?
How thought of early days the yearning bosom thrills !

But the signal 's given, and for the fight they brace
Their steely sinews, and sternly, defiantly face

Their adversaries with the Roman sword and shield,
And the deadly cestus, to die, but never yield.
Then leaps from the ponderous scabbard fiercely bright
Those deadly weapons that glitter in the light.
Then with a mighty clash of steel they come to guard,
And foot to foot and eye to eye they thrust and strike and
And like lightning they deliver blow on blow,   [ward,
And fair women's faces turn as white as snow.
Like crashing of the hail on shielding window pane
Fall the mighty strokes on shield and helmet, but in vain.
Streams of flaming fire from their weapons fiercely fly,
Falling fast like fiery meteors from the sky ;
And they leap and spring lightly aside to and fro
To avoid the deadly thrust or savage blow.

Ha ! one is reached, and he totters, sinks and dies.
See ! the light is fading fast from his glazing eyes,
And his proud conqueror leans panting on his sword.
But not long hath he to wait ; another soon is gored
By the deadly cestus, and piercèd through and through ;
Then the winners seek each other, and the fight renew.
They advance and recede like waves upon the shore ;
Another, and two others are stricken to the floor !
The sixth's sword is shivered, his shield cleft in twain ;
In vain had been the struggle 'gainst the deadly rain.
And the two survivors stand panting there for breath
Before closing in the dreadful *finale* of death ;
And a look of pity stole o'er each speaking face,
And in their eyes, late stern in battle, you might trace
A gathering tear ; and the bowed, weary head,
Spoke of their sorrow for their gallant comrades dead.
But they were aroused from their reverie of pain,
And looked upon each other and the dead again.

Ah ! who are they, these that survive the bloody strife ?
What fate awaits them in the struggle life for life ?

'Tis Julian, the Roman, that slew the forest king,
And the brave Athenian, of whom all Rome doth ring.
They turn and face each other, these men of perfect mould,
And all eyes are tearful with sympathy untold.
But 'tis over now, and sweeps a lurid flame
Over each stern and lofty brow ; and again
Their Roman swords are lifted up, and they engage—
The champions rouse to dreadful battle's ruthless rage.
How the thrusts and strokes fast crash on shield and helm !
How they leap and rush and glide to overwhelm !
And the sparks of fire stream again from screaming steel,
And they deliver and recover, and they reel
'Neath the ponderous blows that on their strong shields
      fall.
O Cæsar ! why not thy stern mandate now recall ?
Save those noble gladiators from such direful fate ;
Speak, most noble Cæsar ! ere it be too late.

Still those dreadful swords in fierce fiery circles scream !
How the eyes of those grand combatants glow and gleam !
For the tempting laurels they contend, and fair fame,
And the cruel pride of conquest, and a fadeless name.
Too late ! too late ! O Rome ! see, see the crimson tide
Is streaming from the intrepid Athenian's side !
For Julian had delivered an upward, lightning stroke,
And his adversary's scarce ready guard was broke.
And sorely wounded he can thrust and ward no more,
But staggers backward on the ensanguined floor ;
And the pallor of death steals o'er his noble brow,
And a weary smile—he is weakly sinking now.
Julian, the conqueror, had retired a pace,
And a look of regret stole o'er his noble face.
Now he springs to the support of his wounded foe,
And o'er his paling cheeks the streaming tears do flow,
And he tenderly clasps and holds that sinking form
That had weathered many a dread battle's storm.

" Forgive ! O Phalereus ! forgive this bitter hour !
We are but puppets in Rome's imperial power."
And those two clasp hands, and in mournful accents low
Phalereus speaks, and his face is whiter than snow :
" Tell my loving mother at Athens, far away,
That I have e'er missed her so, and every day
I have thought of her, and the dear remembered home,
And the peace of happy childhood forever flown.
And, Julian, there is another, a fair Greek girl,
Patiently awaiting me—precious, priceless pearl,
I have ever loved her so.   Say, Julian, will you
Tell her the wayward wanderer was ever true ?
Farewell, comrade Julian ! hold my fast failing hand
Whilst I glide outward into the strange shadow land."

Round the dread arena but sigh and sob is heard,
And eyes are dimmed with tears and every heart is stirred.
Ah ! 'twas a battle royal, those famed men four and four —
A trial unto death, to death and nothing more.

Now the throng glide away ; chilled is every breast,
And stillness wraps the scene ; all Rome hath sunk to rest,
And naught disturbs the silence but the watchful sound
Of the sentry of the legion on his lonely round.
Art satiated, remorseless and relentless Time,
By mankind's sorrow and life's tragedy sublime ?

CHAPTER VII.—THE FALL OF IMPERIAL ROME.

Thou beheldst the Cæsars in their sceptred power
Dominate the known world ; but their kingly dower
Was vast Imperial Rome—the Romans' love and pride ;
Her chivalric people were honored far and wide.

Where now is the Forum where Cicero thundered ?
And the enrapt throng that listened and wondered ?
Death-stilled !   But though insatiate time doth sever,

Cicero's fame shall live, and live forever.
Where now is the grandeur of the Appian Way,
And the proud Roman legions in their grand array,
As home they march with banners proud unfurled—
The stern, invincible conquerors of the world?
The barbarians of the north upon their grandeur rolled,
But the relics remain of those " brave days of old."

Thou hast looked upon Rome in all her glory—
Grand Imperial Rome, that lives now but in story;
Thou hast seen her rise resplendent as the day,
And droop, and fall to ruin, moulder and decay.
Now by the yellow Tiber, flowing on its way,
Is but the mere mockery of a grander day.

CHAPTER VIII.—ANTONY AND CLEOPATRA.

Forgotten of Rome! Antony, thou true son of Mars!
The invincible leader of so many wars;
A loiterer at Alexandria on the Nile,
Lost to the witchery of a fair woman's guile.
Cleopatra, thou famed wonder of the world !
For whom men went mad of love, and, reckless, hurled
Honor and fame and manhood at thy peerless feet—
Very slaves if they but win thy soft smile, replete
With fascination ; and as the bees about a flower
Of poison petals, benumbed is every power.

Are there no modern Cleopatras in our day
That enslave, and even men's honor steal away ?
Just as wily and just as cunning in their guile ;
Just as witching and just as false their winning smile.
And they lure and beckon onward just as well,
Insidiously leading down to death and hell.
Are there no Antonys from lofty heights to fall,
That listen to the witching, wily siren's call ?

Lovely woman ! thy thralling power 's half divine.
Thou canst lift weak man up to heights that are sublime,
Or hurl him down from duty's high and wide estate,
And destroy the powers of the gifted, good and great.
Why not use the subtle influence given thee
To ennoble and sustain in blameless purity ?
And thus walking blameless a beacon on life's shore,
" A thing of beauty and a joy for evermore."

CHAPTER IX.—RETROSPECTION.

Let us retrace our steps along the phantom shore
Of the dead centuries, two thousand years or more,
And look upon a nation whose fame will never cease—
A learned and noble people—grand, heroic Greece.
A freedom-loving nation never could be slaves,
And many desperately fought fields are pent with graves
To freedom.   Attest Marathon and Thermopylæ,
Where millions rushed to conflict on that fatal day
When Leonidas with his three hundred Spartans fell
In an immortal struggle in the jaws of hell.

Not in vain their fall—they died for freedom's glory ;
Greece remembers still—all time shall tell the story.
Persia was ruined at Platæa and Salamis,
And Greece's voice exultant was raised in praise and bliss.
Shall we not, too, O Time, those dauntless deeds extol ?
Though marred by thy stern hands, Greece shall be brave
      of soul.

Alexander at Arbela grasped immortal fame,
And for the Macedonians an undying name;
And Babylon lay at his conquering feet,
And the conquest of the proud Persians was complete.
But the Tigris and Euphrates ran red with gore,
And Darius, all ruined, could not restore
Confidence from disaster, so fled swift away
From Arbela, crushed by disaster in a day.

Swiftly the grand Roman legions marched away
To the field of Metaurus, where waiting lay
The Carthaginians under their leader, Hasdrubal,
Hannibal's famous brother—idol there of all.
Stealthily the Roman legions swift onward go,
And at Metaurus at the dawn fall on the foe—
A wave of Roman valor with resistless flow
That swept the Carthaginians from the field,
After a heroic struggle compelled to yield
To the fiery Nero, all mangled and torn,
And almost destroyed since the opening morn.
All Rome went mad with joy when news of victory came,
And a wild enthusiasm, like a quenchless flame,
Pervaded all.   Imperial Rome would not be denied ;
She swept her foes away, and a world defied.

Why should we, O Time, repeat or enumerate
The world's decisive battles, or the remorseless fate
Of nations that went down on fields of strife and blood
Forgetting the cause of freedom and even God ?
The shadow of thy wing fell on them like a pall
Of destiny when tottering unto their fall.

Thou wast with Cambyses at Pelusium on the Nile,
When the earth shook with the collision, and the vile
And cruel Pharaoh met such a sore defeat,
And Egypt lay defenceless at her captor's feet.

Thou sawest Arminius, the German, put to flight
Varus and his proud Roman legions, and the sight
Should have stirred e'en thy unsympathizing soul—
A people freed from tyranny, winning freedom's goal.

The Romans and the Visigoths at Chalons stood
Face unto face with Attila, the "scourge of God."
The carnage of that field the world remembers still,
And the fame of Attila and his daring will.

At Tours, in Gaul, the Saracenic leader came,
And many fine cities of the Franks were in flame,
And Moslem fury raged, pillaged everywhere,
And Christianity was in great despair.
But their noble Christian king to the rescue came,
And all Christendom doth revere and bless his name.
The furious Moslem Arabs were put to flight,
And slain was Abdurahman in the awful fight.
Charles Martel's name 's inscribed on the tower of fame,
And thy savage waves, O Time, beat on its base in vain.

The last of the Saxon kings at Hastings field fell—
Heroic Harold ! England's noblest loved thee well.
Nobly Britons faced the ruthless Norman pride ;
Fearlessly, desp'rately they fought and died.
Valorous souls ! death were preferable to yield,
And they sank to one pent grave on that decisive field.

O'ercoming all obstacles that beset his way,
Marlborough with Eugene for the Danube made way,
Where at Blenheim Marshal Tollard was deployed,
And the French that great day were utterly destroyed.
Immortal Marlborough ! thy arm never failed,
And despots, usurpers, before thy power quailed.
Imperishable is thy talismanic name—
E'en yet the thought of thee sets Britain's heart aflame.

Plassey, Jena, Wagram, Borodino, Fontenoy,
Were maelstroms of butchery, nations to destroy.
Even the " blue, lone sea" hath known man's ruthless might,
And torn hath been her bosom by the guns in fight—
The fight of navies, drowning the sea's tumultuous roar,
Shaking the very ocean, reddened by their gore :
Camperdown's fierce conflict, Copenhagen and the Nile ;
Trafalgar, crowning glory of Britain's dauntless isle.
But that field of fields that stirred the whole world through,
The battle of the battles, deathless Waterloo—

The brightest gem that shines in England's diadem ;
'Twas fought for liberation and the rights of men.

Unbidden they rise up, so many dreadful days—
The world is red with carnage and dreadful affrays ;
Millions of tears hath fallen, despair unspoken
Hath deluged millions of hearts, and millions broken.

CHAPTER X.—THE FLIGHT THROUGH SPACE.

Insatiable Time !
I grow weary in a vain attempt to follow thee,
Or tell the past, so full of deepest mystery ;
I cannot cope with thee, for thou art everywhere,
And knowest well that I am weak with a despair
Of ever telling of thy wondrous flight
Through the vast realms of space, by the glorious light
Of day, and the weird, lonesome silence of the night,
Or through awful voids of space, dead to human sight.
None but the Maker can measure the flight of time ;
Thou art man's Nemesis, from a power divine.

But in thought I'll flit with thee through realms of space,
And by the silvery moonlight we may dimly trace
Our way in passage to the dazzling god of day.
I'm blinded by its fierce and glittering ray,
For we are drawing nigh, like lightning through the sky,
So swift is finite thought to mount, to soar, to fly.
Now in affright, and awesome dread falls on our soul—
How its vast fiery billows leap, and mount, and roll
Over the awful desolation of its deeps,
Where a whirlwind of sulphurous flame forever sweeps
In seething eddies over its frenzied plains.
What maintains the equilibrium of its loss and gains—
Immeasurable yawning gulfs that glow and glare ?
Are Satan and his dreadful realm abiding there ?

And was it here the fallen angels found their hell?
See! see! the molten tides that sink, and rise, and swell,
And the volcanic bursts that leap frightfully away,
Lighting up the far phantom voids intense as day.

O Time! let's flee away from this maddening sight,
And by more mildly lighted planets take our flight.
Gliding swift onward over soundless, unknown seas,
What stupendous voids the mind in its terror sees!
O shoreless, frightful, endless, vast infinitude!
And by dread amaze unspeakable pursued;
We flit by the way where 'tis neither night nor day,
Amid a deep eternal silence; and I pray
For strength of soul my appalled senses to retain,
A calm the phantom seas may beat upon in vain.
Save us from the calamity of a mind o'erthrown,
Sunk in shoreless darkness with light and reason gone.

Oh, what glory bursts to our view on every side
As we through glowing rosy spaces swiftly glide,
And see the grandeur of a million burning stars
All bejewelled and bedight with golden bars!
In orbits so vast they swing in ellipses round
A grand centre, a controlling power profound.
From the gleaming and glowing centre of the day
Let us glide across the far paths the planets stray.

Hail, Mercury!
All hail! thou "swift winged messenger of the gods,"
Nearest the mighty central heart that burns and throbs;
Holding thee nearest, perhaps the best and dearest,
Obedient to the will thou lovest and fearest.
And so swift thou rollest along these liquid seas,
The poor finite mind amazed but dimly sees
The splendor of thy far panoramic glory,
And failest in an attempt to tell thy story.

13

Beautiful Venus!
Time and I are drifting by thy luminous shores,
Lost in admiration as the soul in rapture soars
Around the intense splendor of thy outward form.
Surely the great Creator sought but to adorn
Thee in a halo of radiance ; a golden sheen
Veils thy beauty, of which we mortals may but dream.
Ah ! to penetrate the veil and look upon thy face,
Which surely is benignant with a warmth and grace
Of which we terrestrials have never dreamed nor known—
We of an orb more chilling, of a sterner zone.

And perhaps, Venus, thou hast a more happy clime,
Continents more generous, scenery more divine,
And seas that are more sunny, sweet winds ever bland,
And purer streams and rivers purling through the land ;
And thy lovely valleys and undulating hills
Are glad with a grander nature, a life that thrills
To the rich, fair fulness, profuse on every side,
Where being is a blessing, full, and deep, and wide.

Do thy flora and thy fauna ever fade away ?
Are thy seasons e'er balmy as a summer day ?
Does the sternness of the winter ne'er come to thee ?
And from death and sin art thou absolutely free ?
Does love and friendship through thy years live on the
        same ?
Man's most needed blessing, a never dying flame.

Farewell, Venus ! we are sweeping fast from thy sight.
Radiant orb, farewell ! We resume our outward flight
Across the yawning chasms of eternal gloom,
In which dead worlds, perhaps, have found an unknown
        tomb,

CHAPTER XI.—MARS.

Across a lessening void we mark a red glare
Rising fierce above us, menacing everywhere ;
And we approach with fear and trembling, and the stars
Grow dim, as bursts on us the wrathful face of Mars.

Hail to thee, stern " god of war " !
Terrestrials have looked to thee through distance afar.
Down the centuries thou wast held in dread and fear
Through the predictions of astrologer and seer.
Holding a strong influence o'er the life of man,
The oracles communed with thee when war began.
But their predictions are found wanting, and a time
Of profound investigation and thought almost divine
Is dispelling the curse of ignorance.   And the mind,
Once groping in grossest darkness and sorely blind
To truth, is emerging into the marvellous light
Of day, and preceded by superstitious night.

And we hail thee, Mars ! we greet thy great glowing face
With wonder and delight, and by its glory trace
Thy continents and seas—so like, so like our own—
Thy towering mountains and atmospheric zone.
Thy undulating hills and valleys seem so fair,
Say, is thy clime more genial ?   Is life a blessing there ?
Thou hast thy clouds and sunshine, thy vapor, mist, and
    rain,
And seasons so like ours, that come and go again.
The sweep of storm and tempest, seas that rage and roar—
Are there ships upon thy oceans that come no more ?
Are there hearts in waiting crushed by weary pain,
Grown hopeless in the cruel watching all in vain ?
Or hast thou a higher strata, man a happier state,
Free from danger and the uncertainty of fate ?
A life of love and plenty, and heaven very near,
Intense in soul, and perfect, devoid of all fear?

Does slavery and wrong never come unto thee?
Is man to man there equal, and absolutely free?
And do they live on there, nevermore growing old,
Exempt from decay and death, and the grave so cold,
Where merely a blest transition to man is given
Through thy gates to the immaculate courts of heaven?

Companion Time! can we not nearer, nearer glide,
To get a view more definite of Mars in all his pride?
To view those seas and oceans breaking on their shores,
And hear the thunder of the billow as it roars?
To hear the winds murmur in the lovely bowers,
Caressing the hills and woodlands, rife with flowers?
To hear the strange, sweet songsters carol light and gay,
And watch the glad coming and going of the day?
To trace the streams and rivers, and hills that die away
In blue ethereal distance, where the mountains lay
Cloud-capped in shadow, or in dazzling light,
And the dreamy splendor of the moons of Mars by night?
To look on a race perhaps superior to our own,
A type of our first created, ere man was o'erthrown
By sin—a calamity, the direful deed of Eve,
For which our benighted world hath ne'er ceased to grieve?

Tumultuous thoughts and strange, beyond our weak control,
Flood o'er the startled mind and agitate the soul,
As, gliding by Mars' shores on our tour outward bound,
Assured by thoughts prophetic, almost profound,
That a nobler race of beings abideth there,
More blest, perhaps, and sinless—a world supremely fair.

Farewell, thou glowing orb! it may be ne'er again
To look upon thy face in pleasure or in pain;
And we bid thee now adieu, and sever thus the spell
Upon us cast by thee; forever, Mars, farewell!
And that saddest of all words floated out, away,
Down the weird and shadowy silence dim and gray;

Up from eternal distance echo repeated, Farewell !
Shudderingly receding in an appalling knell,
Still muttering in hollow phantom tones, Farewell !
From the outer verges of the universe, Farewell !

And vague doubt and terror seizes on us once more
As we dare the frightful chasms, hovering o'er
Abysses, hiding secrets only God may know,
So vast, so deep and shadowy are the seas that flow
Between Mars and Jupiter.   But let 's bear away
And calmly move along where unknown dangers lay.

Ha ! we move on apace,
Swifter than the lightning in a weird, wild race
Toward Jupiter, passing by the lone asteroids,
Whose phosphorescent lights but glimmer in the voids.
Hail, Ceres, Pallas, Juno, and Vesta ! known afar
By the vivid light, the glittering, brilliant star.
Like oases in the desert, to rest the tired eye,
To refresh the famishing, wearily passing by ;
Like harbors by the ocean, or isles far away,
The mariner's haven when skies with rack are gray ;
So ye, too, have your mission ever to disperse
A portion of the darkness shrouding the universe.

But we flit by the planetoids
And observe a deep'ning glow of translucent light
Pouring along the aisles of space, intensely bright,
Heralding the approach of an orb stupendous,
Of which the luminous shadow is tremendous !

CHAPTER XII.—JUPITER.

Jupiter is before us !   Stay, O Time, thy hand,
That we may gaze on an orb superlatively grand !
And we are rapt in astonishment and amaze
At a form so colossal, wrapped in an outward blaze

Of resplendent glory, whose illuminating stress
Penetrates the verges of the known universe.

Hail, Jupiter! of the solar orbs the greatest,
And thou art, perhaps, the grandest and the noblest.
In thy orbit three thousand million miles or more,
By the confines of Saturn's strange, luminous shore;
Or looking on the unfathomable unknown,
Peering into the nebulæ of systems strewn
In the eternal mystery of solitudes
Unspeakable, where scarce even thought intrudes.
But thou art a glorious sight when thy brilliant moons
Light thy radiant face in the night's resplendent noons!

And surely untold millions roam thy mighty plains,
Where existence and progression ever reigns
In peace perpetual, and friendship as true as gold—
A higher life and purer, of love and joy untold.
But thou'rt a mystery still, beyond our eager gaze,
Shadowed by clouds, or belts, and red and purple haze.
We believe man ne'er shall see but the outer line
Of worlds only known to celestial sight divine.

CHAPTER XIII.—SATURN.

Awake, Time!
If ever thou sleepest.   Draw out thy car once more,
And cleave the outer realms of space, beyond the shore
Of noble Jupiter.   Out fearlessly! away!
Trusting a power that sleepeth not night nor day.
Now receding from the greatest, let's seek the strangest
Of the planets on a line remote, where rangest
In untold splendor in an orbit round the sun
Of amazing distance, luminous, stately Saturn.
But we tremble, and we shrink with an awesome dread,
At the yawning distance underneath and o'erhead!
Right and left forever the soul may madly soar,
Seeking for a limit till lost for evermore!

Look up! look up! weak and unhappy doubting soul;
Let the promises of heaven thy acts control;
Then calmly away, where 'tis neither night nor day,
Over the tremulous seas, by the spectral ray
Of stars and systems scintillating down the voids;
Back o'er the desolate sea of the asteroids, ·
Floating outward still, and with mind grown more serene,
Though poised o'er a yawning chasm lying between
Jupiter and Saturn, five hundred million miles! a span
To chill the bravest, and the fearless to unman.
But we win our weird way, and intercept again
A peerless planet, with eight attendants in train.

Noble, mysterious Saturn!
We have no sight to penetrate thy outward glory—
None but the Infinite may tell thy story.
We may know thee when the soul casts off its clog of clay
And sees with spirit eyes when the mist clears away.

By persistence we're nearing thee, and pierce the light
Of thy mighty outward glowing rings, and the sight,
Together with thy brilliant coterie of moons by night,
Puts the rivalry of sister planets all to flight.
What a sphere of luminous glory circles thee,
Floating ever in a tremulous crystal sea!
And were more loving hands extended unto thee
At creation's dawn? In illumined beauty free
And perfect, subject to gloom and shadow never?
Happy thought! "A thing of beauty, a joy forever."
Who could gaze unmoved upon thy lovely face
And not desire grander powers to minutely trace
Thy inner life, which surely is noble and good?
Peerless, mysterious orb! of a sisterhood
Of grand planets, for thee our song shall ever swell.
Peerless, mysterious orb! farewell! farewell!

CHAPTER XIV.—URANUS.

Get our bearings, Time !
Ballast well, and trim thy wondrous aerial car
For another dread abyss, lying there afar
Outward, bordering Uranus's remote, lonely shore—
A shore of frightful silence, brooding ever o'er
Appalling solitudes, o'er which e'en God may weep !
And as we launch away vague horrors o'er us creep ;
But like many a threat'ning danger bravely faced,
The soul is calmed if it by right be braced.
And thus we reason as we dare the dismal deeps,
And a sense of kindest protection o'er us creeps.
And thus we win our way unerringly again,
And these tragic recesses yawn at us in vain ;
And out from the dim, weird spaces, with stately tread,
Moving in majestic order, with uplifted-head,
Appears stately Uranus !
We salute thee on our far journey outward bound,
And invade thy orbit—an elliptic way profound ;
But though thy great moons in all thy pride are beaming,
And the tremulous stars in vague distance dreaming,
We can but view thee vaguely—thy shades sternly hide
Thy cold, averted face, and mien of lofty pride.
Perhaps a race more haughty, more selfish than our own,
In arrogated power is fixed on this far zone.
Strange that the system's otherwise immutable laws
Revolve thy moons from east to west—wherefore the cause ?
Has some fierce convulsion disturbed thy outward form,
O'erturning thy satellites in a planetary storm ?

Because thou art so remote we do not know thee well,
And untold millions may on thy surface dwell.
We leave thee in thy vast area of solitude,
Never again on thy presence to intrude.
And the deep, shoreless, interminable ocean
Of gloom closes round thy evanishing motion !

And I shrink on the verge of an appalling sea
Of chaotic abysses and wastes before me !

But it passes away
As for strength and deliverance we fervently pray ;
And faith and full trust have returned unto me
On the verge of that dreary and desolate sea.
Look not beneath us ; look up ! aye, up and away !
And let not these weird terrors affright or dismay.
Like a meteor we glide in the sure car of Time,
Peering after the secrets that still are divine.

CHAPTER XV.—NEPTUNE.

Now we seek a lone station far outward, alone,
On the confines bordering on the vast unknown ;
An elliptical way of an orb that's sublime—
The sentinel of our system, on the outward line.
Like a flash from the sun we are piercing our way,
But the light from the stars flickers out in the gray
Desolation of oceans eternally stilled,
Like the seas at the poles by Arctic night chilled.
And phantasmagoria bewilderingly plays
Through the weird, sunless glens and the pale chilly haze,
Where spectres derisively grin through the gloom,
Beckoning us downward as to a dread doom !

But the victory is ours—before us they flee—
And we rise from the gloom of that desolate sea ;
And the light from the vast orb we seek meets our gaze,
Translucently illumined by a pale, cold blaze ;
And it flares up before us with one pallid moon—
A stern, lonely wanderer—majestic Neptune !

Strange Neptune !
Pacing thy lone rounds through the evanishing years,
From creation's wonderful dawn guarding our frontiers :

Peering into the distance and watching the deep
Of horror and dangers deadly that never sleep
Creep stealthily from the impenetrable sweep
Of frightful desolation, and there fierce awaits
To hurl their fell attack on our far outward gates.
But an alert sentinel, ever on his rounds,
Is faithfully guarding our remote outer bounds.

And we draw up in the shadow of thy stern form,
Grown gray in fronting the cruel battle and storm—
Draw up beside thee, weary, strange, and travelworn,
Half bewildered, o'erwhelmed, and anxiously torn
By conflicting emotions.   So grim and forlorn
Are the desolate scenes of a weird, spectred form.
Here on the measureless verge of infinitude
We shrink from the indescribable solitude
That hath lain in those bottomless gulfs of dread doom—
The black annihilation of a cold phantom tomb.
Ah, how we shrink from dangers vague, undefined !
The unreal, more than the real, disturbs the finite mind.
O All-wise Father ! give us faith to trust in Thee, ·
All fearless to sail over life's troubled sea.

CHAPTER XVI.—THE CONSTELLATIONS.

Ho, comrade Time !   Thy car !
Let 's toward the constellations glimmering afar !
Take Pegasus for thy guide ; mount upward, away!
Through the glory of the spheres fairer than the day.
Ah ! the thrilling ecstasy of this transcendent view,
Surpassing light and shading, we are passing through.
Upward and upward, higher, higher, we aspire
To reach the bright'ning stars, aglow with heavenly fire.
Ah ! we leave those horrid, grinning chasms far behind,
And they shall no more affright our frail, trusting mind.
Let the soul, that is not clay, lead the vivid way,
Thrilled by the silent song the constellations play !

What a panoramic splendor unveils before us !
Cygnus, Perseus, Lyra, Orion, and Capricornus ;
Taurus, Virgo, Andromeda, and Tarandus—
A few clusters named of glowing, brilliant gems
From creation's vast wealth of priceless diadems.

Ha ! what lurid light is this glaring from the left—
Up over the rim of creation ?   Strangely cleft
Is the gloom and shadow menacingly lurking there ;
Startlingly it increaseth in volume everywhere.
Is 't the conflagration of a great world afar ?
'Tis the lumination of a wandering star ;
And it mounts toward the zenith with a bright train
Of curved, transparent light, gliding all amain,
Upward, passing Aldebaran and Pleiades,
Vanishing, perhaps forc'er, in unpenetrated seas.

Now we have won the spheres of the far starry realms,
And their gleaming glory and vastness overwhelms.
All transcendent are those huge flaming, central suns,
And through vast areas their intense splendor runs.
And these centres are surrounded by stately trains
Of worlds, thrown out on those purple, measureless plains,
And with attendant satellites escorted through the voids :
Interspersing lone spaces are untold asteroids.

And astonishment and awe falls upon our soul
As twice ten thousand mighty planets onward roll :
The lesser and the great—innumerable, untold—
The near and the remote, their glowing orbs unfold.
But beyond is more—the dim silence of a shore ?
A myth ? an eternal mystery ? nothing more ?
But beyond is surely something more.   O God, where ?
Our finite mind is stricken dumb with despair.

For those weird and nebulous systems so remote,
In unsearchable abysses they dimly float ;

And their faint and tremulous light to us is blown
Like faint flickering wands, out from the dread unknown.
How they glimmer in the dense deepness far away,
Those scintillescent starlets in countless array !
Is Centauri, Cigni, beyond our upward flight ?
Lyra, Sirius, and Arcturus intensely bright ?
So far we may not venture in our magic car,
To mount those glitt'ring heights, deep, deadly, and afar.

Art in a reverie, Time ?
Look up ! view the transcendent glory of the scene !
Calmly I wait thee, soothed in spirit, and serene.
Look up ! and view the wonders of infinitude,
Where only thou and I, perhaps, have dared intrude.
All in grand harmony these systems move along,
Singing to their Maker a praise of silent song ;
And a burning thought comes to us, and reason sees
Unity controlling these systems, voids, and seas
To us unknown, vast, lonely, and undefined ;
But still as one great whole in unity combined
They swing round an infinite, all-powerful centre,
And ecstasy of soul comes to us, and doth enter
Our being the thought (it may be divinely given)
That that vast centre, supreme and fair, is heaven—
The centre of Divine government, holy and great,
Keeping ceaseless guard o'er creation's wide estate.

Oh, to reach that glowing centre of eternal life,
Blessed and liberated from sin, and death, and strife !
Never again to suffer loss and grievous pain,
Or mourn in loneliness the years that seem'd in vain.

CHAPTER XVII.—CHAOS.

Upward, Time !
Outward and upward in desperate flight once more,
Let 's peer into a region we dare not, cannot cross o'er.

Ah ! the light is fading fast on our right and rear,
And the deep'ning pallid gloom fills our minds with fear ;
Still upward those nebulous regions float away
Into eternal mystery, solemn, grim, and gray !

Hold, Time !
Stay, in mercy stay the dread rushing of thy car ;
For on our front and left, deep, deadly and afar,
Rise walls of appalling blackness that grimly bar
The way, and no faint twinkle of flickering star
Lights up the impenetrable horror of gloom,
Chilling the very soul, like an impending doom.

Is this the lone region of death and fell despair ?
And is hell with all its fury lurking there ?
Do Satan and Apollyon roam those deadly deeps,
Gloating o'er the suffering of the damned that ne'er sleeps ?
Was 't there the rebellious hosts of heaven found their doom,
To shriek in nameless torture in so dread a tomb ?

Hist ! hist ! did ye hear it ? that shuddering roll
Of frenzied anguish, creeping up from damnation's goal ?

O relentless Time ! Let 's flee away from this dread sphere ;
Surely death and annihilation wait us here !
With the help of heaven let us retreat ! away,
Or we're lost ! Loose thy car on our returning way !
Get thy bearings, and, like a swift heavenly ray
Of light, stream downward by the spaces and the voids,
Like a meteor by the planets and asteroids.

Ah, this fearful sense of falling brings a pall
Of impending danger ! yet ecstasy withal
Comes to us in this thrilling, evanishing fall,
And up the starlit space I hear the faint, far call
Of heavenly choirs to the legions of the blest.
All worn in mind the spirit sinks to peaceful rest,

And dreams of home come to me where all life is free ;
The years that knew no care return again to me.
But Time, that never sleeps nor rests, wakes me once more ;
And we're descending still, and near our pale moon's shore.
It seems a fitting space for so fair a silver queen,
Floating in luminous splendor, smiling and serene.

CHAPTER XVIII.—MOTHER EARTH.

Ho ! Comrade, our planet !
Behold thou the glorious and inspiring sight,
Illumined thus in the solar orb's grand light !
And how his mighty seas and oceans gleam and glow,
And the summits of his mountains crowned with snow ;
His rivers and his streams, like threads of silver gleam ;
His hills and lovely valleys are fair as poet's dreams.
And his undulating plains are rife with golden wains
Of summer's gladness, that in peace and sunshine reigns.

But the night hath closed around us fair and sweet ;
Our world in hazy, rosy dreaming 's at our feet.
A scintillating glory illuminates the sky,
By star worlds glowing in the firmament on high.
Suddenly, from the shadowy splendor of night,
Bursts a shower of meteors in phosphorescent light ;
And darting from the deep abysses far away,
They illuminate our pathway as bright as day—
Fitting escort to our aerial journey nearly o'er.
Lone deeps and starry oceans, adieu, for evermore !

Gently, Time !
Let thy car settle slowly to the earth again.
Say, has not our far quest for knowledge been in vain ?
We sought the mighty planets, systems, voids that chill,
But the mystery of creation 's a mystery still.
But with enlarged ideas we seek the solid ground,
And leave to solve the problem wisdom more profound.

Ah ! at last
'Tis done ! we alight safely from the car of Time,
And we give thanks for the protecting Hand Divine.
Welcome, *terra firma !* Mother Earth, we welcome thee,
Our terrestrial home.   We hail ! we hail and bless thee!
And now, comrade Time, temporarily adieu !
Leave me and go thy way until my hour is due.
I've mark'd thee well, thou scourge, and thy cold looks of
    scorn ;
Thou hast no sympathy for man's lot all forlorn.
I saw thy derisive smile when dangers round us fell ;
And I suffered in doubt and fear, and knew well
Of thy indifference as to what became of me
In life, in death, and even in eternity !

Hast thou not e'er since thy repellent course began
Been the dread foe of nations and the fate of man ?
In vain the pleading prayer to stay thy ruthless hand
For a moment longer of life at thy command :
A mother for her son—a child 'tis hard to spare—
And poverty and wrong aboundeth everywhere.
Oh, the red fatal fields thy cruel feet have trod,
And the millions of ghastly slain beneath the sod,
And the graves of nations thy savage hands have made,
And the tomb of friendship, and hope by thee betrayed !
What is the fate of nations, man's calamity, to thee ?
From vague dread and uncertainty none, none is free.
Thy mandates mar all life, driving man's joys away ;
The shadow of thy wing appals the fairest day.

CHAPTER XIX.—THE FATE OF TIME.

Inexorable and insatiate Time !
Thou, too, shalt die, and dread annihilation meet !
The soul shall happier be when thy ruin 's complete.
Listen, then, thou scourge ! " And the angel which I saw
Stand upon the sea, and upon the earth, lifted up his hand

And sware by Him that liveth for ever and ever
That time should be no longer." Never, no, never,
In the night of eternity shall thy face be seen;
Thou shalt not break in to mar existence more serene.
In the deeps of outer darkness shall be thy doom,
In the desolate voids of black, eternal gloom.

Farewell, then, Time!
By the ruin of the dead centuries, farewell!
By the ensanguined fields of millions slain, farewell!
By the countless tears of broken hearts, farewell!
By the mother's agonizing prayer, farewell!
By the children's want and orphan's cry, farewell!
By the repentant sinner's groans and tears, farewell!
By the sick and weary wanderers, farewell!
By the tortured, dreary lives of slaves, farewell!
By the Saviour's persecuted life, farewell!
By His agony and death thou sawest, farewell!
Aye, thy cruel flight shall at last reach death's shore,
And the soul shall rejoice when thy stern reign is o'er.

LOST AND WON; OR, WINTER AND SUMMER.

O SUMMER! thy regal splendor
  Hath borne the spring-time away;
Thy proud and passionate wooing
  Hath won thee a bride to-day.
Her sweet smiles and tears and sunshine,
  Her glory of flowers and streams
Are gone, and alone I ponder
  O'er vain, delusive dreams.

Her beautiful, tender presence
  Is lost in thy eager embrace;
Thou kissest the dewy fragrance
  From her lovely, lovely face.
And I, who was near unto her,
  Have lost my all to-day—
The chill of the grave is on me,
  My sky is cold and gray.

I stand without the cold portals,
  And through my frozen tears
I mark the bliss that e'er crowns you.
  My own poor broken years
Lie dark in a land that never
  Will bloom with fruit or flowers;
Chill is the bleak wind that sweepeth
  My desolate, haunted bowers.

And thou, with thy priceless treasures,
  In the land of love and song,
Amid full voluptuous pleasures,
  Thy years glide proudly on.

14

Alone, with my vast surroundings,
 Shunned is my weird abode ;
An outcast, with but the bitter ;
 Forsaken by all—but God.

GRANDSIRE.

OLD and feeble, bowed and weary,
 Trembling near the dreaded stream ;
Night approacheth, and the sunset
 Casts a last expiring beam
On the silver-headed wanderer
 Waiting by the turbid tide,
List'ning for the phantom boatman
 O'er the Lethean waters wide.

Yet, amid the gathering darkness,
 And the chill of coming night,
He croons a song that reaches heaven,
 E'en in trusting and delight.
And he seems to catch a murmur,
 Wafted from the other shore,
Of sweet-voiced friends that are awaiting
 Where the night comes nevermore.

Poor old grandsire, patient ever,
 Thou hast known neglect and care,
And hast felt the dreary heartache,
 Ingratitude and dark despair.
But thou 'st ever been uplifted
 And sustained by One who knew
All the sorrow man is heir to,
 And to man's relief that flew.

Oh, ye careless and forgetful !
    For your own and father's sake,
Cheer his feeble, trembling footsteps ;
    Do not let his old heart break.
Take his withered hand and bless him,
    He hath given e'en life for you ;
He will soon glide o'er the river ;
    God grant in peace his last adieu.

ADVERSITY.

WHY should our tears fall down ?
    And why should the heart sink low ?
And why should our courage fail
    When adversity's chill winds blow ?
Bow not thy head, my brother,
    Though slander's poisonous dart,
Hurled by an assassin hand,
    Find lodgment in thy heart.

And though they strew thy pathway
    With thorns that wound thy feet,
Press bravely on thy journey,
    Dare thy proud foes to meet.
Why should we grieve so, and mourn,
    When old friends pass us by
With cold and averted face,
    And we heave the weary sigh ?

Still move on, though sore wounded ;
    Fight thou sternly for the goal;
Heed not thy vile traducers ;
    Be firm, thou, and brave of soul.

Aye, still move steadily on,
　Though all the world should forsake ;
Though you sink beneath your load,
　And the heart at last should break.

Heed not the stony glances,
　Nor the cold, sarcastic tone ;
Press on through storm and darkness,
　Though you stand on the hills alone.
Still fight onward and upward,
　There are mountains still to climb,
And heights to win, my brother,
　That in grandeur are sublime.

Should you fall by the wayside,
　And never reach the goal,
'Tis brave to die 'mid the struggle,
　Displaying a hero's soul.
And as you near the sunset
　Proud peace you may gain at last ;
When the skies are aflame with glory
　You may rest from the weary past.

FULLMER'S LANE.

AFTER years of feverish wandering,
  Long years of loss and pain,
It comes like the tenderest wooing,
  The memory of Fullmer's Lane.
There was a winding way through the forest
  That I lovingly recall again—
A wild wealth of nature's loveliness
  Leading onward to Fullmer's Lane.

And how often, O heart! how often
  In the bright years that have flown away,
When all life was a sunny gladness,
  A full song of the summer day,
We went with a light-bounding footstep,
  At morn or the calm afternoon,
Along the way so sweet and so fair,
  Wreathed o'er by a billow of bloom.

There was a wealth of song from the glades,
  And by upland and shadowed hill;
By lonely tarn and the winding stream,
  And the tiniest silver rill.
The robin, bluebird, and bobolink,
  And the sweet redbird soft and low;
The quail, with its festive shout "Bob White,"
  Broke in on the rhythmic flow.

And we burst from the shadowy wood
  Overlooking the meadowy plain,
And gained the home by the pebbly stream
  Bordering on Fullmer's Lane.

Dear friends awaited our eager feet
   In that rural home so dear ;
Alight with love and the jewel content,
   And the essence of right good cheer.

And we quaffed from the delicious spring
   Bubbling up from the dark ravine ;
And played on the banks, sloping away,
   And bathed in the running stream.
We chased the squirrel from tree to tree,
   And joined in the bobolink's song
That rose from the meadows joyously
   And gaily followed along.

We saw the sun in the west sink low,
   And the warm moon rise over the plain,
And listened to the winds go by,
   And knew not a shadow of pain.
But partings come, and the world rolls on,
   'Tis ever, aye, ever the same ;
And relentless fate dissevered the ties
   That drew us to Fullmer's Lane.

After the flight of pitiless years,
   With heart grown heavy with pain,
I seek for the beautiful winding way
   That led us to Fullmer's Lane.
The stately forest is swept away—
   Not a vestige of it can we trace
As we look for the entrance to Fullmer's Lane
   And the old familiar place.

The day is as lovely as ever June
   In its wealth of roses can be,
But no friends are left by the pebbly stream
   To cheer or to welcome me.

The tear will fall for the lovely past,
   And the fond heart will murmur its pain ;
Farewell ! for strangers but mock us here ;
   Farewell, then, to Fullmer's Lane !

AUTUMN WINDS.

O WINDS ! why sound so mournful ?
   'Tis the grand autumnal time ;
The world is dressed in splendor,
   And all things are sublime.
There's a fulness in the vales,
   Fraught with blessings rich and rare ;
Ripe fruits bedeck the uplands
   And hillsides everywhere.

O winds ! why sigh so mournful
   Through the forest's golden sheen ?
More touchingly beautiful
   Than all the summer's green.
'Tis true the leaves are falling,
   The forest glades along ;
The birds are fleeing southward,
   I hear their farewell song.

O winds ! I, too, am mournful
   O'er the things that cannot be,
And thoughts that crowd my bosom
   Sob like waves along the sea.
O voices, long, long silent !
   O faces, long hid away !
Your presence breathes around me
   With the mournful winds to-day.

THE BATTLE OF BATOCHE.

WE were waiting for the signal
    In our lines before Batoche ;
Ready, eager, and expectant
    For the grand and final rush.
For three days we had been fighting—
    On the rebels' pits we'd rained
A furious and pelting fire,
    And our advance maintained.

All along our lines 'twas whispered
    " We storm the pits to-morrow,"
And a thrill of valor swept our ranks,
    Dispelling care and sorrow.
We laid the smoking rifle by
    When the shades of night drew on,
And grouped about the camp-fire's light
    To await the morrow's dawn.

And some sang songs of home and love,
    And some of martial glory ;
And merry laugh responsive came
    To pun, or stirring story.
The sentries paced their lonely round ;
    All silent was the scene
Save for here and there a dropping shot
    From pit or dark ravine.

The soldier sank to peaceful rest,
    The earth his slumber-bed ;
The night winds crooned a lullaby,
    The stars beamed o'er his head.

And all, perhaps, were thinking then
  Of loved ones far away—
Brave hearts, that ere the morrow's eve
  Should perish in the fray.

From Nova Scotia far they came,
  Quebec, and Ontario;
Manitoba's fearless sons were there,
  Ready to face the foe.
All there to stamp rebellion out
  And the grand " Old Flag " to save ;
" A united empire " for us all,
  And to traitor hordes a grave !

The thunder of the frowning gun
  Roused up that soft May dawn ;
The bugles blared the reveille
  Beside the Saskatchewan ;
And there was forming in " hot haste,"
  Beside the flowing stream.
The sun shone on our gleaming steel
  All peaceful and serene.

And Williams, with the Midlanders,
  Formed on the left with cheers,
And Grassett on their right deployed
  His Royal Grenadiers.
The valiant Ninetieth in support
  To the right the line prolonged,
And Boulton, with his mounted men,
  Near to their right wing thronged.

The Surveyors' scouts moved to the right
  To prolong the line again,
And Boulton's mounted infantry
  Formed near the open plain ;

And French's scouts held the extreme right,
    Poised like eagles for their prey;
Montizambert with his guns moved up,
    For a moment held at bay.

Howard and Rivers their gatling
    Placed by the Ninetieth's side,
And prepared to sweep the plain
    With their missiles far and wide.
And down the stream the *Northcote* lay
    With the Infantry School corps,
To upward move and draw the fire
    Of the foe from either shore.

And bravely Major Smith performed
    This trying duty that day,
Though fiercely assailed he sternly held
    The wild western shore at bay.
A gallant corps, deserving well
    Of our country and our Queen;
History records your daring deeds
    On that far storied stream.

The infantry brigade was led
    By the gallant Straubenzie,
Full of resource, with eagle eye
    Safe vantage ground to see.
At the zareba Haughton stood,
    Cool, intrepid under fire;
His men his spirit emulate
    In chivalric desire.

And thus formed up that fearless line,
    As steady as on parade;
The light of battle on each face—
    Of such are true heroes made.

The signal at last is given,
  The bugles ring out "advance";
The general 's in position;
  We're under his flashing glance.

With a ringing cheer we greet him,
  That war-worn veteran gray,
The hero of a hundred fights
  In strange lands far away.
His hand directed wise and well;
  For him the heartfelt shout;
His strategy and deep resource
  Put the rebel hordes to rout.

"Forward!" now along the line
  Rings our leader's fearless tone;
And with quick bursts of rousing cheers
  We enter the fire zone.
And the Metis open upon us
  From pit and dark ravine;
Pelting like fierce hail about us
  Comes a deadly leaden stream.

We pause, and return upon them
  Such a fire as shakes the hills;
Montizambert's guns tear through them,
  And our lines with confidence thrills.
Jarvis's battery joins the left,
  And thunders beside the stream;
And Howard's gatling is raging—
  From its lips the missiles scream.

'Twas dreadful, the roar and tumult,
  But our men rise above fear;
Ha! the Midlanders and Grens rush on,
  Winning the first line with a cheer.

"Forward, now, with the bayonet!"
  Rings out along the whole line,
And a cheerful, responsive cry
  Rose from a valor sublime.

Forward, now, dauntless Midlanders,
  And brave Royal Grenadiers!
And, gallant Ninetieth, sweep the plain;
  Ring out, ring out defiant cheers!
And, Boulton, with your mounted men,
  Rush on the doomed rebels, too:
Ye're not the corps to pause nor shrink
  When there's daring work to do!

Ho, scouts! to the front; forward, too,
  Rush like mad upon the foe;
A French leads on, ye need not doubt;
  Strike with might a crushing blow!
Montizambert, let your guns rage,
  And Howard's gatling gun scream,
And rend the rebel pits and lines,
  And shake the trembling stream!

The decisive moment had come—
  Forward! forward! side by side;
"Charge home!" the general ordered,
  With manly, confident pride.
And the ring of our flashing steel
  Greeted his lionlike eye,
And we swept like a besom on
  With a thrilling battle-cry.

Gallantly and swiftly onward
  With a mighty rush we go,
And burst like a pent-up torrent
  On the desperate fighting foe.

Like chaff by the wind we swept them
  From pit and from dark ravine ;
The bayonet was effectual,
  And withering as a flame.

Aye, we struck the pits and ravines
  In our fiery onward roll,
But not for a single moment
  Was the charge beyond control.
Hand to hand we taught them a lesson
  They ne'er will forget again,
And broken and beaten they fled
  Over the wide death-strewn plain.

From line to line we pressed them,
  Turning their right on our way ;
Clearing their works with our lines of steel,
  And thus deciding the day.
From every point we charged them,
  Till Batoche lay at our feet ;
The rebels were utterly ruined,
  And our victory complete.

And we pulled their bunting down,
  And hoisted the Old Flag again,
And a storm of heartfelt greeting
  Rolled in thunder o'er the plain.
And we cheered for Queen and country,
  And our chief we loved so well,
And silently dropped a tear
  For those who in fighting fell.

Mournfully to the muffled drum,
  At the smile of another dawn,
We put our gallant dead away
  By the dark Saskatchewan ;

And we wept as never before,
  And silently marched away,
Leaving them there at peace and rest
  Till dawn of the judgment day.

My country, forget thou them not,
  Nor the close of that sad scene ;
They dared their all for the flag they loved,
  And died for country and Queen.
Revere, then, that hallowed place ;
  Their life was no idle dream ;
Honor the brave dead far away
  By the dark and storied stream.

FALLING LEAVES.

Poor falling leaves ! I have watched you
  Fading slowly, with heavy heart,
And as you patter around me,
  Vain tears to my tired eyes start.
Drearily the rain is falling,
  And my soul is heavy with pain ;
O winds, thy desolate sobbing
  Hath wakened old dreams again !

Short-lived, but ah ! how lovely
  Were the peaceful summer hours !
Sweet golden days in the wildwood,
  Reposing 'mid fairest bowers.
The skies were grand in their beauty,
  And the earth was never more fair ;
The hills and vales filled with rapture,
  Caressed by the perfumed air.

As a child of nature I revelled
　By hillside, cool streamlet, and sea ;
Tender and kind were the voices
　That whispered in love unto me
Of a time that had no seeming,
　When life was all joyous and gay,
And the years, with roses laden,
　Passed soon like a dream away.

I knew when the autumn shrouded
　The world in a strange, sad veil,
And heard in the lonely woodland
　The hollow, mysterious wail
Of the wind in sad meanderings
　By forsaken bower and stream,
Searching out the dim recesses
　Where the summer had dwelt supreme.

Whence cometh these weird, sad longings ?
　Ah ! wherefore this dreary pain ?
I'm tired as a weary child,
　And would rest and forget again ;
But the drip of the weeping rain,
　And the moan of waves on the shore,
And the pitiful falling leaves
　May cease in the heart nevermore.

THE SEA.

Ah ! but thou'rt beautiful, sapphire sea,
　When the sun in splendor along thee smiles,
And thy sparkling wavelets rise and fall
　In murmurs afar by a thousand isles,
Where whispering winds speak soft and low—
　O gentle isles, kissed by thy restless feet—
Where the spices and palm and olives grow,
　And odorous blossoms so fair and sweet.

But why dost thou moan so, O great, sad sea?
　Such a weary, pitiful, pleading moan,
Like a soul all dead to the hope of heaven,
　Drifting out and lost in the vast unknown.
And why dost thou sob through the moonless night?
　Such passionate sobs rend thy deep, dark caves,
Throbbing up from thy bosom ne'er at rest,
　O sea, with thy million lone hidden graves !

Thy deep soul ever appealeth to me
　In the lonesome night on the wave-worn shore ;
But I cannot tell all it says to me
　Of voices and dreamings that are no more.
Sometimes thou murmurest soft and low,
　When the summer glorifies earth and sea ;
Thy pathetic voice is borne on the wind,
　The sweet south wind toying kindly with thee.

And thou seemest to woo in tender tones,
　And would clasp and hold the warm, shining shore ;
But thou failest, O sea, and thy sad voice
　Is sobbing and sobbing forevermore.

O wonderful, majestic, awesome sea !
    Surely the Creator speaketh in thee ;
And a sorrow so deep, so mysterious,
    Appealeth in sobs eternally.

When the wild typhoon sweeps thy heaving breast,
    And thy billows threaten the angry sky,
Thy merciless fury knoweth no bounds
    As the doomed ships before thee madly fly.
In vain the appealing flag of distress,
    In vain the minute guns peal o'er the sea,
In vain are prayers and the pleading cry—
    They sink ! they sink to eternity !

But the storm rolls by, and the waves subside,
    And the sun in glory bursts forth again ;
But oh ! there are many breaking hearts,
    Weary of waiting in hopeless pain.
Aye, ye're watching in vain through dimming eyes ;
    Ye've waited so long by the storm-swept shore :
The seasons will come and the years will go,
    But the loved will come no more, no more.

Art troubled, O sea, that ye rest not, nor sleep,
    Nor cease thy dirges by night or day ?
The loved and lost of the pale, dead past
    Strew thy drear chambers and desolate way.
And they slumber in utter loneliness ;
    No friend may kneel by their dismal tomb ;
They never know of the spring's fair hours,
    Or the songs of birds.   The summer's bloom

Decks not their mystical, sea-fret graves,
    But they await the illumining ray
Of light from heaven to pierce the cold gloom—
    An everlasting celestial day.

15

I love thee, O sea, in thy every mood—
  In passion rent, or in gentle tone;
Thy awesome voice is a mystery still,
  But never at rest is thy weary moan.

ONLY A FADED LEAF.

'Twas only a faded leaf
  That settled down on my hair,
The last from a poor bare bough
  In the crisp October air.
I gathered it tenderly in,
  And could not restrain the tears
As I thought of summer hours
  And the silent faded years.

O beautiful fallen leaf!
  Russet and crimson and gold,
With a tinge of emerald still,
  Smitten by the frost and cold.
A souvenir of the past,
  Telling of spring's fair hours,
Of the bloom and sighing winds,
  And June's ambrosial bowers.

But still this dear autumn time
  Is tender and subtly sweet,
Though littered by fallen leaves
  Rustling sad at my feet.
As lives that are good and true
  Fade out like an autumn day;
More beautiful at the last,
  They serenely pass away.

So all the hills are enwrapped
  In the hazy, dreamy light
Of the Indian summertime —
  A season of calm delight.
Ah ! little pale fallen leaf,
  Type, thou, of man's short hour—
To bud and bloom for a span,
  And fade as the leaf and flower.

ASTRAY.

I HAVE not a cent in the world,
  And I've left my father's home
Out in the hard world to wander,
  Friendless, poor, and alone.
I have sought in vain for a place
  To earn my daily bread,
A shelter from the winter's storm,
  And a place to lay my head.

But cold are the bosoms I meet,
  Aye, cold as the drifting snow ;
I'm turned away from their doors,
  And I know not where to go.
All day I've struggled along
  Through the weary wastes of snow,
And I'm tired almost to death,
  But who will care now, or know ?

The night is closing around me,
  And fierce is the angry sky ;
I'm hungry and faint and helpless—
  Must I sink by the way and die ?

'Tis strange in this terrible hour
   That thoughts of my childhood's days
Should pass like a dream before me
   In all their innocent ways.

Ah! sunny home by the hillside,
   Song-birds of the long ago,
I hear your glad, wild, sweet singing,
   And the murmuring brooklet's flow.
Ah! happy days in the wildwood,
   Revelling in nature's bowers ;
Bluest skies, and soft wind sighing
   'Mid the tall trees and flowers.

Ah! songs I sang with my mother
   At evening's golden glow,
Voices of father and brother,
   Why are ye haunting me so?
Ah! years that came with temptation,
   And lured me away from right,
Till hope was gone, and in frenzy
   I fled from its wiles in fright.

Weep, hearts, for there on the morrow,
   By the sun's wan light ye may trace
His weary way, and find there
   Frozen tears on his poor dead face.
God in His infinite mercy
   Knew when all hope was slain,
And closed his eyes, and in pity
   Relieved him from earthly pain.

A SPECTRE.

Away, gaunt fiend !
Take thy tyrannous presence from my cottage door.
  Too long thou hast held me captive at thy will,
  And I cannot bear thy blighting touch so chill,
For I am weary, and my heart is bruised and sore.
Too long thou'st mocked me with thy hideous face ;
  When all the world seemed dark and cold to me,
  Thou'st jeered and taunted in thy fiendish glee,
That I was homeless and had scarce a resting place.

Vile spectre, avaunt !
Take thy evil visage from my humble cottage door,
  And thy lacerating talons from my shrinking heart.
  O ! I have prayed that thou would'st pity and depart,
And leave me peace at last that I might want no more.
Why hast thou all these weary and burdened years
  Shadowed every hope and left but toil and pain,
  Clutched at my very life, and made all vain
The aspirations that died in sorrow and in tears ?

Down, black phantom !
Filled with blighted hopes, vain dreams, and dead men's
        bones,
  Thou heedest not the pleadings of the souls that die,
  The widow's want and prayer, the orphan's cry
For help, earth's poor that struggle on 'mid sighs and
        moans.
Thou hast still'd the voices that rang light and gay,
  And hushed the laughter that will gush no more,
  And brought the gloom of night along the shining shore
Of souls once bright with bloom and sunny as the day.

Insatiate ghoul !
I'd snatch thee from thy infamous pedestal,
    And hurl thee writhing down the glaring vaults of hell,
    That man might walk redeemed, with head erect, and
        dwell
In plenteousness when capital's divided well.
But I'll arise and smite thy grinning, dev'lish face;
    Aye, I'll fight thee unto death's grim, ghastly gate,
    And, though I perish by thy cruel fangs and fate,
'Twere best to fight a hero's fight for liberty and place !

Malignant foe !
Thou shalt at last be put to ignominious flight,
    For life is but a span, an echo on the shore,
    Where burdens are laid down and sorrow is no more.
Thy doom shall be " cast out in endless, shoreless night."
Thank God, there is a sphere to which thou canst not rise,
    A radiant place of fadeless bloom divine :
    Man's home supernal, far beyond the reach of time,
Where weary ones may rest, O wondrous paradise !

A REVERIE.

THE golden sun all mellow was falling
    Adown the far aisles of the flaming west,
Bathing earth and sea in fading glory
    As it sank majestically to rest.
Murmuringly the summer winds were breathing
    A song of love to the birds and flowers,
Wooing low the streams and distant woodlands,
    And toying with gems in fairest bowers.

Low were the tones, mysterious and soothing,
  That came from the depths of the throbbing sea,
Whisp'ring the soul of the great Eternal,
  Far, far beyond, where bright spirits are free.

Gently the twilight came stealing around me,
  Mantling earth and sea in dreamy array ;
Palely the night orbs o'er me were twinkling,
  Silv'ring the waters away and away.
Serenely the queen of night in her beauty
  Looked on the sea and the isles afar,
Pointing her rays o'er the quivering foliage
  To the far gates of day just left ajar.
Sweet were my dreamings alone in the gloaming
  On that summer's eve of the long ago,
Loving and trusting in meek adoration,
  Quaffing from nature's mysterious flow.

I paused by the murmuring sad voiced sea,
  Dreaming of love, with the world at my feet ;
So trusting is youth at the flush of its morn,
  Soaring high on the wings of hope complete.
But darker and denser the shadows grew,
  Deepening to gloom as night grew apace ;
Ghostly clouds hid the stars, sky, earth, and sea,
  And the crescent moon hid her beautiful face ;
And the wandering night winds sighed and grieved,
  And the waves sobbed low along the dim shore,
And a voice like a prayer, full of tears,
  Wailed pitifully, " Nevermore ! "

And I softly wept, yet I scarce knew why ;
  Vague doubts and fears touched my passionate soul,
Like the approaching tempest heard afar
  When its muttering thunders onward roll.

I wandered away o'er the pitiless world,
   Fighting life's battle with might and with main,
And amid toil and tears through long sad years,
   So weary of waiting, and all in vain.
All scathed and worn by the battle's fierce flame,
   With the day uncertain and incomplete;
Bright hope, love, and fame, and friendship so dear,
   Lie a pitiful wreck at my tired feet.

I've come once again with the summer time,
   At the evetime's mystical afterglow,
To the lonely sea, 'neath a waning moon,
   Where the waves still restlessly ebb and flow.
I look far out o'er the shadowed deep,
   Seeking its dreamland isles afar;
But I scarce can see for the blinding tears
   The beautiful sunset gates ajar.
But I seem to view up its golden aisles
   A fairer world 'neath immortal skies,
All bright with bloom, and the friends I loved,
   On the fadeless hills of paradise!

IN MEMORIAM.

List! The year was slowly dying
   In the dark December days,
And the winds moaned low and sadly
   O'er the lonely winter ways.
And the hills and vales were lying
   As when life's last flush hath fled,
Folded in a snowy mantle,
   Silent, dreamless, cold and dread.

Whilst the winds without were grieving
  O'er the meads and frozen streams,
Hearts within were filled with mourning,
  Near the firelight's fitful gleams.
On a couch of painful anguish,
  Meek and patient, pale and wan,
Hand clasped hand in solemn parting—
  Dying mother, stricken son.

" Dearest mother, are you trusting
  In the name of Jesus now,
As you near the Stygian river
  With the death damps on your brow ?
Oh, so cold and dark the waters !
  Do you fear to enter in ?
Mother, I shall sadly miss you
  In this world of care and sin."

" Yes, my boy, I'm fully trusting
  In the Saviour's mighty love ;
And I know His hand will guide me
  Safely to His courts above.
Ah ! I hear such holy voices
  Chanting on the other shore,
Filling all my soul with rapture
  As I'm swiftly sailing o'er."

Thus she passed beyond the river,
  Far beyond the gleaming bars
Of the sunset's golden glory
  And the pathway of the stars.
And they laid her last cold relics
  'Neath the dreary drifting snow,
Whilst the winds moaned saddest requiem,
  Prayerful, solemn, grieved, and low.

ONLY DREAMS.

ONLY dreams, aye, dreams forever
 Haunt my soul and fill my brain
With the loved that I may never
 Meet in this great world again.
Springtime seems but fraught with sadness,
 Though the birds sing just as gay ;
And there's still as much of gladness
 In the blooming, balmy May ;

And the soft winds play as lightly
 O'er the verdure and the flowers ;
And the sun beams just as brightly
 Over nature's lovely bowers ;
And the streamlet and the river
 Murmur onward to the sea,
Singing low with silver quiver
 Just the same, but not to me ;

And the twilight dews of even
 Just as sweet a fragrance shed,
And the pale night orbs of heaven
 Beam the same, though years have fled—
Years that brought so many changes,
 Years that stole my flowers away ;
Now in fancy only linger
 Dreams that once were bright as day.

Visions of the cot and wildwood
 Flit before me evermore,
But the friends that blest my childhood
 Meet me at the stream no more.

Thus it is that dreams will haunt us—
  Forms and scenes we loved so well ;
Smiling faces, tones and voices,
  Time nor change can e'er dispel.

THE BATTLE OF CUT KNIFE HILL.

O'ER the vast rolling prairie,
  And afar in the " Great Lone Land,"
Otter's column 's advancing
  Amid dangers on every hand.
Yet forward, steadily forward,
  A day and a long night they go,
And just at the morn's pale dawning
  Sweep down on the savage foe.

And under the gallant Otter
  Swiftly they form up and well,
Dash forward over the streamlet
  Into coulee, ravine and dell.
Moving into the fighting line
  With a rush the fierce gatling goes ;
Forward, into the hot centre,
  Dealing death on the dusky foes.

And the intrepid Shortt moves up,
  Placing his guns on either side,
To sweep coulee and dark ravine,
  And the Cut Knife Hill far and wide.
With " B " Battery in support
  Of Rutherford's raging guns,
Shaking the dark, trembling stream
  That by the base of Cut Knife runs.

On either flank of the batteries
  The Mounted Police were placed,
And steadily they extended,
  And proudly the dark foe faced.
To the right and rear were the Guards,
  And the proud Infantry School corps,
Cool and steady as on parade,
  Under Gray and the stern Wadmore.

To the left, on a ledge of the hill,
  Extending near unto the stream,
Was the ever-gallant Queen's Own
  With but an interval between
The stealthy approach of the foe.
  Protecting the ford and right rear
Was the good Battleford Rifles—
  Brave men, deterred not by fear.

Opening along the whole line,
  The roaring guns shake the hill,
And the infantry's fire crashes,
  And all hearts heroically thrill.
Thus cool, collected, and steady,
  Dealing out grim death on the foe,
By coulee and hill and ravine,
  And the trembling stream below.

Here the foe rushed for our gatling,
  But were met by a scorching flame
From the Police and artillery,
  And driven confused back again.
Shortt gallantly led the brave onset,
  And the foe were punished sore,
And the deafening guns raged madly,
  In one incessant roar.

The right rear was now menaced,
  But there came a defiant cheer
From the ready Battleford corps
  As the savage foe drew near.
And the gallant Nash with his corps
  Cleared the ground that was threatened so ;
The Queen's Own and the Guards assisted,
  And delivered a telling blow.

The left rear, too, was threatened,
  But instantly now to the fore
Went the fearless Queen's Own Rifles
  And Nash with his gallant corps.
Hot and furious was their fire,
  Holding there the red fiends at bay,
And their coolness and their valor
  Added lustre to the day.

Meanwhile, Ross, the intrepid scout,
  With his resourceful, daring band,
Stole around the dark foeman's flank,
  Making untenable their stand.
Thus at eleven o'clock of the day,
  After six hours of strife,
Our flanks and our rear were clear of the foe,
  Though severe was the loss of life.

But the object of the reconnaissance
  Was admirably attained,
And Canadian and British valor
  Was at Cut Knife Hill sustained.
The wounded and dying were cared for,
  And the gallant dead borne away
To the slow, sad tread of comrades,
  At the close of the dying day.

Honor Otter, Herchmer, and Shortt,
　　Wattom and the gallant Pelletier,
Nash and McKell, Sears and Mutton,
　　And Rutherford hail with a cheer.
They fought for this grand land of ours,
　　For our union from sea to sea;
Placing their lives in the balance,
　　They won, and Canada is free.

And shall not a grateful country
　　Honor the living and dead?
We, so blest in our true freedom,
　　Remember the blood that was shed.
As long as the years roll by us
　　May the Old Flag over us wave,
And conspirators and traitors
　　Find a ready dishonored grave.

THE SILENT VOICE.

O songless, lost, and silent voice,
　　Steal back from pale oblivion's shore,
And breathe the songs so loved of old,
　　That echo down the years no more.
O voice, lost voice, that pined and died—
　　A solace with the changing years—
I miss thee so, my more than friend,
　　That soothed to rest life's cares and fears.

We were so gay, lost friend and I,
　　When life was young and all a song;
And tenderness steals o'er us now,
　　As thoughts of old around us throng.

We played at dawn by field and glade ;
　The wild birds joined us with their song ;
And oh ! the days were fair and sweet
　That to the dreamy past belong.

We were so merry when the hills
　Were mantled o'er with emerald green,
And summer winds blew soft and low,
　And bloomed the lilies by the stream.
And how we sang by lane and mead,
　And wandered through the forest aisles,
By brook and rill and lonely tarn,
　Where nature in profusion smiles.

And tasks were lightened by our lay,
　And dear to us was the old farm—
Our own dear home beside the stream,
　Where hearts were sunny, true and warm.
The ev'ning heard us singing still—
　A solace 'twas for every care—
Ah ! feet will seldom go astray,
　If cheered by song and mother's prayer.

We had a lay for every theme,
　And sang of home, of life, of heaven,
Our country and our country's cause,
　The sinner, and his sins forgiven.
We sang of friendship and of love,
　Of plighted troth and true hearts slain,
Of heroes and their noble war
　On many a hard-fought battle plain.

But time flows on, and bears away
　Our youthful dreams, and on the tide
Of stormy seas we too are borne,
　Drifting and drifting far and wide.

And still we sing, though oft through tears
　　We scarce can trace the lonesome way,
Or count our grievous loss or gains
　　As closes down the dreary day.

And we have known adversity,
　　Saw love and friendship take their flight;
And very weary grew our feet;
　　Alone we looked upon the night.
And sad and sadder grew our lay,
　　But still it soothed the heart to rest;
Teaching us patience to abide
　　The years in trust and tenderness.

But when our voice grew weary, too,
　　Chilled by the winter's sleet and rain,
And stilled in death's embrace it lay,
　　Our head bowed low in dreary pain.
We are forgot, our voice and I,
　　That once could wake the smile or tear,
And stir the heart to tenderness,
　　And drive away its every fear.

And now our feet must go alone;
　　Our day is passing, night is near;
If we should sink beneath our load,
　　Ah! who will drop a silent tear?
A thought comes to us, and it cheers,
　　It makes the lonely heart rejoice,
That in a sphere above the stars
　　Awaits a more melodious voice.

FORGOTTEN.

A LITTLE apart from the rest,
   Unnoticed and alone,
No crypt or costly monument,
   Nor rich engraven stone.
A little lonely weed-grown mound
   But marks the silent spot
Of all that now is left of her,
   The fair, so soon forgot.

The summer hath kindly given
   A few wild fragrant flowers
To deck her lonely, neglected grave
   In meekness from her bowers.
And nature's song is there trilling
   A soothing lullaby,
And in the rustling foliage
   The wind breathes sigh for sigh

To the voice of wavelets murmuring
   In whispers deep and low,
Of a maiden fair as summer
   That perished long ago.
Meek and loving and gentle,
   Pure as the angels are
Was her every thought and feeling,
   Her soul was bright as a star.

I'm filled with a deathless longing,
   Aleene, kneeling by thee ;
But the years are slowly waning
   Into eternity.

16

And shall we be reunited,
    Where love and life ne'er dies,
In a land of summers fadeless,
    In the vales of paradise ?

———

INNER LIFE.

What is this that subtly stealeth
    Over my soul to-day,
Just as the last sweet day of summer
    Fleeth swiftly away.
Weird and strained is this tender silence
    That broodeth o'er the lea,
Over the streams and lonely woodlands,
    And along the shrouded sea.

The fields are shorn of their golden yield,
    The harvest time is o'er,
And the last sweet day of the summer
    Is gone for evermore.
I hear only the crickets chanting
    A ceaseless, haunting strain,
And the plaint of the wandering winds
    Filling my heart with pain.

Regret for the past that was so fair
    Steals back with phantom tread,
With beautiful dreams and faces dear
    Hid with the silent dead.
And I bow in tender reverence
    Beside their sacred tomb ;
My soul is full of a fond desire
    For rest, sweet rest, and home.

But still in these mystical dreamings
  Comfort and strength is given ;
These soulful, loving, and tender thoughts
  Bring us nearer heaven.
And nature is full of subtle charms
  That speak to the soul alone ;
And they soothe and purify and bless,
  Nearing the setting sun.

SPRING-TIME.

A MONOTONE of love and song,
  In cadence mild, serene
As unseen harps borne on the wind,
  Breathes over all the scene.
I love thee yet, beauteous time ;
  Yet oh, so far away
Adown the dim forsaken past
  Thou lead'st my thoughts to-day.

So grand, awak'ning from death's sleep,
  So regally adorned
Art thou, O nature's queen ; and I
  Thy absence long have mourned
As for the dead who come no more.
  Across a wintry sea
I look in vain ; only in dreams
  Do they return to me.

The melody of other times,
  In many an olden song,
Echoing down the vanished years
  In interminable throng,

Steals o'er my soul, and I would wake
　　The dear old strains again,
Though fraught with many banished hopes,
　　Delusive dreams, and vain.

———

WE HAVE MISSED THEE.

A SONG.

WHEN the low, sweet winds of summer
　　Play among the wildwood trees,
And the waves of ocean murmur,
　　And the flow'rets ope their leaves ;
In the evening's dewy hours,
　　At the twilight's dreamy ray,
In the morning's balmy bowers,
　　All the long, fair summer's day.

CHORUS.

Shall we never hear thy gentle voice at evening ?
　　We've been pining for thee, Allie, all the day ;
And our sad hearts o'er the lonely seas are gliding,
　　Seeking vainly where our darling's footsteps stray.

We have missed thee, ever missed thee,
　　With thy sweet and tender smile,
And thy bright and glowing beauty—
　　Nature's pure and winning guile ;
And thy voice's glorious music
　　We, alas, do hear no more
In the vale where Allie wandered
　　In the dear old times of yore.

When the golden sun his splendor
  Pours along the summer sea,
And the southern winds are dying,
  Allie dear, come back to me.
We are weary and so lonely ;
  Ah, this life seems but in vain
Since our Allie hath departed—
  Dearest one, return again.

THE RESCUE.

A Thrilling Incident, and a Gallant Rescue off Leamington,
Ontario, in the Winter of 1895.

Bitterly all day the north-east gale
  Swept with a wild roaring moan,
Hurling particles of glist'ning ice
  That cut to the very bone ;
And a leaden and lowering sky
  Threatened the frozen world ;
The storm king was sternly approaching
  With frosted banners unfurled.

Ever darker and denser it grew
  As the day wore on apace,
And the swirl of the merciless winds
  Tore on in a fierce, wild race.
It was a day to seek the shelter
  Of home by the warm fireside ;
God help the homeless at such a time
  That wander far and wide !

Suddenly in hushed tones through the town
  Ran the word from Pigeon Bay,
That the harvesters of ice were drifting
  Helplessly out and away—
On an ice-floe helplessly drifting,
  Detached from the wind-rifted shore,
Out over the bosom of Erie
  'Mid the tempest's ruthless roar.

"To the rescue! the rescue!" was shouted,
  And we paused with bated breath,
Close beside the rage of the waters,
  Black and menacing with death.
And many a stern face grew whiter
  As we saw thro' the deadly gloom
Our friends drifting out, swiftly drifting,
  Helplessly to their doom.

"Launch the 'lighter'! quick, launch the 'lighter'!
  And drift to the floe away,
O'er the swirling, desolate waters,
  Out over wide Pigeon Bay."
Thus cried the dauntless Robinson,
  And instantly to his side
Sprang Conover, Miller and Cullen,
  And Frank Ives in manly pride.

"Pay out the long shore-line now swiftly,
  We'll save them at any cost;
Pay out till we reach the ice-floe,
  They must not, shall not be lost."
And they drifted before the tempest,
  And gained the edge of the floe,
But the very last inch of the shore-line
  Could let them no farther go.

And before the rescuers could reach them
  They drifted swiftly away,
While the gallant crew of the "lighter"
  Were now helpless on the bay,
With the black waves leaping over them,
  Icy, and cold as death,
Stiffening their garments about them,
  And congealing the very breath.

We knew that their efforts were futile,
  And looked in each other's face,
And scanned the wild waste of waters,
  As the gloom of night grew apace.
"Launch the sail-boat! launch the gallant *Davie!*"
  The hero Johnston cried,
And Ives and Ralph and Herman Robson
  Instantly stood by his side.

And they hoisted their ice-cold canvas,
  Spread their wings and swept away,
Full three miles through the wild tempest,
  Engulfed in a deadly spray.
They reached and saved the perishing,
  Landed them safe on shore—
At the imminent risk of their own lives,
  Gave them to their friends once more.

And we hauled away on the shore line,
  Hauled the "lighter" back through the gloom
Of the storm and approach of night-time,
  Saving all from a dreadful doom.
Some cheered, and others were weeping,
  And through the old town there ran
The news of the intrepid rescue—
  Man's venture for fellowman.

The Humane Society awarded
　　A medal for each manly breast,
And we pinned their badges of honor
　　On proudly, for such a test
Of stern endurance and heroism
　　Is seldom, aye, seldom seen ;
And we cheered for them as ne'er before,
　　For our country and our Queen.

———

A PRAYER.

FATHER, I've trespassed in Thy sight,
　　But I'm weak and poor and sad ;
My days are long and dreary,
　　And my soul is never glad.
My nights are dark and lonely,
　　And my dreams are full of pain ;
I've wandered, oh, so long,
　　And toiled so long in vain.

I'd feel Thy forgiving hand
　　Rest kind on my stricken head
Ere the last sad sigh is breathed,
　　And I sleep with the quiet dead
In a dreamless, perfect rest ;
　　No bitter, cankering care
To trouble my deep repose,
　　Or fill me with dark despair.

Forgive, for my burden is heavy,
　　And grievous, and hard to bear,
And I have no home to-night ;
　　And around me everywhere

The chill and blight are falling,
  And the way is rough and cold ;
The summer of life is faded,
  And I am growing old.

Forgive, for my tears are falling ;
  I kneel at Thy sacred feet ;
Lead from " the deep, dark valley,"
  Where but ruin reigns complete.
Forgive, for all around me
  Is the winter's fret and moan,
And I long for summers fairer,
  Near Thy great white throne.

THE FAREWELL.

I stood to look a last farewell
  Upon our dear Dominion shore,
Ere I should turn afar to roam,
  Perhaps to view it nevermore.

I looked upon the waters bright ;
  The scene recalled the times of yore,
But who can tell how I have loved
  Thy waves and sands, oh, peaceful shore ?

The crescent moon shone o'er the sea
  And lit the dark and vaulted sky,
And touched the waves that rose and fell
  In gentle murmurs like a sigh.

Ah ! days, sweet days, ye've flown away
  With Aleene by the shining sea ;
It was a time too fair to last—
  Only a mem'ry now to me.

For time's relentless years went by
　　On voiceless, viewless, sable wing :
Ah ! lost Aleene ! that drooped and died
　　In the sweet fragrance of the spring.

She's resting now, to wake no more
　　When moon and sea are gleaming bright ;
She sleeps, and I am weary now.
　　Away, these tears ! I go ; good night !

———

FAREWELL TO SUMMER.

FAREWELL, thou beautiful summer,
　　Gliding swift from our land away ;
Thy viewless winds have a murmur
　　And cadence of sadness to-day.
Adieu to thy laughing sunlight,
　　And thy skies so supremely blue ;
The sigh of the breeze at twilight,
　　And peaceful glades starlit in dew.

Farewell, thy streams softly purling
　　Like silver threads over the lea ;
Great rivers rolling onward,
　　Right grandly toward the sea.
Shadows steal out from the woodlands,
　　Lengthening day by day ;
The sun sinks low in southern skies
　　As the summer-time drifts away.

The fairest and tiniest flowers
　　Have closed their delicate leaves,
And the harvesters have garnered
　　The last of their golden sheaves.

Afar in the lonely wildwood,
  By hillside, bright bower and plain,
The reddened brown leaves are sifting
  Fast earthward in red, red rain.

And burns the vast flaming sunset
  In crimson and tawny-barred gold ;
Athwart the advancing night-time
  The star-gemmed skies unfold.
Sadly, aye, sad and regretful,
  I list to the wild, glad strain
Of the song-birds flying southward,
  Filling my heart with pain.

And the winds are melancholy
  That tread o'er the withering lea ;
And mysterious tones in unison
  Come up from the restless sea ;
And my yearning thoughts are tender,
  And fair hopes that ended in pain
Rise with the summer's departure,
  Like pale ghosts, to haunt us again.

And I sigh for summers olden,
  For a time that cometh no more.
The years of the past were golden :
  On memory's dreamland shore
I buried them in deep silence ;
  And I shed there some burning tears,
And ever the days creep slowly
  Into wearily fading years.

There's a clime of fadeless sunshine
  Where the chill and blight ne'er come,
And perpetual bloom of summer
  Is surrounding a great white throne.

I wonder, approaching the sunset,
    When life and its cares are all done,
If we, though sinful and outcast,
    May enter that beautiful home.

———

REMEMBRANCE.

I'M thinking of thee to-day, Jennie,
    While the spring is young and fair,
And nature's glad songs are ringing
    Along the perfumed air ;
And the winds are lightly playing
    O'er earth and the far blue sea,
And floods of warm golden sunlight
    Crown forest, and vale, and lea.

My heart is young to-day, Jennie,
    Though years and years have flown,
And delusive dreams have perished,
    And many dear friends are gone.
Yet to day I revel in fancy
    At memory's fadeless shrine,
And the thoughts that stir my bosom
    Are tender and half divine.

Over the hills to-day, Jennie,
    The blooming, sun-crowned hills,
My footsteps lightly go, Jennie,
    Where the pure sparkling rills
Merge in the stream's soft murmur
    The wind in its voiceful glee
Joins in the mystical music
    Of nature's own harmony.

Oh, how I sang to-day, Jennie,
  The songs we loved so well ;
Songs of the olden time, Jennie,
  Ere we had said "farewell."
I'm looking beyond the years, Jennie,
  To a far-off golden shore,
Where life, like the fairest spring-time,
  Will bloom on for evermore.

THE WORSHIPPERS.

I stood in a wide-arched portal
  That led to the house of God,
And gazed on the assembling people
  As up the aisles they trod ;
And as with lofty bearing,
  In ranks of proud array,
With garments all resplendent,
  The worshippers bowed to pray.

And the lights streamed out the windows,
  Streamed out like shining spears—
Sparkled gaily and scintillated
  From the gleaming chandeliers—
Out on the desolate tents of night,
  All tempest-tossed and wild ;
Out on the glistening frost and snow,
  Where drift on drift was piled.

Oh, proud worshippers there assembled,
  Sumptuously clad and warm,
Do you think of the homeless wanderers
  Out in the pitiless storm ?

Do you extend them a helping hand?
  Have you sheltered, clothed and fed,
And cheered by sympathy's magic
  The soul that was almost dead?

Do you think of the hopeless poor?
  Their dwellings are chill and bare;
They are comfortless and all forlorn,
  With little to eat or wear.
Do you visit them in their sorrow?
  Do you help them from your store?
For Providence has ever blest you
  With enough, to spare, and more.

Do you help the struggling widow
  In the fight for daily bread?
Do you succour the orphan children,
  Scantily clothed and fed?
Do you visit the sick and needy,
  And soothe their heartache and pain?
For encouraging words and kindness
  May lift them up strong again.

The tall spire pointeth to heaven;
  The worshippers pass within,
Heeding, perhaps, but slightly
  The want, the despair, and sin
Of the great world's unfortunate poor,
  Helpless and hopeless and worn;
Tempted, fallen, and tired of life,
  Its bitter neglect and scorn.

I turned away from the portal
  Thinking what might have been
Had you kept the example set you
  By the lowly Nazarene.

The eyes of the world are upon you,
   And faith in your precepts is flown,
And because of example and teaching
   Many have sceptical grown.

AT MIDNIGHT.

I stood tearless and lone at midnight
   Near a grave by destiny made ;
Deep in a vale by a lonely stream,
   Where the branches drooped and swayed
In the soft night wind that breathed a sigh
   To the flowers in the sheen
Of the pale moon, and the world at rest
   Seemed fair as an angel's dream.

But sorrow enwrapt me at midnight
   Beside my beautiful dead,
And I buried it deep for evermore,
   And hope with its white wings fled.
And I wept alone at the midnight
   A passion of burning tears —
I knew the way would be rough and long
   Through all the untried years.

I stole away from that sacred place,
   Where never a form was laid,
But the fairest dream my soul e'er knew
   Rests in that sylvan shade.
In many lands and o'er distant seas
   My restless feet have strayed ;
I've faced the storm and battle's rage
   With courage undismayed.

In every clime and on every sea
   I vainly sought to forget,
But memory still remained the same—
   A changeless, fadeless regret.
I have come again at the midnight,
   After changeful, weary years,
And the scenes of the dear long ago
   Fill my eyes with tender tears.

And I steal sometimes at the midnight
   To that quiet, sacred place,
When the wind's breath kindly caresses,
   And the moon unveils her face.
I dream of the future at midnight,
   A fadeless, celestial shore,
Where the lost shall be reunited,
   And weariness come no more.

CHANGE.

Sunny were the days of childhood,
   And the old home was aglow
With love of the happy faces—
   A dear dream of long ago.
And the household then was perfect,
   With no vacant, appealing chair,
Like a long sweet day of summer,
   Breathing joyance everywhere.

Like songs of birds in the spring-time,
   Or the fragrant flowers of May,
Or the blooming of the summer,
   Or the seasons that glide away;

Like dreams our life is, and fleeting,
　　Aye, a dreaming, and nothing more ;
True life is beyond the gloaming,
　　Full and free on God's fadeless shore.

———

THOUGHTS.

Aʜ ! why is it ever thus ?
　　These mystical thoughts and tears
Are ever present with me
　　As a dream for years and years.
Is 't the voice of weary winds
　　In plaint o'er the blighted lea,
Rustling the autumn leaves
　　Adown from each faded tree ?

Or the flight of little birds,
　　As they pass from us away,
With their sweet notes of gladness,
　　That we miss from day to day ?
The crickets' ceaseless chanting
　　In the serried grass and flowers,
Wakening olden memories
　　Of the long, long silent hours ?

The sombre hues that gather
　　O'er purpling hill and dell,
The flowing stream and fountain
　　Seem e'er haunted like a spell.
And many hearts are haunted,
　　Saddened and thoughtful grown ;
Dead leaves are around them lying,
　　And the warmth of life is flown.

17

Is it the moaning billows
  That surge o'er the lonely sea
Whose mournful tones are ever
  Pleading sobbingly to me
Of a brother that I loved?
  Lost where the wild tempest sweeps,
Unfathomable and lone
  Is the bier where he now sleeps.

And when we walk at even
  Along the dim-lit shore,
We hear weird voices whisper,
  "Nevermore! no, nevermore!"
There in the holy silence,
  Bowed to a tender power,
Passionate dreams enfold us
  In that pale, mystical hour.

We gaze far out and upward
  Toward God's great vaulted dome,
Where stars in their bright splendor
  Are gleaming one by one.
They seem so pure and holy
  In their calm, silvery light;
We feel subdued and lowly
  'Neath their pathless flight.

I think it is thus with us:
  The great Creator's power
Is ever present with us
  In leaf, and tree, and flower.
The sighing of the lone winds,
  And the moaning of the sea,
All join in one grand anthem
  Of the great eternity.

SPRING.

THE spring has come! Once more I hear
　　The song-birds carol free,
The gentle winds play o'er my brow
　　In whisp'ring melody.
A glad refrain from hill and dell,
　　From mountain, stream, and sea,
Pours joyously o'er all the land,
　　From winter's shackles free.

Alternate suns and April rains,
　　Distilling dews at even,
Will deck in verdure all the land;
　　And just as fair as Eden
Will bud and bloom the forest glades.
　　Vales and leafless bowers
Will spring into new life again,
　　Enwreathed with fairest flowers.

Sing on, sing on, glad voice of Spring!
　　Wake, wake, the song again!
A jubilee of joy shout forth
　　From mountain, stream, and plain.
O human hearts, by care oppressed,
　　Rise up! rise up! and o'er
This joyous time, so pure and young,
　　Renew thy strength once more.

REGRET.

A TENDER, delicate kiss given me long ago,
   A wistful look from the deep blue eyes,
That set my sensitive yearning heart aglow
   With dreams of an earthly paradise.
But we drifted far apart, my love and I,
   For the world is cold and hearts must break ;
And in vain were tears and the weary sigh—
   They said it was best for her dear sake.

IN MEMORIAM.

ONE more tender, fragile flower
   Faded from our sight to-day,
Just as spring-time's buds and blossoms
   Ushered in the bloom of May.
She had lingered, fading slowly,
   Till the op'ning of the day ;
'Mid its radiant, dewy fragrance,
   Her sweet spirit soared away.

We've sung her last sad requiem,
   Closed the eyes that lost their sight—
Eyes that beamed with love and beauty,
   Eyes that shone with holy light.
Ah, how many hearts will miss thee,
   Miss thy smile and gentle tone ;
Life's but emptiness and shadow
   When the loved and lost are gone.

In the graveyard on the upland
  That o'erlooks an inland sea,
Where the flowers bloom in beauty,
  Where the birds sing wild and free :
In the grave we sadly laid her
  At the quiet eventide,
And the thoughts that filled our bosoms
  Breathed of prayer and faith sublime.

She's not dead, she only sleepeth
  From the cares of earthly strife;
She'll arise more fair and perfect
  To a grander, nobler life.
If we follow in her footsteps,
  We, too, may the goal attain :
Just beyond the Stygian river
  Blooms a life that 's not in vain.

THE PARTING.

I NEVER deemed we thus should sever,
  Two hearts that vowed to love forever ;
I never thought in this proud, selfish world,
  That love so soon her soft white wings furled.
Our parting I remember yet too well :
  The budding spring was decking earth once more,
The birds were singing in the quiet dell,
  The south winds sighed along the rippling shore.

We stood where fragrant violets grew
  Beside thy cottage door ;
The early dawn soft glances threw
  The lovely landscape o'er.
I took thy hand, it quivered not ;
  Thy face was calm and cold ;
You knew not then the storm of grief
  That o'er my spirit rolled.

One impassioned kiss I pressed
  Upon thy lovely brow,
But thou turn'st coldly from my side—
  How strangely changed wert thou !
We parted, and we ne'er have met
  Since then, long years ago ;
But still I dream, and dream of thee—
  Sad thoughts will backward flow.

Since then I've wandered far and wide
  O'er earth and stormy sea,
And mingled in the world's deep strife,
  But still I think of thee.
The human heart I trust no more ;
  Sweet smile or voice's tone
Are but an echo on the shore
  Of dreams that long have flown.

Thus it is with many a one
  In the world's hurry and strife :
Deserted and ever alone,
  They end a weary life.
Hoping not and trusting never,
  Waifs on the sea of time ;
Longing, aye, longing forever
  For something more divine.

TO THE WANDERER.

It is years since we met, my brother,
  Years of more loss than gain ;
I wonder as I sit by the fire
  If we e'er shall meet again.
I'm tired of time's ceaseless changes,
  And longing as ne'er before
For the faces I knew in childhood,
  And smiles that greet me no more.

And I sigh for a time long vanished,
  And weep o'er my life's lost cause.
Ah ! the battle was long and doubtful,
  With never a lull nor pause
In the long strife fierce and vengeful ;
  And swept from the fateful field
Was my torn and toil-stained banner
  When at last I was forced to yield.

I am thinking to-night, my brother,
  We two may clasp hands once more,
And sing the songs of the olden time,
  And wander there as of yore
Over the hills long, long forsaken,
  And by paths that are o'ergrown ;
By many a nook and quiet vale
  Bordering our dear old home.

We may seek the stream in the meadow,
  And wander on through the glade,
And revel again in joyousness
  In the woodland's grateful shade ;

And hear in fancy our father's voice,
  And our mother's cheerful call
To the noon-tide rest and welcome cheer
  Lovingly prepared for all.

Ah! to-night in this dreary northland,
  How the wild wind sweeps and moans
Through the lone forest bare and ghostly,
  That awesomely rocks and groans!
Madly it leaps o'er the white, dead hills,
  Sweeping fiercely the plain afar;
And there is no light of pale, cold moon,
  Nor yet of wandering star.

Far away in the sunny southland,
  Where the breeze steals o'er the sea,
Toying with foliage and flowers,
  And where wild birds carol free,
There, brother, thy feet are wandering;
  And over my stricken head
Old memories are fondly crowding
  Of the living and the dead.

LULA BY THE SEA.

A SONG.

In the loveliest springtime,
  'Neath a willow tree,
There we laid poor Lula
  Near the sighing sea,
That the birds might warble
  Sweetly o'er her tomb ;
That the flowers in beauty
  There might ever bloom.

CHORUS.

Yes, by the sobbing sea we've laid her,
  Near its waters flow,
Where the sad waves are ever breathing
  Music deep and low.

When the shadowy twilight
  Gathered o'er the lea,
And the stars of heaven
  Were beaming on the sea,
Then with gentle Lula
  Oft we silent strayed
By the murmuring waters
  Where the moonlight played.

Now no more with Lula
  On the ocean's shore ;
When the breeze is dying
  Lula comes no more.

Gone to rest forever
   In her beauty's bloom,
'Neath a dark green willow,
   In the silent tomb.

I am growing weary
   Watching here alone,
For my darling Lula
   Nevermore will come.
Yet a voice is ever
   Whisp'ring unto me
That there are no partings
   Beyond life's mystic sea.

TIRED.

TIRED of the past and present,
   For the slowly fading years
Have brought so little of joyance,
   So many sorrows and tears.
Tired of fighting life's battle
   Between evil and the good ;
Tired, so tired of living
   And being misunderstood.

The path of life to the present
   Has been hard and rough all the way ;
My feet are worn and bleeding,
   And burdened from day to day
With a load that never grows lighter ;
   And hope dying with the years
Of toil and disappointment,
   Life's bitterness, pains, and tears.

Tired of the cold surroundings
　　Of folly, ambition, and pride ;
The glint, the glitter, and falseness
　　Alluring on every side.
Tired of my own sad longings
　　For blessings I never knew :
A love that is deep and changeless,
　　A friend that is ever true.

Tired of the stony glances
　　Of eyes cold as pale death,
Where charity never lingers,
　　And with their icicle breath
They blight and wither the blooms
　　Enshrined in the human heart ;
The bright hopes and aspirations
　　Of our life a very part.

Life 's like the sea, ever restless,
　　Limitless, deep, and wide,
Where many gallant ships go down
　　Battling 'gainst storm and tide ;
Whilst others sail gaily afar
　　'Mid beautiful isles of song,
O'er blue and sunny wreathed seas,
　　Where pleasures innumerable throng.

Tired of watching and waiting
　　The dawn of a happier day ;
Will the night with gloom and sadness
　　Nevermore pass away ?
If there's aught in the mystic future
　　Of reward for the dreary past,
Will the wayworn, weary wanderer
　　Find rest and peace at last ?

THE LOST FLOWER.

WHY do I ever dream of thee ?
In vain are thy dreamings, O memory ;
Why sit in sorrow—others are gay—
Restless and grieving, as day follows day ?

Bright as the morn sparkling in dew,
Blooming with roses' beauteous hue ;
Pure as an angel, artless and true,
Smiling in gladness, loving me too.

When o'er the lea with silent wing
Summer was stealing flowers of spring,
In a sweet valley, where willows wave
O'er faded blossom, made we her grave.

I'm only waiting for that blest hour
When I shall rest with my lost flower,
Waking at last where the perfect day
In loveliness shall fade not away.

DRIFTING.

THE day has gone and the night is come,
    Dreary, dreary, dreary ;
And hope is dying within my breast,
    Weary, weary, weary.

The pitiless winds sweep the earth in wrath,
    Drifting, drifting, drifting
The fierce white snow, with a wail of woe,
    Over the wild, dark reaches sifting.

I sit by the dim, forsaken hearth,
    Thinking, thinking, thinking
Of a love that ne'er can come to me ;
    Shrinking, shrinking, shrinking
From the cold clasp of a fateful hand
    That shadowed all the years.

Dreary without, and dreary within,
    Dying, dying, dying
Is the last hope of a broken life
    That can love and trust no more.

LONGING.

I HAVE grown weary of voices,
    And I long for silence and rest,
And the peacefulness of night-time,
    When no care doth my soul infest.

And I've grown weary of faces
    That have never a thought for me ;
Of eyes all cold and repellent
    I would be forever made free.

And I've grown weary of thinking
    The thoughts that my being possess ;
The finite and the infinite
    Forever my bosom oppress.

I'm very weary of hoping,
  And e'er waiting from day to day
A happy and bright consummation,
  An illusion still far away.

I'm weary of vacant places :
  The dear hands that clasp mine no more
Have drifted o'er the dark river,
  And gained the eternal shore.

Ah ! how I miss the dear faces
  Of old friends long years since made free ;
But only their vacant places
  Forever are calling to me.

And so I'm saddened and lonely,
  And trying to trust and to wait,
Dreaming and longing for rest time—
  'Tis the passion and burden of fate.

THE LAST SONG.

I HAVE sung my last song, and am ready
  To go at the dying of day ;
Ere the gloom of night comes to sadden,
  My feet shall have passed away.
No more when you meet at the twilight
  Shall I mingle my voice with the strains
That tell of home, of love, and heaven,
  And the past with its pleasures and pains.

And when again you are carolling
    The old songs I love so well,
Will you steal a thought for the absent,
    For the one who is saying farewell ?
Or must I then, too, be forgotten
    When my voice shall be nevermore heard ?
Will regret ne'er trouble thy bosom,
    Nor memory ever be stirred ?

Sing on, happy hearts, in the gloaming ;
    Sing of home, and of heaven, and love ;
Heed not the feet that have wandered
    Far away, like the voice of a dove.
An echo I hear sweetly tender,
    That seems ever to whisper to me
Of a meeting of friends long severed,
    In a life made all perfect and free.

THE FIRST SNOW.

I'm walking to-day with mem'ry
    Through the woodlands weird and still,
With ghostly shadows around me,
    Haunting, and strange, and chill.
Ominous clouds are gathering
    O'er a ghastly, threatening sky ;
The voice of the wind is grieving
    In the treetops bare and high.

And the streams are stilled and sleeping,
    And under my onward tread
The fallen leaves are rustling ;
    And from the pale, silent dead

Come stealing back phantom footsteps
  By many a ruined bower;
And tender, mystical murmurings,
  From many a pale dead flower;

And a subtle song of summer,
  Of beautiful seasons fled,
Of faces, voices, and ruined hopes,
  Sweet dreams, and the tears we shed;
And sweet as the angels' singing,
  Or the summer's soft twilight,
Or love asleep in fragrant bloom,
  Or the peaceful, dreamland night;

And a love that waked to never die,
  A radiant and fadeless bloom
That waning years cannot efface,
  An endless and golden noon.
I revel at will with mem'ry
  By streams and rippling rills;
My heart is wrapt in ecstasy,
  As I climb its shining hills.

But list to the dirge of the wind
  Through the ever deep'ning gloom;
See! 'tis falling, the death-white snow,
  Awak'ning my soul too soon.
It whitens the lonely moorlands,
  And the forest glade and glen,
The dreamy hills and silent vales
  Where the summer late hath been.

And see how it swirls and eddies,
  Searching fiercely everywhere;
It clasps in an icy embrace,
  Flurrying fast through the air.

'Tis so desolate and dreary,
　And thought grows heavy with pain,
For it may be that never for me
　Will the summer come again.

PEACE.

At last, when the sun is setting,
　And the beautiful golden bars
Reach upward through purple splendor,
　And mingle their light with the stars ;
The winds are hushed to a whisper,
　Caressing the leaves and flowers ;
And song of birds are rippling
　Sweetly in twilight bowers ;
I ponder o'er past and present,
　And rest from the care and strife—
At peace with all, and storing strength
　For the daily battle of life.

ARMAGEDDON.

CHAPTER I.

I KNOW not if 'twas in a vision, or a spirit dream.
'Twas at the noon of day, when fairest summer time serene
Clothed all the world in loveliness ; when dazzling light
Streamed o'er the Himalayas, and the grandeur of the sight
Lay all before me, as I stood on that far peerless height,
And saw through spirit eyes the whole world at my feet.

Magnificently grand was that far panoramic view,
And I was lost in wonderment as swift-winged vision flew
From sea to sea, lake, river, stream, and tiny rippling rill,
Far mountains tow'ring to the skies, and rolling plain and
      hill,
And a thousand verdured swells that like billows roll away
Beyond the horizon's mystic rim and the far gates of day.

From tropic seas I pierced the veil where Arctic oceans
      roll,
By a thousand isles that gem the deep and flit from pole
      to pole,
And swift return by milder climes of rich perpetual bloom,
No more to look on that wild waste of mystery and gloom.

I saw the cattle on a thousand sloping emerald hills,
Heard the dream-songs of shepherds that through the dis-
      tance thrills
The list'ning ear ; and saw millions of tillers of the soil—
The support of kings, nations—earth's suffering sons of toil.

A thousand cities glistened in the near and far away;
All domed and minaretted, by a thousand streams they lay.
I heard the din of commerce and the rush of countless feet,
And the cry of untold voices, and babel reigned complete;
And pomp and power were trampling the poor and weak
    ones down,
And kings looked on from palace halls with ne'er rebuke
    nor frown.

I saw giant nations flaunting diverse banners to the breeze,
All bristling o'er with armament, and frail thrones at their
    knees;
Lust of power was rampant, jars and threat'nings every-
    where,
Deep mutterings of the rising storm fell across the air.
The seas were white with commerce, with the ships that
    o'er them sweep,
Watched by the navies of the world, vast guardians of the
    deep;
I heard the cry of Christian, and of ruthless Moslem bands
Flaunting their crescent banner with cruel bloodstained
    hands.

One flag I marked on every sea, in every clime and zone—
The meteor flag of Britain, proudly, defiantly outthrown.
It seemed to tower over all, bidding tyrants to beware,
Of the nation's rights its bright folds guard to have a
    proper care.
There were mutterings and combinations adverse to
    Britain's fame,
And from the horizon's darkening rim burst shafts of
    ruddy flame.

But a couchant lion rose and shook his majestic, tawny
    mane,
And roared with a roar that shook the seas and braced his
    giant frame;

And the Empress of the Ocean stood on her seagirt shores
In the panoply of war, where her royal banner soars.
Serene and noble there she stood, in majesty and pride,
And beckoned, and millions of men uprose, and far and
    wide
Her dauntless ships moved out, and covered all the sea,
To guard the nation's sacred cause and Christian liberty.

The German nation heard the call that echoed o'er the
    deep,
And her mighty heart was thrilled, and with one generous
    sweep
Hurled all differences to the four quarters of the wind,
And swiftly ranged by Britain's side, as one in heart and
    mind.
And Italia's answering cry rose up, regenerated, free,
As she joined the alliance with a shout for Christian unity.

The Austrian nation was moved as by a mighty throe,
And prepared to strike by Britain's side the now advancing
    foe
Of Russ, and Gaul, and Moslem hordes converging for the
    fight
That is to shake the astonished world in horror and affright.

Converging to the gates of India in columns vast they
    come
To the martial blare of trumpets and roll of fife and drum,
The half a million horse—the van—in wild clangor clears
    the way
For three thousand frowning guns in formidable array,
With vast masses of infantry—six millions of the foe,
To deliver a vast attack, an irresistible blow;
To sweep Albion from the Ind, and the German power to
    break;
To win the Orient, even the world to dominate

For the passes of the Himalayas on and on they sweep,
Making the very earth to vibrate beneath their marching
feet.

But hark ! on the expectant and sharply startled ear
Bursts a fiercer blare of trumpets and a still more rousing
cheer.
I turned my vision southward. Oh, welcome, glorious sight !
Five million men advancing in the glowing golden light
Of the sun of Ind, that fell athwart the grand array
Of Albion and her illustrious allies.   And far away
I saw another army moving swiftly to the right
(As if detached from Albion's hosts), and disappear from
sight
In the foothills of the Himalayas—some deep strategy
evolved
By Wolseley and Roberts, who war's problems oft have
solved.

Too late, the rushing foe the barring mountain passes gain,
And swift debouch in mighty mass and unfold along the
plain.
An awful front is formed, reaching leagues and leagues away,
Deployed in seven battle lines in stupendous grim array,
With three thousand guns at intervals frowning there
between
Vast corps of horse and infantry, such as the world hath
ne'er seen.
Intermingled were strange devices to hurl storms of shot
and shell,
Hot and furious as the deadly, insatiate maw of hell.
Bicycle corps with protecting shields flashed everywhere ;
And balloons, like eagles, poised on high, borne along the air ;
Swooping like eagles for their prey, searching the far and
nigh,
They fearless rise above the clouds and soar along the sky.

Swiftly telegraph lines reach every part of the vast line,
Entrenched by corps of engineers skilful of design.
And central, in rear of that stupendous and waiting host,
The White Czar of all the Russias with his staff takes
    post.

With the Russians forming the centre, gigantic, deep, and
    wide,
And the corps of France the right wing, a mass of fiery
    pride ;
And the Sultan's hordes of Moslems form the left, and
    there await
The awful pending struggle, the doom of a boding fate !
And thus they wait the adversary, Gog and Magog.

CHAPTER II.

Again I turned to the southward, thrilled by the glorious
    sight
Of vast battle lines advancing all beautiful and bright ;
With flashing steel, like countless stars, bannered, bedight
    they come,
Great waves of scarlet, blue and gold, fearlessly rolling on,
Preceded by a reconnaissance of cavalry and balloons,
With deadly explosives to hurl by hot platoons.
Five million men advancing in the panoply of war,
With Albion in the centre ; and prolonging the right afar
Are the Italians and Austrians facing the Moslem bands,
The followers of the crescent from far Orient lands.
Deployed to the left are the Germans, a stately array,
Once more to grapple their ancient foes, defiantly at bay.

Seven leagues ! seven leagues ! an awful front
    Albion and her allies form !
Five battle lines advancing in parallel,
    Fronting the dire impending storm,

With vast masses of brilliant cavalry
　　At intervals on each wing,
And supporting divisions in reserve,
　　They half a million sabres bring.
Intermingling are three thousand quick-fire guns,
　　And destructive and strange machines—
Cunning devices for the attack and defence—
　　Under cover of light steel screens.
And covering the front are bicycle corps,
　　And steel-armoured motor cars ;
Swift and frightfully deadly, well befitting
　　The grand intrepid sons of Mars.

As a very god of vast war sits Wolseley
　　On his charger, unmoved, serene,
In rear of the centre, with a brilliant staff,
　　Intrusted with the command supreme.
And the stern Germans are with their great war
　　　　lord,
　　The Kaiser, eager for the fray ;
Believing the God of all battles will win
　　Them this last great decisive day.
And the Austrians and dauntless Italians
　　Passionate enthusiasm bring,
And are grandly, unflinchingly coming on
　　Under Emperor and King.

Oh, the dread majesty of that gigantic,
　　Glorious panoply of war !
Advancing with the awesome roar of the sea
　　When its deep wrath is heard afar ;
Advancing upon the giant adversary
　　To the swift help of the Lord.
To put the proud, inveterate followers
　　Of Satan to the pending sword ;

To free the benighted world from tyranny,
  And the hard yoke and scourge of sin,
They roll on, and onward, fearing neither death
  Nor hell, all eager to begin.

Now pauses the colossal, mighty advance,
  When near to the gigantic foe,
Ere hurling a destroying and vast attack,
  Ere delivering the first great blow.
To perfect his wonderful dispositions
  Wolseley, with lightning speed,
Distributes his detail of final orders
  By wire, 'cycle, and fiery steed.

The engineers along the intrepid lines
  Throw up works of shelter and defence;
And wires and 'phones to every abiding corps
  Waiting the issue grim, intense.

It was an awful and a trying moment.
  Should heaven now, or hell, prevail?
I feared as the masterful Christian hosts
  Prepared the foe to assail.

CHAPTER III.

Hist! what's this horror stealing o'er the serenitude of
    heaven ?
A weird panoply of cold, metallic light had driven
All the deep-toned azure of the summer skies away.
A spectral terror seems to chill the very noon of day.
And see! those strange, dark phantoms falling on the
    earth and sea,
Portending calamity.   An appalling mystery
Envelops all the horizon, and a pending doom
Seems inevitable to man ; and nature's woof and bloom
Is smitten by a poisonous and hot simoon.

But see! it changes.   A wondrous crimson flood
Hath enveloped earth, sea and sky in lurid robes of blood!
And from out the awful threatening deeps, and voids on
    high,
Marshalling legions of phantom armies go sweeping by!
And they wheeled in vast evolution on high o'er where I
    stood.
The hosts of heaven, in the glorious panoply of God,
Wheeled into huge lines of columns fronting on the foe;
In golden chariots and equipments strange, and burnished
    so.
I bowed in awe; I could not bear the dazzling sight
Of that mass of immaculate glory, intensely bright.
But I thought with ecstasy, that heaven would fight this
    day
For the Christian hosts in the vale, and bear the foe
    away
To destruction, desolation, and bind Satan with a chain,
And cast him down headlong, to trouble man never again.

But hark! from the threatening vale below
    Comes a rumbling commotion,
A sullen roar, as when storms sweep across
    The wrathful face of the ocean;
And from Albion's front move two thousand guns
    Sternly rolling upon the foe,
With vast corps of riflemen in support;
    And swiftly forward flashing go
The bicycle divisions, and quick-fire guns,
    A destructive torrent to pour.
And aloft are the airships and balloons;
    Like great eagles they rise and soar
With dire explosives and deadly machines
    To hurl death on the lines below—
The awful lines in manœuvre vast
    In the strange light glittering so.

Suddenly along those ponderous fronts
    Bursts the roar of the dreadful guns,
Causing the very earth to tremble
    As through it the vibration runs.
And peal on peal incessant staggered
    The great mountain on which I stood;
And the responsive, bellowing thunder
    Of the adversary froze the blood.
Thus, loosed from the leash, the dogs of war
    Burst in nameless fury on the foe,
And death was hurled from the clouds above
    To the hosts in the vale below.

And I saw lines of airships advancing,
    Soaring like mighty birds of prey;
And rent asunder were the lurid clouds
    That obscured the red god of day.
And I saw them glide on to each other,
    The opposing lines up on high,
And the trumpet call from balloon to balloon
    Manœuvred them through the sky.
And still dropping their horrid explosives
    Below to the shattered plain,
They seek by quick aerial manœuvres
    Advantageous positions to gain.
And thus rising, poising, and advancing,
    Pausing in close column and line,
The strange scene was awesome and wonderful,
    And immeasurably sublime.
Fiercely on each other with quick-fire guns
    Destruction they now madly pour,
And infernal machines and magazines
    Add their terrible, deadly roar.
And out on the vast aerial spaces
    It echoed and rolled away,
A shuddering and horrible tumult,
    Lost in distance grim and gray.

And contending there for the mastery,
    Some collided with ruinous clash,
And fell from the fierce crimson clouds above
    To the earth with a horrid crash.

And thus they fought in the aerial plains
    To cover their own below,
And to hover o'er, and hurl destruction
    On the contending mammoth foe.

I looked on the fearful scene below,
    And the earth was pent with the slain ;
And the deafening and tumultuous roar
    Rolled o'er the embattled plain.
And from the hot lips of six thousand guns
    Leaped whirlwinds of smoke and flame,
And the fiendish missiles tore divisions
    Asunder, in ruin amain.

In majestic evolution vast masses
    Of infantry enter the fire zone,
And whole fronts of magnificent columns
    Into eternity are blown.
And the bicycle corps and quick-fire guns
    Into the maelstrom of battle go ;
Flashing in and out all along the fronts,
    They deliver their blow on blow.
Vast clouds of cavalry charge on the wings
    At intervals along the line ;
And the mighty reserves *en masse* abide
    Magnificent and sublime.

And these enormous adversaries sway
    In furious struggles to and fro,
Repelling, receding, and advancing,
    Like the vast sea-waves' ebb and flow.

Incessant charges of the cavalry
    Sweep like whirlwinds over the plain,
And though thousands fall in the mad *melee*,
    They charge and recharge again.
And they shore whole lines into fragments
    Where confusion had entered in ;
Where the foot and horse had suffered most,
    They drove their wild charge within.
Again and again they too were hurled back,
    Broken, beaten, and swept away
By the deadly guns and the magazines
    Of the infantry's ceaseless play.

And explosives drop from the fierce red clouds,
    Hurling death and dismay around,
Making ghastly rents in the shattered ranks,
    Chasming the trembling ground.
And the infantry charged fierce and wild
    With the bayonet's resistless play,
And their deadly work in the mad *melee*,
    Added horror to the ghastly day.
Thousands of banners waved through smoke and
        flame,
    And wild cheers rent the glaring sky ;
Along the lines for leagues and leagues
    Rose the dauntless battle-cry.
And oh, the incessant tumultuous roar !
    On the shuddering world it fell ;
It seemed to rise from the infernal pit,
    The red bellowing maw of hell.

CHAPTER IV.

And so the night fell redly down,
    Such a night as man ne'er hath seen—
One vast crimson glare through the universe,
    And weird phantoms flitting between

The stars that glowed in the vast far voids,
   Falling prone on the earth and sea.
Horrible convulsions ran all amain,
   Staggering the mountains under me ;
And lightning leapt from the fierce red clouds,
   And the appalling thunder shock
Seemed to rive the firmament in twain,
   Crashing from mountain and rock to rock.
And fiendish voices shrieked through the air,
   Mocking and gibing at man's doom ;
And the pale, dead legions heaping the plain,
   Peering out of the gory gloom.

And the battle ceased not ; through the night
   It raged with the fury of hell,
And the ponderous blows that Albion dealt
   Like a destroying angel fell.
They pressed the Russians from line to line
   By the bayonet and sabre stroke ;
On and on with a deathless valor,
   Through their vast divisions they broke.
And the left of the line stands firm, where
   The Germans are sternly at bay,
Assailed by the Gauls in furious hate,—
   They must not and will not give way.

But the right is threatened and sorely pressed
   By the Sultan's valiant corps,
For like rocks they abide before the fire
   The Italians and Austrians pour.
Avalanches of smoke and raging flame
   From the batteries belch far and wide ;
Like a misty veil cover all the field,
   And creep up the great mountain side.

'Twas as a mist of blood, obscuring but
   Slightly the struggle ; and on high
The bright aerial ships still hovered
   In conflict along the fierce red sky.

Suddenly, with terrific, awful throe,
   The earth was rent at the mountain's base,
And hot sulphurous fumes uprose, and
   Demoniacal cries, and the face
Of Satan, with horrible equipments,
   Crawled up o'er the red rim of hell ;
And twelve flaming legions of fiends—lost souls—
   Sprang after, and into phalanx fell.
With flaming harness all scaled, bedight,
   Hideous blazoned shield and lance,
With Satan, Lucifer and Apollyon,
   They prepared their direful advance

To the help of the mighty adversary,
   Gog and Magog.   They clanged their shields,
And raged and uttered such blasphemous,
   Malignant, and discordant cries
As only the infernal conclaved
   Regions of the damned could vomit forth.
And frightful shapes—scorpions, lizards, vampires,
   Dragons, and serpents—wriggled up,
Hissing, and spread along the scorched ground
   Their poisonous slime and horrid breath ;
And all things venomous, of which to touch,
   To breathe, is loathsome, instant death !

I was horrified and appalled,
   And raised my eyes in prayer ;
And oh, the sight that met my affrighted gaze,
   In the red cloud's tremendous glare !

The celestial army, by some wondrous
    Evolution, poised o'er the foe—
Poised central—and hurled annihilation
    To the Satanic hosts below ;
Hurled vast streams of glaring lightning,
    And rending thunderbolts roaring fell,
And countless blinding meteors scathed
    And ruined Satan where they fell.
Avalanches of ponderous aerolites
    Tore the maw and counterscarp of hell !
Nameless armaments beat Satan's cohorts down,
    And a hideous, discordant knell
Of rage, despair, smote the shuddering hills,
    With'ring the verdure all amain,
And rolled in nameless horror along
    The lines of that ensanguined plain.

Nearer and nearer swooped the celestial
    Legions in majesty and might,
Until, all ruined and beaten down,
    The demon foe were put to flight,
And Satan seized and bound with a chain,
    And hurled blaspheming back once more
Down the accursed, eternal void of
    Damnation's frenzied awful shore !
Closed and sealed was that deadly maw
    Of desolation and of doom,
That man might escape the horror of an
    Everlasting suffering and gloom.

All through the lurid night the conflict raged
    With furious, unabated breath,
Swaying backward, forward, with frightful carnage
    In the cruel revelry of death.

And the flame and light of that vast battle,
   And the veil that shrouded all the sky,
Made light as day upon the earth and sea,
   And where the air ships fought on high.
All the night Albion had pressed the huge
   Centre of the foe from line to line,
Pressing onward, aye, steadily onward,
   With deeds of chivalry sublime.

CHAPTER V.

The intrepid Germans have not made way,
   But like the rocks they firm abide,
And the fiery Gauls dash swift upon them,
   Like the rise and sweep of ocean's tide
In frenzied fury hurled forward,
   And rolled backward over all
The stern rocks they seethe and roar upon, ere
   Hurled in ruin to their fall.

The far right of the line's in peril sore
   At the dawn of another day,
And though sorely pressed by the Sultan's corps,
   They will die, but never give way.

This I saw as the glaring sun uprose,
   And the conflict still shook the world ;
And in mighty mass all along the front,
   The vast foot and horse were hurled.
And the earth was heaped and pent with the slain,
   And their blood like a river ran,
And ne'er was witnessed such a battle-scene
   Since ever this strange world began.

And I see through the red rays of the sun
  A glad sight that my bosom thrills :
'Tis Roberts, debouching in rear of the foe,
  From the sheltering Himalayan hills.
'Twas he that had disappeared to the right
  Ere the dreadful conflict began ;
'Twas Wolseley's masterful, strategic stroke—
  A card in his vast battle plan.
With the flower of the Ind and British Guards
  He fell on the brave Sultan's rear
With half a million of horse and foot,
  With a prolonged, thunderous cheer.
And they shattered the Moslems from right to left,
  And rent and tore them asunder
By the infantry's fire, and sabre stroke,
  And the batteries' awful thunder.

Crushed to atoms between the two lines,
  The Sultan's ruin is complete,
And he lays his flaming scimitar down
  At the invincible Roberts' feet.

The critical time had now arrived
  To deliver a crushing blow,
And Wolseley redoubled all the fire
  Of his guns on the suffering foe ;
And the infantry close up, and again
  They a devastating fire pour,
And the bicycle corps and quick-fire guns
  Added their fierce and incessant roar.
And from the crimson clouds his aerial ships
  Hurl their cruel and deadly rain,
Shattering the foe in the lines below
  And rending the stormswept plain.

19

A grand *coup de main* he had prepared—
    A thousand electric motor cars,
With a hedge of spears on their outward shields
    That flashed like countless silver stars ;
Each with a quick-fire gun, and a score of men
    Held with the reserves in the rear.
He sends with a rush all along the lines
    Those intrepid souls without fear.
Forward in line at intervals they sweep
    With resistless hedge of steel,
And the writhing lines of the foe they reach—
    See ! see ! they in wild horror reel
From the death rush of those wonderful cars
    That cut them to pieces there,
And confusion enters those suffering lines,
    And a wave of sullen despair.

And Wolseley seizes the fateful moment,
    And rolls forward now the whole line—
Seven leagues ! seven leagues of front !
    Irresistible and sublime.

" All along their front let the cavalry charge!
    Crush now their faltering powers !
Let the reserves sweep the foe from the field !
    Complete this day of days, which is ours."
And they swift unfold and sweep o'er the plain,
    Resistlessly forward everywhere,
A fiery mass of heroic chivalry,
    So glorious and so fair.

Like destroying angels they fall on the foe,
    Rending, destroying all amain,
And they reel back in despair, still struggling there,
    But ever and ever in vain.

And the cavalry charged in mighty mass,
   And the earth rocked beneath their tread,
And they shore whole lines into mere fragments,
   And the fragments in terror fled.

The infantry volleyed, and swept the guns,
   And charged through the flame and smoke,
And rent and ruined those wavering lines
   As through and through them they broke.

Thus Albion and her allies rolled on
   Till from every position driven,
Bleeding and torn, ruined, and all forlorn,
   The foe were cast to the four winds of heaven.

Oh, mourn! oh, pity! and weep, all the world;
   At the close of that awful day
Two million of fearless, heroic dead
   Were hidden forever away!

And the sinister skies were cleared again,
   And the phantoms that fell on the sea,
And the fierce crimson clouds faded away,
   And heaven's blue shone again o'er me.
I heard a song, as of seraphic choirs,
   And it floated down from above,
A most wonderful song of ecstasy,
   Of rejoicing and infinite love.

And the celestial host soared upward,
   Away, repeating the chorus; it ran:
" For the world is redeemed; joy! joy! joy!
   Peace on earth and good will to man."

CHARITY.

Seek but to benefit thy fellowman:
　Let smiles, not frowns, his rugged path assail.
Better with blinded eyes his faults to scan,
　Than let the sin of wrong and scorn prevail.

O Charity ! unfold thy pure white wings,
　Teach us to suffer and to forbear ;
To hurl no darts, no evil, bitter stings,
　For life is needful and full of care.

Then fold us, fold us, in thy pure white wings,
　Shield us from ourselves, and let us see
Only good in others, and the joy that brings
　Peace to us in life and in eternity.

THE END.